RESISTANCE

BOOK 1 LIBERTY

EILIDH MCGINNESS

'Surely the day will come when colour means nothing more than the skin tone, when religion is seen uniquely as a way to speak one's soul: when birth places have the weight of the throw of the dice and all men are born free, when understanding breeds love and brotherhood.'

Josephine Baker

This novel is a work of fiction. The village of Saint-Antoine-de-Double in an imaginary one. However many of the events described in the book are based on actual events although these have in some circumstances been altered for the purposes of the story.

I include a bibliography of sources used in my research at the end of the book for anyone wishing to learn more about the history of Dordogne during the occupation.

I love to hear from readers and can be contacted on facebook, twitter and at www.eilidhmcginness.com

I also have a Pinterest account with photographs of many of the places described in the novel.

Best wishes

Eilidh McGinness

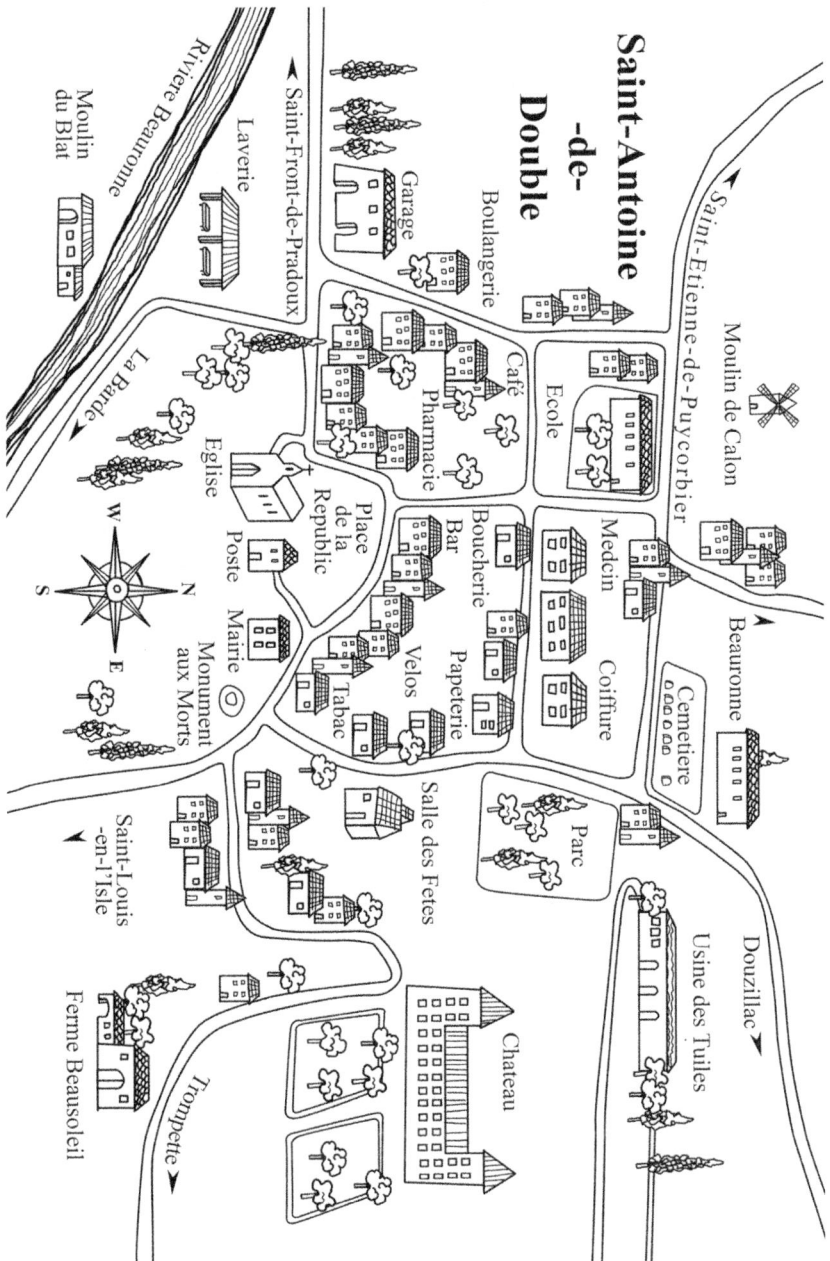

Saint-Antoine -de- Double

Moulin du Blat

Rivière Beauronne

Saint-Étienne-de-Puycorbier

Moulin de Calon

Laverie

Saint-Front-de-Pradoux

Garage

Boulangerie

Café

Ecole

La Barde

Pharmacie

Eglise

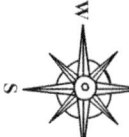

Poste

Place de la Republic

Mairie

Bar

Boucherie

Papeterie

Velos

Tabac

Medcin

Coiffure

Beauronne

Cemetiere

Monument aux Morts

W

S

N

E

Saint-Louis -en-l'Isle

Salle des Fetes

Parc

Douzillac

Usine des Tuiles

Ferme Beausoleil

Trompette

Chateau

Zone occupée   Zone libre

Angoulême

Nontron

La Rochebeaucourt

Mareuil-sur-Belle

Thiviers

Brantôme

Vertellac

Excideuil

Allemans

Riberac   Tocane-Saint-Apre

Saint-Aulaye

Saint-Astier

Périgueux

La Jemaye

Echourignac

La Roche-Chalais

Saint Antoine de
Double

Neuvic

Vergt

Villamblard

Isle

Mussidan

Montpon-Ménestérol

Villefranche-de-Lonchat

Libourne

Saint-Martin-de-Gurçon

Montpeyroux

Bergerac   Creysse

Sarlat

Lamothe-Montravel

Dordogne

Chateau des
Milandes

N

Villefranche-de-Périgord

Ligne de démarcation

0   10km   20km

Chapter 1

CASTILLION-SUR-DORDOGNE, JULY 1941

Was this to be his coffin? Was he to die here? Legs screaming. Gasping for breath in air saturated with alcohol and the musty odour from the boots strung around his neck. His legs, feet, and ankles marinaded in a rich, blood red Bordeaux. Hérisson wedged his elbows into the ancient oak panels of his hideout and waited. Silence. Better than any of the alternatives. Thankfully the cooper who had sealed him in his cylindrical prison had done so with all the skill of his trade. Otherwise the constant pressure from Hérisson's body would have caused a seepage, alerting the German guard, who even now was examining the cart and its cargo, that all was not as it seemed.

Voices, too muffled to discern. His heart pounded against his chest. Then a jolt, making the barrel shudder. The cart began to move forward. At last. Hérisson mouthed thanks to every deity he could summon from the mists of his memory.

How many times had he crossed over the bridge at Castillion-sur-Dordogne? So many. But never like this. Never knowing that if he were discovered, he would be executed immediately, without trial, without even his name. After what seemed a lifetime he felt the cart draw to a halt. They had reached the other side of the bridge. The control point for entry into Vichy France. The inspection here would be a formality. In a few moments he would enter the Free Zone.

The cart shuddered as it began to move again. With nothing to occupy his thoughts but the pain in his legs, time passed interminably. After an eternity, the swaying and jolting stopped. Voices. Close by, and urgent. He felt the wine draining from around him as the barrel was emptied from the tap at its base. Then vibrations and the shock and spark of hammer on metal as another cooper set about freeing him.

The head hoop was removed, then the quarter hoop, allowing the staves to fall open and the barrel head to be lifted, revealing him like a jack-in-the-box. Except he was a hedgehog-in-a-barrel.

He staggered forward. The driver and the cooper grabbed his arms, steadying him. 'Give yourself a moment lad. It's not an easy journey.'

'I'm fine. Get the others out.' Hérisson gripped the side of the cart, struggling to adjust to his surroundings as he forced his cramped limbs to straighten. Slivers of dusty light fell from the bullseye windows high on the walls, revealing the paraphernalia of the wine producer's trade that lurked in the shadows of this vast *chai* furnished for the production of wine. Enormous casks fit for an ogre's feast lined the far wall. A wine press with its gigantic iron screw guarded a narrow doorway leading perhaps to cellars below. In front of the press, a table with rickety chairs scattered around it. A line of carts presumably used for collecting the grape harvest at the *vendange* were positioned beside the tall, arched, double doors. Rows upon rows of dust- covered bottles, empty or full he could not tell, lay stacked beside the carts. Everywhere the odour of wine-soaked wood. The mule that had pulled the cart stamped and brayed its impatience to be free.

With a clang of metal, another barrel hoop was removed, then Loup emerged. Further clangs heralded the arrival of Pinot and then Cerf. The friends gathered by the cart, wine dripping from their sodden trousers. They hugged each other. They had done it. They had escaped from the Occupied Zone. ' You've made it to the Free Zone. Congratulations', the driver said.

Each youth shook hands with the driver and the cooper.

'Here lads,' the cooper handed over a pail. 'Some water to wash yourselves. We have to partly fill the barrels because sometimes the guards check to see there really is wine inside.'

'What a waste', Pinot commented.

The driver laughed, holding up a bottle he was filling with the liquid drained from the barrel.

'No waste. This fine blend will be on a *Boche* table tonight.'

They all laughed. Then the driver produced a wicker basket with some bread, cheese, wine and sausage. The group settled themselves around the table and hungrily set about the provisions.

'Here, take these', the driver invited, holding out the remaining contents of the basket. 'You know the route.'

'Yes', Hérisson confirmed, tapping his jacket pocket.

'Once you reach Saint-André-de-Double, ask for Pete. No one else, mind. If you're careful you shouldn't have any trouble on the way.'

They all shook hands again. The driver opened the side door of the *chai*, checking first one direction then another. With a wave over his shoulder, he signalled the four young men that it was safe to leave. They sidled out of the building and set off in the direction the driver had indicated, along a potholed track lined on either side with immaculate rows of vines. Hérisson glanced back as they left the *chai*. The cooper was already engrossed in reconstructing the barrels. In a few hours their driver could cross back over the demarcation line into the Occupied Zone, but then all his barrels would be empty.

'It's a good day's walk', Hérisson warned, 'but with a bit of luck we'll get a lift.'

The track stretched before them, dry and dusty. Here and there in the distance they could see the figures of workers clipping excess shoots from the vines. Most would be women, or children. Youths of Hérisson's age had become rare. He puffed out his chest and stepped forward. If felt good to be taking action. He and his friends were on their way to join the Resistance. He hoisted the straps of his backpack which were already beginning to dig into his shoulders. The sun climbed slowly across the sky as they tramped onwards. Soon they shed their jumpers and jackets as it became hotter.

It was approaching midday when they saw a farmer, a beret precariously perched on his head, drive a horse-drawn cart, heaped high with fresh hay, out of a field. They ran after it, waving and shouting. The good-humoured driver, face wrinkled either by age or the sun, cheeks reddened with a lifetime's consumption of wine and Ricard, allowed them to climb aboard. The lads relaxed, lying in the sweet-smelling hay, heads propped against their backpacks, as the wooden wheels turned and bumped, taking them onwards towards their destination.

The next part of the journey was more dangerous. They had decided to avoid entering the town of Montpon-Menesterol. It, like Castillion-sur-Dordogne, was a border town on the demarcation line. Men of their age would attract attention.

Following the advice of the *passeurs* who had assisted their crossing, they had destroyed all their identity papers. If they tried to pass through a control point, the consequences would be disastrous.

Hérisson had found the burning of their papers liberating, and not just because of the wine-drinking and joviality that had accompanied the ceremony the previous evening. He had a sense of being reborn. He was a new person. Able to forget his background and everything associated with it. He was someone with no past. No duties. No obligations. No expectations vested in him. Only a future. A future filled with adventure and an important goal. His mission. To free France of the Nazi poison pumped though her veins by the beating heart that was the Vichy regime. Once liberated, his homeland would be reborn, like him, in a world where the communist dream of equality for all would take root and flourish.

The friends skirted Montpon-Menesterol, deciding to swim across the river just outside the town in order to avoid walking the extra kilometers to the bridge at Saint-Laurent-des-Hommes. First they sheltered from prying eyes and the relentless sun under the fronds of weeping willows that lined the river banks. Then they hungrily picnicked, grateful for the food and bottle of unadulterated wine they had been furnished with, all of which tasted even better after their long march.

The lads joked as they stripped off their clothes and tied their belongings into misshapen bundles. Hérisson entered the river first, his only possessions in the world raised above his head. Pinot and Cerf followed, squealing as the cold water swirled around them. 'Girls', Loup taunted as he followed them. But then he slipped on the pebbled floor just managing to balance in time to save himself from an icy dip. They scrambled ashore on the opposite bank amid peals of laughter, then dressed quickly, grateful for the hot sun as it warmed their goose-pimpled flesh. It was time to begin the ascent into the Fôret-de-la-Double.

'My feet hurt', moaned Cerf, 'I hope we get another lift.'

'Not much hope of that. The roads are empty."

'No one's got any fuel. Except the police, and we can hardly get a lift from them.'

'There'll be more opportunities once we get into the forest', Loup assured optimistically.

'Let's hope we catch a farmer or a forester going towards Saint-André.'

Hérisson barely listened to his friends. He searched the changing landscape for evidence that the intelligence he'd been given was genuine.

Once his membership of the Communist Party had made him a target for the roundups, which had become part and parcel of life in the Occupied Zone, he had resolved to join the Resistance. It was the logical choice, based as he was close to the demarcation line. That line had sprung up between the Occupied Zone and the Free Zone after Marshal Petain's signature on the armistice agreement with Germany. In the Free Zone, by definition, Hérisson's movements would attract less attention. Consequently, Resistance activities should have more impact on the enemy. The underground press reported that the Resistance units in the Fôret-de-la-Double were becoming increasingly active. What's more, they were rumoured to have contacts in London – contacts able to guarantee arms supplies and vital intelligence. The temptation had proved irresistible. When Hérisson had cautiously shared the plan with his friends, also members of the Communist Party, they'd been determined to join him. And so their escape from the Occupied Zone was born.

That morning, their journey had begun amongst neatly tended vineyards. Now signs of ordered civilisation had disappeared. Cropped fields had been replaced with dense forests of oak, chestnut, elm, and birch. The trunks sank into dense blackthorn and bramble. Ivy twisted and strangled even the greatest oaks. The landscape was savage and wild. Narrow roads mutated to still narrower tracks, tunneling through the tangle of trees and dense vegetation. Visibility was severely restricted. Anyone foolish enough to stray from the road could become lost after even a few meters. It was perfect terrain for the guerrilla tactics favoured by the Resistance. Hérisson felt a shudder in his spine as he breathed in the forest air. He could taste the rebellion. It throbbed through his surroundings as tangibly as the blisters forming on his feet.

On they tramped, their pace slower now. Finally, as dusk fell, they approached Saint-Barthelemy-de-Bellegarde. Luckily, a farmer's wife, sympathetic to their pleas for some water from her well, took pity on them. She provided some thick vegetable broth, together with some heavy home-made bread. Her husband watched silently from his armchair by the fireplace as they tucked into the food. In return for an hour spent splitting logs, the woman allowed them sleep in the couple's barn.

The building was not like those constructed from the impressive blonde Girondine stone Hérisson and his friends were accustomed to. The barn was built from vertical wooden *colombages* , with the spaces between the oak pillars interspersed with red clay *bricos* and mortar. The tiled roof was in need of repair and the rear section smelt strongly of something unpleasant but not readily identifiable. Tired hay lay abandoned in a corner. The four lads made dusty pallets to sleep on, close to the main door. Loup passed round cigarettes and they went outside to smoke.

'Do you know where in the village we have to go?' Loup asked Hérisson.

'We'd better not talk out here. They might hear us.' Hérisson nodded towards the cottage as he spoke.

'Don't be ridiculous', Pinot joked. 'That old couple? They're harmless.'

'We don't know that.' Hérisson hissed.

'He's right', Loup agreed. 'We don't know anyone here. We don't know who to trust or who might be an informer.' He tossed the stub of his cigarette to the ground and carefully trod on it, making sure it was extinguished.

'We'll be fresh tomorrow. We can set off at dawn.' Hérisson told the others. Cerf muttered something about his feet and went back inside.

'I wonder when we'll get guns', Pinot said, his voice wavering.

Hérisson studied his friend, wondering, not for the first time, how committed he was to their adventure. Pinot had always been reticent and timid. Not one of the most obvious recruits for a secret army, but what choice had there been? They had all openly broadcast their belief in the principles of socialism. As a consequence, they had immediately become targets of the Nazi regime, once Hitler broke his agreement with Stalin and invaded Russia.

Circumstances had forced them either to take action or wait for the inevitable knock on the door, which would signal the beginning of a journey to a work-camp, a prison, or the firing squad.

When war broke out they hadn't been called up because of their status as agricultural workers. In truth, Hérisson hadn't even considered joining up. Firstly the prospect of a French defeat had seemed impossible. Hadn't they been assured that France's army was the strongest and most disciplined in the world? Hadn't the government committed a fortune to constructing the Maginot Line in the years before the war? The Line, an underground system of fortresses that stretched the whole length of France's Eastern Border was impenetrable. At least that's what they'd been promised. Secondly his Party leader had insisted the instructions from Moscow were not to resist the German invasion, and had assured them that the time for socialism in France was close at hand. Germany's invasion of Russia had shattered that illusion. Hérisson's soul had burned with shame for France when Petain had signed the armistice agreement with Germany, dividing his country into two. He refused to accept Nazi rule or the Nazi vision of a super race. Now he was ready to fight for France and for the principles he believed in. Now he was taking control of his future.

Chapter 2

LA BARDE, SAINT-ANTOINE-DE-DOUBLE, JULY 1941

'Damn that animal', Sabine muttered as she put down the milk churn and ran towards Coco. The goat had yet again managed to escape the paddock, and was already chewing on the white linen tablecloth billowing on the clothes-line. The other goats would soon follow, forgetting their allocated grazing, once they too discovered Coco's escape route. That goat had to be taken in hand and urgently.

'Help', Sabine yelled. Within seconds she was joined by the rest of her family, as *Maman* and her sister Josette emerged from their cottage, and Papa and her brother Tomas, still holding their pitchforks, from the field where they had been turning hay.

As the family surrounded the goat, she took one last defiant tug at the tablecloth before leaping onto the cart which stood in front of the barn. Then she skirted the well and began to trot down the lane. Sabine managed to grab one of her horns as she passed but the animal jerked sideways, knocking over the churn with a clatter of hooves before turning towards the forest. Sabine felt like bursting into tears as the lid rolled free and milk splashed over the cobbles, turning muddy brown before seeping away in the dry earth.

Papa whistled, sending his hunting dog, Tintin, after the

escapee. The *Griffon Bleu de Gascogne* cross bounded effortlessly after the goat, overtaking her and flopping to the ground blocking her escape. Coco turned towards the *potager*, tempted perhaps by the prospect of fresh lettuce, but was immediately flanked by Papa and Tomas. Responding to his master's commands, Tintin rose and herded the goat back into the courtyard. Finally an out-manoeuvred Coco was forced into the barn. Papa and Tomas ran into the building. The goat emerged a few minutes later, secured by a rope around her neck. Papa and Tomas each holding one end. They led the goat back to the field and tied her to the gate. Then they separated, in order to search for the gap in the fence that had made the goat's break out possible. Papa muttered as he collected the wire and cutters to carry out the necessary repair. 'We have to get rid of that goat. She's too much trouble.' Sabine was in no mood to defend her lead goat. Not after the morning's milk had been lost. She picked up the toppled container, replaced the lid and walked back to the milking shed. There would be no cheese-making this morning. Sabine decided she would take advantage of the unexpected disruption in her routine and visit her friend Mariette, who lived in nearby Mussidan.

Sabine changed into a dress and shoes. She refused to wear in public the *sabbots* or wooden clogs they all wore when working on the farm. For her, the hated footwear designated the owner both as a peasant and a person with no understanding of either fashion or style. She checked her hair. Mariette was always impeccably turned out and Sabine refused to give her friend any excuse to think she wasn't equally sophisticated. She collected her bicycle from the barn and set off. It was already a hot day, but it was exhilarating cycling down towards Mussidan. The return journey, mostly uphill, would be much more difficult.

Sabine crossed the bridge over the river Isle and continued through the centre of town. She was about to turn left, in the direction of the grocer's, when Madame Deloitte, distinctive in her wide-brimmed navy hat, appeared suddenly, stepping from the shadows of the church. Sabine swerved sharply , skirting the queue outside the butcher's and diverting down the cobbled side street leading towards the bakers.

Maman had asked her to try and get some slices of ox tongue, but, as expected, there was a queue. The mutterings from those last in line indicated little prospect of receiving anything even if she did bother to wait, despite being in possession of the requisite ration cards.

Sabine slipped along the street then back across the square in the wake of Madame Deloitte. Now she could catch up with Mariette.

A few minutes later she was secure in her friend's attic bedroom, spying on the townsfolk from the discreet window that provided a view over the square. As they'd done so many times before, Mariette and Sabine gossiped over the movements of the townsfolk as they went about their business.

Was it the result of too much alcohol, or an old war injury, as he so often claimed, that caused Monsieur Robert to stagger and sway when he walked?

Were the doctor's visits to Madame Dupont entirely medicinal?

Was it love letters the post-boy was so careful to deliver to the very beautiful Genevieve?

The scenes played out before their eyes in full colours, not in black and white like the news reels and films they watched avidly at the cinema. On the surface the goings-on of their neighbours and friends had changed little since the first time they'd sat together at their spy-hole. The town and its life continued, but the world had changed around them.

Their friendship had spanned years. The first time they'd met, they'd both been twelve when Sabine had begun to attend *college* in Mussidan. The years had passed, and the girls had matured from playing with dolls to dreaming about boys, and then men. Mariette had left *college* at the first opportunity and found a job in the local textile factory. When she married, her parents allocated her the upstairs part of their house to make a home for herself and her husband.

Sabine shuddered as she glanced at the stack of her friend's magazines. Once well-leafed, they now gathered dust beneath the polished oak chest of drawers. They were a remnant from life before the outbreak of war. From a time when they had chatted about their dream husbands. In those days it had been love and weddings that had formed the mainstay of their conversations. That innocence had been stolen from them. Those dreams of weddings and endless love had been born in a different world.

'You don't agree with this Petainist government do you?' Mariette's voice hardened as she asked the question no one dared utter too loudly in their frightened new world.

'No, of course not.'

'I can trust you, can't I?'

'You know you can.'

Mariette crossed the low room, as silently as the snowy owl, which wintered in Sabine's family's barn, swooped upon its prey. She slowly pulled her wrought iron bed from its place by the window. With a knife, she dislodged a plank of wood from under the sill and pulled out an object wrapped in muslin. With a triumphant expression, Mariette carefully unravelled the package. 'Here, hold this', she urged, holding out a gleaming black revolver. Sabine shuddered. Although she was used to guns—hunting was part and parcel of her Papa's life—the sight of the shiny black steel sent a shiver down her spine. This weapon was not designed for shooting game; its purpose was infinitely more menacing.

She took the gun, felt its coldness penetrate her skin. An overwhelming need to vomit overcame her and she dropped the gun as if it had burned her. Mariette laughed. She picked up the weapon and produced bullets from their hiding place beneath the window. She swiftly clicked open the cylinder, her deft hands loading and unloading it as if it were an exercise she had been carrying out all her life.

Sabine looked on in awe—not just at the speed with which her friend managed the task, but by her cold indifference to the fact that it was a murder weapon she held in her hand. Sabine glanced at the sampler on the wall behind Mariette's bed. She remembered her friend neatly embroidering the words *Amour dans la Coeur, joie dans la maison.* on the intricate design as she dreamed of her future husband. Who could have imagined that those hands, which had patiently and skillfully sewed the knotted cornflowers and poppies which bordered the slogan of love and happiness would soon use their nimbleness to load a lethal weapon?

'What are you doing with that?' Sabine asked her friend.

Mariette laughed, suddenly pointing the gun at Sabine.

'What the hell are you playing at', Sabine yelled, diving onto the floor, experiencing genuine fear as her friend twirled the gun carelessly around her finger. Mariette laughed enjoying her friend's alarm. 'You saw me empty it. You know it's not loaded.'

'Didn't your father tell you never to play with guns', Sabine muttered angrily as she pulled herself to her feet, simultaneously taking care to keep out of any possible lines of fire should the weapon unexpectedly discharge.

Mariette, at last more serious, put the gun down.

'I want you to take this somewhere for me.'

'You're mad. I'm not taking that thing anywhere.'

'Sabine, listen to me. You want to make a difference don't you? You want to do something?'

Sabine nodded, mesmerised by her friend's intensity.

'I've been recruited into a small resistance group here. I can't tell you more. Security. It's our first defence. I've got to get this gun to Saint-André-de-Double. It would be really suspicious for me to go there. But you. You deliver cheese to the village bar. I remember you telling me.'

Sabine nodded. After hard negotiation between her father and the Department of Food and Supplies, she had been allowed to maintain her deliveries of cheese to a number of local restaurants. 'But what's it for?'

Mariette dipped her eyes, refusing to meet her friend's gaze.

'I can't tell you that. But It's vital it gets there. '

Mariette met her eyes now. Staring into her soul.

'I wouldn't ask you otherwise.'

Now Sabine's eyes fell. She was unable to answer.

Germany could not win the war. Not now they had attacked Russia. At least that's what everyone said. But shouldn't she do something? Didn't she hate how Papa refused to act? If she did nothing now wasn't she just like him? But fighting. She'd always been taught that was the man's role. Except she resented that too. She wanted her own place in the world. The right to make decisions. Her eyes lifted, meeting Mariette's full gaze. She reached out and took the gun. This time she did not flinch at the touch of cold steel. She rubbed her thumb over the cylinder. *Click, click, click* went the metal as it revolved. She felt power, strength, and confidence flood through her being. For the first time in her life she was in command, not bobbing and floating and swirling, directionless as a piece of flotsam on the Beauronne as it twisted and turned on its way from Saint-Antoine-de-Double to Mussidan, where it joined the Isle.

France would win the war. The tide was turning, and she could be part of the forces that made it happen. Sabine noticed then the iciness in her friends' eyes. A coldness swept through her own body as new questions invaded her thoughts. How would they be changed? How far down this road would they have travelled by the time they reached the end? Would they have gone too far to ever go back? She knew she could never recapture the innocence she'd once possessed before the war began.

And what of her friend? Mariette frightened her. She burned like a zealot, with an intensity that was both terrifying and inspiring. She surely could never return to the meek creature she'd been before the war. Like Sabine's cheese could never again become milk. They could never return to their former lives or their former selves.

~

It was with nerves dancing and singing that Sabine set off for home. Her handbag, slung casually over her shoulder, sagged under the weight of the gun and ammunition it now held. The queue for the grocer was shorter now, and the baker was closed. The game of boules in the square was continuing. A few refugee children, barefoot with heads shaved, played marbles on the kerbside. No one paid any attention to her. Except the boy delivering the papers who whistled at her as she cycled past.

Couldn't they all see she was carrying a gun? Couldn't they tell she was different? A sense of excitement swept over her and, energised, she cycled faster, speeding across the bridge over the Isle and into the village of Saint-Front-de-Pradoux. Past the bakery and the hairdresser. She took the fork towards Saint-Antoine- de-Double. Soon she would be home. And no one had paid any attention to her. Mariette had been right. This was easy.

When she reached the *fermette*, *Maman* was gathering tomatoes from the potager. Papa and Tomas were loading hay onto the cart. They moved with urgency, as Papa was concerned that the gathering clouds signalled rain. Josette peered around the barrels in the *chai*, in search of the nest of a rogue hen. Sabine put her bicycle away and entered the cottage. Usually, she would have hung her handbag in the *chai* with her coat and boots, but she could hardly leave it there with its lethal contents. Surreptitiously she slipped past *Maman*, the bag tucked hidden under her arm, and awkwardly climbed to the attic room she shared with her sister. If she slipped her package under her bed, there would be no risk of anyone finding it.

Night began to fall and the family gathered for their evening meal. While the others intently discussed Josette's discovery of a nest of some dozen eggs, Sabine's thoughts were too distant to join the conversation. Even her family hadn't noticed she was different now. They had no idea that she'd carried a weapon that was vital for an impending Resistance operation, or that even now the deadly armament was lying upstairs on the knot holed floor of the bedroom she shared with her sister.

That night she could barely sleep. She lay in her bed, staring through the tiny arched Perigourdine window, at the only permissible light in their blacked-out world, the stars scattered over the night sky. She, Sabine, whom nobody thought capable of anything but making goats cheese, had been recruited into the French Resistance. What was more, the adventure had only just begun.

Chapter 3

THE FOREST

The road seemed steeper today. The rain, which had amounted to only a few droplets when Sabine left on her errand, grew to a steady drizzle. She would have turned her bicycle round and returned home had it not been for the urgency of her delivery. The gun had to be at the café in Saint-André before midday.

Giving up the struggle as the gradient of the road increased, she climbed down from the bicycle and continued her journey, pushing her burden up the hill as quickly as she could manage. She still had a couple of kilometers to go before she reached her destination.

Hearing a crunch of branches she stopped and turned to look behind her. The empty road formed a twisting tunnel beneath the canopy of leaves as it wound its way down the hill. She roved her gaze over the dense forest, searching for a source of the noise. It could have been a deer surprised by her sudden appearance, but she didn't think so.

Crunch.

There it was again, amongst the trees. Level with her. Fear crept through her veins and she became conscious of how very alone she was. She hadn't told anyone where she was going. The gun, now hidden beneath her delivery of neatly packaged cheeses, became a source of alarm. What if she was searched? What if someone tried to take the weapon from her?

Again she scanned the forest in the direction of the noise. Was someone there? She couldn't risk losing the revolver. This was her first mission. She wasn't going to fail. But dare she use it? The elation she'd experienced when she'd set out on her adventure vanished. Why hadn't she been satisfied with snapping matches into a V and tossing them down onto the pavement?

Trembling she addressed the forest. 'Who's there?' .

No answer. Even the birds were silent.

She faced forward and began once more to push her bicycle up the hill. But faster this time. As quickly as she could without actually breaking into a run. Soon she would reach the top, then the road dipped downward and she'd be able to put some distance between herself and whatever was there, hidden in the forest.

'Wait!'

She didn't. She ran.

Laughter chased her.

Then footsteps fell behind her on the road. *Thud, thud, thud.* How many were there? She couldn't tell. More than one. She daren't look round.

Powered by an adrenaline rush, she surged forward. Not far now. If only she could make the brow of the hill.

Nearly there.

Strong fingers gripped her arm. She struggled, but couldn't free herself without letting go of the bicycle. She was pulled round, to find herself looking into the face of a young man.

'We just want directions. Don't be frightened.'

She stopped, shaking her arm in his grip. 'Then let me go.'

His hold on her loosened, Sabine looked past him at his companions.

Four of them. All about her own age.

The first bent down in a theatrical bow, delighted to meet you.'

The others followed suit.

Sabine smiled. Infected by their youthful high spirits, she no longer felt threatened by them. Though she was conscious of her damp straggled hair, and of them looking boldly at her body.

They were handsome, vibrant, and full of energy. And they appeared to vie with each other for her attention.

The first one said 'let us introduce ourselves. The names we're using —our *noms de guerre*— are the animals of the forest. That's where we hide until we're ready to attack'. They circled round her, one stepping forward then another. She could not help laughing.

'Hérisson', he bowed again, 'because I seem cute and harmless.'

Sabine looked him over. More thoroughly this time. He was right. The name seemed to fit him. Warm brown eyes instilled trust. And with his dark unruly hair, wearing a brown leather jacket, and carrying a light backpack of the same colour, he could merge into the forest as easily as a hedgehog.

'But I have spines'. Hérisson flashed a stiletto knife he took from his jacket. She gasped as he flicked the blade before her. 'You, though, have nothing to fear...unless you are a traitor.' For these last few words, his voice sharpened and his eyes turned cold. Sabine shuddered.

Loup leapt forward, not to be outdone

'I am named for the wolf, strong and powerful.'

Hérisson jumped-in. 'No, we call him that because he has little girls for dinner.'

Loup gave a knowing grin. 'No, I only eat grown women.' His eyes wandered appraisingly over her body as if he had some authority over her. Sabine blushed. She was not accustomed to such directness.

A third youth came forward, announcing himself proudly. 'Cerf. Because I run like a deer.' Sabine laughed, relieved by the interruption to Loup's undressing of her. For this one too, the name seemed appropriate. His face was long and narrow with wide brown eyes. He even looked like a deer. Wiry, yet strong. No doubting his claim of speed was justified.

The last of the four stepped forward. 'Renard, because I hunt at night.'

'No', the other three chorused, 'Pinot, because of the amount of wine he drinks.' They all laughed again, and Sabine laughed with them.

Loup approached her bicycle and flipped open the lid of her basket. Then bent down sniffing the cheeses. 'Mmm, smells good.'

'Hey, stop that', Sabine scolded, firmly replacing the lid over the basket. In spite of their hints that they were members of the Resistance, the lads seemed harmless enough, but she couldn't risk her parcel falling into the wrong hands.

'Well, it's very nice to meet you all, but I have work to do.'

Sabine continued on her way, but the youths fell in beside her. Hérisson pulled the bicycle from her hands and began pushing it for her.

'Where are you going?'

'To deliver these cheeses.'

She indicated the contents of her basket. Hérisson nodded.

"We want to join the Resistance."

Sabine pretended not to hear.

'We need help.'

'I don't know what you mean.'

'We know there are pockets of Resistance groups in the forest. We're going to join up. We won't accept Nazi rule. We want to be free.'

Sabine laughed again. This time, more derision than enjoyment.

'Why on earth do you think I can help? How do you know I'm not a traitor?'

'I feel it in my heart.' His eyes, deep and soulful, seemed to overflow with sincerity.

'How do I know you're not all spies for the Vichy government?" Sabine asked, pausing for a moment, and taking her bicycle back from Hérisson.

Hérisson laughed.

'Do we look like informers?'

The foursome stood together grinning at her in what she thought they imagined was a persuasive manner. They didn't look sly and shifty-as informers might. But neither did they look like genuine members of the Resistance. They're open, careless manner didn't in any way conform to the strict, cautious, and secret approach Mariette had lectured about only yesterday.

'Look, sorry, but I can't help you.'

'But you're from around here aren't you?'

'I am *Doublais*', she lifted her chin. There'd been Faures living at La Barde for hundreds of years. They were part of the Fôret-de-la-Double, and it was part of them. The *Doublais* heritage flowed through their veins, as vital a life source as their blood. An ancestry she was proud of.

'I'm no use to you. Do I look like a Resistance fighter?' She was conscious again of her dress and how it clung to her body, inviting their eyes to run over it. After a pause, Hérisson continued.

'No, of course not. But we've crossed the demarcation line to join. We must make contact with a group.'

'I really can't help.'

'But the Fôret-de-la-Double is known for sheltering the Resistance.'

Loup stepped forward, aiming a finger at her. 'You said yourself you're a local'. Turning to Horizon, 'She must know something'. His voice was raised now, and his gestures more irritated. Sabine felt uncomfortable, increasingly concerned for the gun in the basket. She really had to get on. Impatiently she shook her head.

'What do you know about the Forest? Nothing, I bet. Way, way back, in Napoleonic times this area was known as a refuge for beggars and thieves. For people who lived by their own laws. Because it was a swamp-land, full of mosquitoes and ridden with the ague. Only the toughest could survive here. The monks at the Abbey in Echourgnac drained it over the years and my forefathers cultivated the land and made their homes here. We have always lived by our own laws. Not the dictates from Paris, or Vichy. Every year, on the first of May, the *Foire de la Latière* is held here in the forest. The local people come in their thousands sell their goods. It actually started as a horse fair, where the thieves got together to sell or exchange the animals they'd stolen. Things don't change much around here. We still gather fruit, nuts, and firewood – even though it's prohibited. The Germans will never take over in this forest. We keep our own time here. Listen.' The bells from the church echoed down sounding the hour. French, not German, time.

'But that's why we've come here', Hérisson pleaded.

'You're not local', her contempt giving an edge to her words, 'Can you skin a rabbit? Trap a hare? Capture a pigeon. You'll never survive here. Go home, boys. To your mothers.'

She mounted her bicycle, intending to speed-off down the hill in as close as she could get to a dramatic exit, leaving these innocents behind her.

Hérisson moved in front of the bike, holding the handlebars. The intensity in his eyes drew hers, holding her gaze like a magnet.

'You have to help us. We've already risked our lives crossing the demarcation line. We're here to fight. We're ready to die for France.'

Gone was her bravado of only seconds earlier. Sabine gulped. The forest was suddenly silent. She didn't know what to do. She looked in turn from one to the other. Each seemed sincere. But could she trust them? If it was up to her alone, she wouldn't hesitate. But she wasn't alone. If even one of these youths was an informer, the wrong choice now could serve as a death warrant for herself and Mariette.

'Come with me.' She dismounted.

'I don't know anyone who can help you. Maybe you can ask in the village. I've a delivery for the restaurant; you can come with me.'

'Thank you', she could hear genuine gratitude in Hérisson's voice. The other lads, clearly invigorated by the prospect of help, walked alongside her.

Seeing the high spirits of her companions returned, Sabine tried to respond with the same light-heartedness to their outrageous flirting and competitiveness. Yet she also tried to hide the anxiety she felt at bringing her new acquaintances to what was supposed to be the meeting point for leaders of various local resistance groups. What if she was walking into a trap? Such thoughts battled for her attention as she rode slowly towards her destination while the lads jogged beside her.

Only too aware of her pounding heart, she chained her bicycle, then led the youths inside. A flood of warm air and the odour of garlic and rabbit from the stew of the day greeted her. The room was dimly lit with lanterns hanging from stone walls and overhead beams. Madame Barrat stood behind the bar, where an elderly man, his beret still on his head, sipping a Ricard, and taking an occasional drag on a cigarette as he read the newspaper. A few workers, seated at tables, were already tucking into their midday meal, glasses of a local red wine in their hands. Others, by the window, also drinking wine, were engrossed in an intense conversation in the local patois. Sabine caught mention of the best method of treating the Colorado Beetle with which they had recently been plagued.

Silence fell as Sabine and her companions entered behind her. It seemed to her they were standing like exhibits at a fair. Everyone in the room examined them with open curiosity. Sabine, in turn, studied them. Middle-aged men and younger boys. Weather- wrinkled faces. Impassive stares. Working clothes. Farmers. Foresters. Who was here to collect the gun? At least one of the men here must be a *Maquisard*. But which one? She had no way of knowing. They all looked like local farmers and foresters having their lunch. Nothing seemed in any way out of the ordinary. Sabine wondered for a moment if she had gone mad. Perhaps her fuddled brain had created a fictional world where she was the unlikely heroine. Perhaps there was no gun. No mission. Maybe she was just a goat girl delivering cheese.

'At last, Sabine.' Madame Barrat broke the silence. 'What kept you, girl?'

'Sorry, Madame, I have your order here.' She lifted the cover of her basket to display the neatly ordered rounds of cheese beneath.

'Thank you, my dear. Come through to the kitchen; you can dry yourself by the stove.' She gestured towards the kitchen.

Sabine followed her through the door behind the bar and into the kitchen where the delicious smelling stew was bubbling on the cast-iron stove. She was led into the press and began to lift the cheeses onto the stone shelves. They'd be stored until used for the *Perigourdine* goat's cheese salad for which Madame Barrat was particularly famous.

'Who are those lads?' Madame Barrat's voice, though low, conveyed urgency.

"I didn't know what to do. They stopped me on my way here. They told me they wanted to join the Resistance and that they'd been told to come to Saint-André-de-Double.'

'You haven't told them anything', Madame hissed.

'No, of course not, but they were boasting about joining the Resistance. I could hardly leave them on the road. Who knows who they might have spoken to?'

'Who knows, indeed? It was right to take them here, of course, child. You've done well. Now leave this in my hands. Have some soup before you leave. And your young friends, too, I think they'll be glad of a hot meal before the day's out.'

Sabine returned to the bar. The tense atmosphere had dissipated. Some of the customers had even began chatting to her newly acquired friends. Sabine noticed the landlady nod to one of the customers, a man in his thirties with a weather-beaten complexion, wearing a heavy coat. The landlady indicated a table next to him and invited Sabine and the lads to sit down.

'We've been offered a bowl of soup each', Sabine explained to the others. They sat down and Madame Barrat brought a carafe of heavy blood-red wine to the table together with a basket of thinly sliced home-made bread. Then she brought a terrine of soup from which they each served themselves. The heavy vegetable broth flavoured with garlic and rosemary was filling. They mopped their bowls with bread, then rinsed them with the wine, before lifting up their bowls to drink the residue, known locally as *chabriol*.

The lads', spirits, raised by the warmth of their surroundings and the delicious meal, began to talk about the Resistance again.

That made Sabine anxious. 'Shush, we don't know who might be listening.' They quietened their voices but Sabine became more uncomfortable. Mariette's lecture about secrecy burned in her consciousness. She didn't know everyone present and she couldn't risk attracting attention from unwanted sources. Rising from the table she said, deliberately loudly, 'It was nice to meet you all today. Goodbye.' As she opened the door to leave, she caught the landlady sending a glance to the man to whom she'd nodded. The man then shook his head in a movement so subtle it was almost imperceptible.

Sabine mounted her bicycle and was already racing down the hill by the time the youths had followed her outside the restaurant.

'What do you make of that?' Hérisson asked, as they watched the girl's fleeing back, coat flying wide, like wings, giving the impression that if she pedalled fast enough she would actually fly.

'Reckon you frightened her', Loup joked

'More likely you. She's very beautiful.'

'Too good for the likes of you', Pinot said thoughtfully. Hérisson glanced at him, Pinot rarely commented on anything at all, never mind women.

'Thought we were onto something.' Loup thumped his fist on the door post.

'Don't you ever think about anything else?'

'I didn't mean that. I thought she knew something about the Resistance. How we could contact them.'

'We'll never know. She's gone now.'

'What are we going to do now?'

'Well, our instructions were to come here. This must be it.' Hérisson strolled across to the blond stone church and then back to where the others were standing at the steps to the door to the restaurant. 'There's nothing here except the restaurant and the church. This place hardly merits being called a village. I'll go in and ask the lady that gave us the meal if she knows Pete.'

Hérisson went back inside and approached the bar. Carefully he whispered. 'We're looking for Pete.' The landlady stood still for a moment, forehead wrinkled as if trying to connect the name with a person. She shook her head. 'There's no Pete here. Only me. I'm sorry, you must have made a mistake.' She turned her back and went over to clear the table used by one of the groups that had just left.

Hérisson followed her. 'But you must know him. I was told to come here.'

Madame Barrat turned and asked the remaining customers. 'Do any of you know Pete?' Hérisson felt the curious gaze of the remaining men. The silence that filled the room was as tangible as a heavy winter fog. No-one responded to the question. Madame Barrat shrugged. 'There you are, *Monsieur*. He's not known here. Maybe if you try Saint-Michel-de-Double.'

Hérisson stood staring around him. The driver had been so sure with his instructions. He had been told to come here. To this village. This was their one chance. Their only contact. 'But you must', Hérisson's voice sounded shriller. He had to make the woman understand. One of the men stood up. A commanding fellow, despite his faded patched jacket. As if it was a signal to the others, the remaining occupants of the bar also stood up. The first man to stand up, his features set in a heavy frown, approached Hérisson. There was a slow menace to his step, and his hands clenched into a fist.

'This bar is closing. It's time for you to leave.' The woman nodded. Hérisson could feel the rising tension in the room. The stony silence and cold stares spoke more clearly than words. He had to leave. Hérisson nodded and turned, stepping out into the sunshine.

His friends gathered round.

'Maybe we should try to go back home.'

'We can't. Once we crossed the demarcation line there was no going back.'

'Forward only, men.'

'But which direction?'

'"We'll have to find somewhere to sleep for tonight.'

The group stood on the steps outside the restaurant, which, together with the church, was situated at the highest point in the village. To the north the lane twisted past a few houses then wandered down into the forest as did the roads to the south and west. Around them in every direction the landscape was covered in a blanket of trees. Somewhere, hidden in that green expanse of thousands of hectares, were the fighting forces of the Free French. The army they had risked their lives to join. The army they were going to have to find if they were to realise their commitment to fight for France.

Hérisson pulled a set of binoculars from his bag and began to survey the landscape. The others wandered around the church and the nearby lanes hunting for some clue as to the location of the mysterious army to which they had sworn allegiance.

Hérisson pointed to the tower of the church. 'If we can get up there, we'll be able to see for kilometers.'

He urged them, 'Come on', as he climbed up the steps leading to the weather-worn oak door with its centuries-old studs. It creaked as he pushed it open and his comrades followed him inside. The coolness of the church interior was a welcome relief from the now hot summer sun. They milled about by the door, on pave-stones that had cracked and worn over the centuries. A gigantic wooden ladder, to the right of the door, sloped up from the pave-stones to a trapdoor set in the ceiling. Hérisson pointed to it. 'That must provide access to the tower.'

'We should ask permission', Pinot insisted, stepping towards the altar, where presumably the priest might be engaged. Hérisson, already well up the ladder, looked down, shaking his head. 'There's no time, and what would we say anyway?' Loup shrugged and followed after him. Hérisson, reached the trapdoor and heaved it open. He climbed onto the gallery surrounding the bell, followed by Loup, then Cerf, whilst Pinot played an anxious lookout at the foot of the steps.

The view from the tower was breath-taking, especially after their experience in the forest, which had been akin to wandering through a vast green maze. Now they stood on the mountain top experiencing panoramic views of their surroundings.

Hérisson studied the village and the lands beyond, with clearer perspective. He knew the garrison town of Riberac lay to the north, and that the village of Saint-Michel-de-Double lay to the south. He could see, or perhaps he imagined, the church steeples of Echour-gnac to the west and Saint-Germain-de-Salembre to the east, winking through the tangle of trees. Loup and Cerf joined him, scouring the landscape for a clue that would lead them to their destination.

Hérisson nudged Loup. 'Here', he passed the binoculars and pointed into the distance. 'What's that? I think it's a coil of smoke'.

'Yes, I can see it. Maybe it's a camp', Loup lowered the binoculars.

'How far, do you think?'

'Maybe four kilometers as the crow flies. There's a track down there. It forks west, but It's impossible to judge the distance using that.'

'We won't be able to orient towards it once we lose the height of the village', Cerf added.

'Don't worry'. Loup produced a compass. 'I can take a bearing. If we follow that track then head west when it forks, we should find it.'

CLANG.

Reverberations echoed around the tower, numbing their ears. Hérisson watched in horror as Cerf struggled to right himself after toppling against the old church bell. The clamour, occurring outside traditional hours for bell-ringing, would serve as an alarm for the village.

'Let's get out of here', Hérisson yelled. The lads shimmied down the ladder, joining a frightened Pinot at the bottom. A priest emerged from the sacristy. Unhindered even by his cumbersome attire, and moving with considerable speed for his age, he shook his fist and yelled, '*Arretez, arretez!*'

Whether the flush on his cheeks was due to uncanonical use of the communion wine or anger, they did not wait to find out. The lads fled. The priest, between pants for breath, stood at the doorway yelling for help. Thankfully the customers from the café seemed to have dispersed. Any occupants of the village who might have come to their *curé*'s aid had either returned to work or were too heavily invested in their afternoon *sieste* to heed the cries of alarm. The lads ran from the village, following the lane they had picked out from their viewpoint. Their pace slowed to a steady walk once it became clear they weren't being pursued.

Confident they were finally on the right track, they marched along their chosen route with renewed vigour, singing the *Internationale*. Soon they would be with a unit which would train and arm them for the battle for freedom that lay ahead.

Chapter 4

LA BARDE, SAINT-ANTOINE-DE-DOUBLE

Sabine smiled as she slipped on the *sabbots*. Before, she had hated the moment when her toes pressed against the unforgiving wood. The touch that signalled her acceptance that she was a *paysanne*. A peasant, dismissed so readily before the war as unworthy of notice by the Parisiens she aspired to emulate. The war, and the food shortages which accompanied it, had brought a renewed respect for the farmers and food producers in rural areas, as townsfolk flocked to the countryside in search of vital supplies no longer accessible in the cities.

Now the *sabbots* represented something different for Sabine. They, like all the tasks she had found so tedious before, scrubbing the table where she prepared the rounds of cheese, washing the muslin in which she wrapped her produce, mucking out the stalls where she milked the goats, were part of her disguise. Who would ever believe that the simple farm girl with the basket of goats' cheese was in fact a member of the Resistance? That concealed about her person was a message of vital importance to the nation. She walked with renewed energy and confidence towards the goat shed. She was a secret agent. A spy.

It wasn't only excitement over her new found profession that caused every nerve in Sabine's body to tingle. The meeting with the young men had been fun. It seemed like a lifetime since she had laughed and joked like that with people of her own age. She wondered if they'd been accepted into one of the Resistance camps. She hoped she'd see them again.

Once the goats had been milked, Sabine joined her mother in the kitchen, where the final preparations for the evening meal were underway. They decided to eat outside under the shade of the teilleul tree, where a light breeze rustled the leaves and brought relief from the heavy humid air. The family gathered round the trestle table, which was set there during the summer months. They sat and broke bread together, beneath the protective canopy of the great tree with grasshoppers chirping and Clemantine the cow contentedly chewing her cud as she grazed in the shade of the oak trees lining her paddock.

Papa passed round a *saucisson*, one of those made by Maman in springtime, as she did every year when they killed the pig. They chewed the salty meat, accompanied with heavy homemade bread. Afterwards they had cheese, served with lettuce from their potager, and Papa allowed them each a ration of their home-made wine, watered down according to their age. Then he ordered the tasks for the following day. As she was responsible for the goats and cheese-making, Sabine was the most autonomous of the family. Josette, not yet accorded such privileges, was to help with the hay. Seeing her sister scowl, Sabine was delighted, though she tried to disguise her pleasure. It often seemed to her that her sister was usually given the lightest tasks when the jobs on the farm were apportioned. The raking of hay and forming it into sheaves was hard work, especially when the weather was hot, as it promised to be tomorrow. Her brother, accorded the same work, grinned with pleasure. For him it was another step further along the route to adulthood. Since he could walk he had aspired to emulate his father. Now nearly fifteen, Tomas had the beginnings of a moustache and a deepening voice, and he seemed to try harder than ever to match the work their father did on the farm.

Maman would probably occupy herself with making bread in the early morning and then help in the field afterwards. Only she, Sabine, would be sheltered from the sun as she worked in the *chai* which was always cool.

As the sun slipped from the sky and the fragrance of honeysuckle permeated through the night air, the family sat sipping wine and gazing over the fields and the forest that had barely changed in hundreds of years. It was easy to forget that Montpon-Menesterol lay less than twenty kilometers away, the closest control point on the demarcation line which stretched from the Basses-Pyrenees in the South to Gex in the north, dividing France in two. On the one side, the *Zone Occupé,* which was occupied by German soldiers, and on the other, the *Zone Libre* or Free Zone where Sabine's family lived. Whilst the government, in Vichy, claimed to administer the whole of France, the Resistance, of which she was now a part, believed that the Vichy government, headed by Marshal Petain, operated as a puppet state for the Nazis and was every bit as evil as the occupiers.

She longed to go inside and turn on the treasured radio, so that she could listen to the broadcasts from London. General de Gaulle, leader of the Free French Forces, transmitted every night. Hidden amongst the messages were coded intelligence briefs for the Resistance. Messages about weapons drops and the arrival of secret agents. Her whole being trembled with impatience. But she couldn't listen to the broadcast. Her father would never permit it. He viewed any attack on Petain as a personal attack on himself. Papa had served under Petain in the trenches of the Great War, at Verdun. He had been awarded a *Legion d'Honour* for his services. A fact which the family was never allowed to forget. The medal took pride of place on the mantelpiece in the kitchen. While *Maman* polished the brasses every Saturday evening, including the inkwell fashioned after a barrel with a cat on top, and kettle that had never boiled so much as one cup of coffee, Papa, positioned in his chair by the fireplace, polished his medal with reverence. 'The Marshal has done what is best for France', he had insisted when news of the armistice had been announced. His voice had trembled and she was sure there had been tears in his eyes as he continued, 'We must accept the situation.'

On occasions when his was tongue was loosened by wine or some of the homemade *eau de vie* which their mother excelled at making, he would argue that the occupation was better than the alternative. Thousands of dead in trenches. Rats crawling over their bodies. When he spoke like that, Sabine became frightened. His eyes would fill with horror and his hands would tremble. His body seemed to shrivel and shrink before her eyes. He was no longer her father, the man who ruled his kingdom with iron will and meticulous order. Instead, he became a timid shadow, who muttered in a voice she did not recognise, and insisted that young men's lives mustn't be wasted. Then Papa would look at Tomas, fear in his eyes, and shake his head.

Sabine had become increasingly frustrated by what she considered her father's blind insistence that their patriotic duty to France was to trust their government and wait. Even when she challenged him. What about the prisoners of war? What about the rounding up of Communists and Jews that were rumoured to take place in the Occupied Zone? What was happening outside their *fermette*, their private kingdom? Didn't he realise that although they were in the Free Zone, customs control points were being established in Mussidan and Beaupouyet. Even though no letters were permitted to cross from one zone to the other and anyone crossing the border without a pass could be imprisoned, that didn't stop the flow of information. Atrocities were happening on their doorstep.

When challenged, Papa would mutter Nazi propaganda in a voice she didn't recognise. Jews? Hadn't their greed caused the Depression? Gypsies? Weren't they better off now? And the Communists? Weren't they more dangerous than the Nazis? No matter how much she tried to persuade her father that his views were wrong, he was intransigent, and would only repeat, unquestioningly, the propaganda they were spoon-fed through the German-controlled media. Sometimes, when his hands trembled and his voice wavered, Sabine wondered if he accepted the situation because he could not stomach the alternative. *Maman* appeared to have no view whatever, acceding as always to her husband's opinions. Tomas, of course, accepted their father's dictates without question, and Josette was not one to concern herself with politics.

So as the sun dipped below the trees and darkness fell, Papa outlined the tasks Sabine and her siblings were expected to perform. Sabine nodded from time to time. She was not listening. She was no longer someone who cheered silently each times news of an act of Resistance filtered through the gossip of her community. Now she was one of the people making things happen. Her thoughts were of her next meaningful task and the adventurous life she had embarked upon.

Chapter 5

THE FOREST

Daylight melted away. The forest began to assume a more sinister air as, shadows innocent in daytime, assumed a more menacing appearance when thrown by a clouded moon. Hérisson experienced shooting pains through his ankle with each footfall. His shoulders ached where the straps of his backpack rubbed against his shirt, and worst of all his stomach grumbled with unrelenting pangs of hunger.

Loup spoke with an edge of exasperation, 'We'll have to find somewhere to kip for the night. We obviously aren't going to find anyone now.'

The others agreed, and they began to search for a suitable place to set up camp.

'We'd better hide ourselves from view from the track, just in case' Loup urged. 'Here, this way.'

He'd spotted a narrow pathway branching off the main track. The four lads agreed it was best to get out of sight, so they decided to follow the path. Brambles and thorns dragged at their clothing as if deliberately trying to impede their progress. Hérisson started at an owl hoot. Loup grabbed both Hérisson's and Cerf's arms, pulling them to a halt as they heard a rustling sound. In a voice not above a hiss, he warned, 'Something's coming this way, and fast.' Hérisson felt his heart pounding in overtime as the crunching of branches became louder and closer. In a blur of leaves and upturned earth, a wild boar burst across the clearing in front of them. Hérisson's breath stopped in his throat as the fierce tusks swivelled towards him. The animal's powerful shoulders made it look even more menacing. Hérisson ducked behind the broad trunk of an aged oak, his companions following rapidly.

'What the hell?' gasped Loup.

Pinot stood frozen, white-faced in the moonlight.

'I can't believe how big it is.' Said through chattering teeth.

'What if it charges?'

Hérisson did his best to sound the experienced hunter. 'They don't, unless threatened.'

The beast sniffed the air, then, losing interest in them, trotted off into the forest.

Hérisson emerged from his hiding place. 'Wh-ew, that was close. I was sure it was going to charge.' Loup laughed, but nervously. The wild boar's sudden appearance and departure was unsettling. Despite their bravado, the animal had made them all very conscious of how ill-equipped they were for their surroundings.

'Let's get a fire lit, and have something to eat. We'll feel better. Then we can make plans for tomorrow.'

Pinot, the self-appointed cook, managed to light a fire and was soon able to produce a pot of ersatz coffee made from the mix of ground walnut and acorns he had brought. They were so hungry and thirsty it even tasted good!

They sated their hunger with rations of bread and sliced *saucisson*.

'How far d'you reckon we've walked in the last few days?' groaned Pinot, examining his blistered feet.

Cerf answered him, after a fashion. 'However far, we're completely lost'.

Loup tried to reassure the others. 'No, we have the compass. Even if I've miscalculated the route, we can easily find a village by the church spires and reorient ourselves.'

Hérisson spread out their map and pointed to an area to the north-west of Saint- André-de-Double. 'I believe we're here, and the smoke we saw from the tower is here. We should arrive tomorrow in the morning, if we set off early.'

'What if we don't find anyone?' Pinot moaned.

'We will', Hérisson sounded confident. 'This whole area is a base of the Resistance. We're bound to come across one group or another sooner or later.'

'I don't know', Pinot worried. 'What if they find us, before we find them?' He looked defeated. Cerf cut in, 'It's obviously not as easy as we'd thought to join up. I'm sure that girl knew something. She must. She lives here. And she wouldn't help us. Our food won't last for more than another day. If we don't find a unit to join tomorrow, we'll have to give up.'

Hérisson jumped to his feet and glared at his companions, banging a fist into the palm of his hand. 'We can't. We won't.'

Chapter 6

MUSSIDAN

The girls embraced. Eyes glittering with excitement, Sabine recounted her journey with the gun and its safe transfer to Madame Barrat. 'Do you know what it was for?'

'No, of course not.' Mariette's tone indicating she considered the question exposed her friend as an amateur. 'We each know the minimum possible. It's the safest way to protect the cell. For the moment you'll receive all your orders from me. I'll be your only contact. That way, if you're captured and tortured, you'll only be able to betray me.' Sabine squeezed her friend's hand. Although Mariette whispered in low urgent tones, the risk in their sleepy corner of Dordogne seemed imaginary. 'Listen, this will be your next mission.'

Exuding excitement, Mariette explained they'd be carrying propaganda leaflets to various drop boxes for onward distribution. 'It's important work – the only way to keep hope alive.' Sabine nodded. Incorporation into Mariette's mysterious family of Resisters, even if she could never know who they were, had given her a sense of belonging.

As the war progressed, she'd felt increasingly isolated from her family. Papa's unquestioning loyalty to the Marshal had become increasingly difficult to stomach as the plundering of France intensified. He, like the others in her family, chose not to see what happened around them, the un-mourned dead from the initial fighting, the trainloads of wheat, livestock and textiles dispatched to Germany. The cement and chalk sent from Saint Astier to Bordeaux. She'd felt the replacement of '*Liberté, Égalité, Fraternité*' by the meaningless 'Family, Work, Homeland', had been a stab to the very heart of the French soul. Those principles of Liberty, Equality and Fraternity had been fought for and won when the peasants of France had risen up and rebelled against a repressive aristocracy. Privileges of birth, carried down through generations for centuries, had been swept away in a few bloody months. After the revolution, the principles of Liberty, Equality, and Fraternity had been written into the French Constitution to protect those who came afterwards. These fundamental beliefs flowed through the life-blood of any French patriot.

As Sabine slipped into the kitchen and viewed her father crouched in his armchair by the fire, intently rolling a cigarette from the potent tobacco he now grew himself, she felt both shame and pride. Shame that the man whose form used to fill the doorway to their house did not have the strength to resist the dark grip of Nazism, which swirled around them like the dank swamplands that had once covered the region. Pride that she was now a member of the secret army which had sworn to liberate France. She was determined to rise to the challenge. Nothing and no one would stand in the way of what destiny had prepared for her. Now she too was a soldier, as her father had once been. She would show them all.

Chapter 7

THE FOREST

The lads broke camp with the dawn and continued their journey through the forest. Shortly before midday, by the shores of a lake, they discovered a ring of stones surrounding a small mound of fresh ashes. The ashes were recent. But they found no indication of who had set the fire. Pinot pointed to a number of recently felled trees and grumbled that the fire was more likely to have been made by foresters.

Loup was sceptical. 'Would members of the Resistance leave a trace like this?'

Despite his friends' objections, Hérisson was convinced they'd located the remains of one of the camps used by units of the Resistance they were so desperately seeking. They ate another meal of sliced sausage and bread, the bread now so hard they had to dip it into the water before they could chew it.

'What now?' Pinot asked, wiping his hands.

In spite of his outward show of certainty, Hérisson was worried – a concern he dared not show. He'd persuaded his friends to embark on this journey with him. As each day passed, he was forced to consider how ill-prepared and naïve his plan had been. Yet he wouldn't contemplate abandoning their mission. He sensed with every nerve in his body that they were close. He could almost smell the *Maquisards* they were searching for. The air of this forest, despite it's proximity to the Occupied Zone, throbbed with Resistance. With power. With strength.

The four comrades studied the map again, regretting they no longer had the advantage of elevation to plan a route. The dense forest was a curtain that hid everything. At this level, they had no prospect of seeing anything that might indicate human activity. Hérisson studied the map again. Because of the lake, their location was relatively easy to pinpoint. He pondered the surrounding terrain. If he planned to hide in the forest, where would he go? His finger hovered over the map, as he were a water diviner with a hazel branch. He circled his finger around their immediate vicinity, finally settling on one of the most isolated locations.

'We'll head there. On our way, we'll keep alert for any signs of the Resistance.'

Loup peered over Hérisson's shoulder at the map. 'We should make it in the next couple of hours if we keep moving.'

By nightfall, after another day of fruitless hiking, the group silently made camp. Their supplies were almost exhausted; they had blistered feet and plummeting morale.

The four lads huddled round the embers of their fire, in the growing darkness. Loup passed around cigarettes.

'I think we should go back to Saint-André-de-Double', he argued. 'I'm certain that something was going on there.'

Hérisson dismissed this. 'I feel the answer's here, and we're close.'

Cerf, eyes nervously darting between Hérisson and Loup, muttered, 'Yeah, let's go back to that restaurant.'

Pinot yawned and stretched out his arms. 'll I want is a glass of wine and a good night's sleep.'

Chapter 8

LA BARDE, SAINT-ANTOINE-DE-DOUBLE

Sabine carefully wrapped the fresh cheeses in soft muslin. Then placed them in neat lines on the stone shelves of the press, beside those she had made the previous day. She was so accustomed to the pungent odour, she no longer noticed it. Satisfied with the quality of her produce, Sabine brushed down her apron and, taking a deep breath, began walking towards the cottage.

As usual, her father was still sitting by the fireside, nothing to indicate that he had moved since the last time she'd seen him. *Maman* had joined him on the opposite side of the hearth. Between them a cauldron hung above the hearth with flames licking around its base. The welcoming odour of pigeon stew permeated through the kitchen. Sabine felt her stomach rumble, more in expectant satisfaction than angry hunger. *Maman* looked up. Before she could ask, Sabine confirmed the cheeses were made and all was well. Her mother smiled, pleased with her daughter's mastery of this most domestic of tasks. How satisfied it made Sabine feel. Before, she had felt stifled by the life that was expected of her. Marriage, children, gentle subservience to her husband's wishes and desires. She had secretly longed for the day when she could leave the farm and experience something other than the rural life she knew, which so often felt as if it were drowning her. The catalogues from Paris, which arrived by train at the beginning of each season, had been, for her, as sacred as her parent's bible. She and her friends had copied the latest fashions from Paris, emulated the appearance of the models in the magazines, living, in their imaginations, the exciting existence for which they longed. The war had robbed them of those dreams, but a chance meeting with Mariette had taken Sabine into an exciting new world. It was far from the one she'd hungered for, that of a socialite in Paris. Still the life of a spy was equally exciting and infinitely more dangerous.

So now when her mother checked with her about whether the cheeses were stored at the right temperature, she could smile meekly and conjure an appropriate response. 'Yes, they are maturing and will be ready soon.' Before, her whole being had rebelled and she'd responded in an angry growl, because it was a question that reinforced how trapped she was. Now her life as a cheese-maker was a necessary disguise. Her cover.

She was no longer a young girl, trapped in the countryside with no destiny other than to repeat the tedious life her mother knew. Now she was a girl who would form her own future. She was a rebel, with a purpose and a future of her own choosing. A true Resister.

Chapter 9

THE FOREST

Jabbing pain shot through Hérisson's foot, racing up his leg, through the fog of sleep, through unconsciousness, more insistent even than the aches and stiffness that seemed to accompany the nights he had spent outdoors.

He opened his eyes, trying, through his befuddled brain, to make sense of what was happening. He realised it was still very early, though whisps of light penetrated the canopy of leaves high above.

What had him more awake was click of a rife being cocked, and then fully so as a solid object made another contact with his foot, sending another sharp pain up his leg. Twisting away from his attacker, he moved to sit up.

'Hands above your head', he was instructed in a heavily accented voice.

He was staring down the barrel of a gun just centimeters from his face. His eyes followed the barrel to the impassive expression of a handsome but weathered face, framed with black hair swept back from the forehead. Looking sideways, he could see his friends were being woken in a similar fashion. The four were ordered to their feet and instructed to stand in the centre of the clearing. A ring of men formed around them, each armed and with their weapons pointed directly at the lads' chests.

The man who had disturbed Hérisson was clearly their leader. He waved his gun menacingly in front of him.

'What are you doing here?'

Hérisson didn't respond immediately – his mind was racing. Could he safely reveal their intention to join the Resistance? If these men were in any way associated with the *Boche*, that would serve as their death warrant.

Although their captors were not dressed in any kind of uniform, they were armed to the teeth. Each carried a rifle and wore a bandolier, full of ammunition. On their hips, each wore a hunting knife with lazorated blade. Their boots were well worn and resembled army footwear. They couldn't be Armistice soldiers or in any way associated with the Vichy police, could they?

'Carlos.' A man raced into their midst, clearly addressing the leader. A stream of foreign words followed, rapidly accompanied by gesturing and pointing of arms. The men began to move. Spanish. Hérisson experienced relief. They must have stumbled upon one of the groups of Spanish soldiers he'd heard about. Men who'd escaped the internment camps into which they'd been thrown after escaping to France from the struggle against Franco. Men who had pledged to fight Hitler until they could return to their homeland and get rid of their own dictator. Thankful for his Spanish grandmother, Hérisson struggled to pronounce the words she had so laboriously taught him. 'We want to join you', he stammered in Spanish.

Just for an instant, Carlos looked surprised. 'No time now', he muttered. With a few rapid hand signals, he directed his men, then signalled Hérisson and his friends to keep quiet and follow. The group, led by Carlos, crept through the forest in single file, crouching low. Once they reached a rocky incline, they crept behind hanging fronds of bracken and ivy, becoming invisible to all but the sharpest eyes. One of the men stood guard, peering downwards from their hiding place.

The sound of several men talking. Words drifted through the

forest, scattered pieces of conversation. From what Hérisson could discern, the men below were charcoal burners investigating the damage to their kiln after a recent storm. They planned the location of their next fire-pit unaware that a gun was trained upon them. Hérisson relaxed. There appeared to be no imminent danger. What's more, their captors, if Spanish, were likely to be Communists – the branch of the Resistance the lads had most wanted to join. Not as prisoners, admittedly, but at least they'd found what they were looking for.

Once the charcoal burners could no longer be heard, Carlos led the lads to another clearing, still under armed escort. He ordered them to stand in line, then walked up and down past them, his stance and bearing consistent with him being a professional soldier. He examined each one with a cold impassive gaze. Then he sighed and approached Hérisson. Speaking in heavily accented French he demanded again, 'Why are you here?'

'We want to join the Resistance'. Hérisson squared his shoulders.

The man laughed.

'Do you have any experience? Have any of you ever fired a gun?'

'No, But we want to fight.'

'You mean you want us to look after you.'

'No, of course not.' Hérisson retorted angrily.

'But you know nothing', Carlos said dismissively. Hérisson stared defiantly at the Spaniard, who took a cigarette from a case in his pocket, then placed the cigarette in his mouth, lit it, took a draw, and studied Hérisson coldly. He continued, 'You don't even know how to survive in the outdoors. Your camp was a disgrace. You didn't have a lookout. It was a piece of cake to capture you. You are boys wanting to play at being men.'

'We're here to fight', Hérisson insisted.

In a flash, Carlos grabbed him, twisted him round and held a knife at his throat while trapping his arms in a vice-like grip. Loup started towards Hérisson, reaching out to grab Carlos's arm but one of the other soldiers leapt forward and pulled him to the ground. Like lightening, he sat on Loup's chest, his legs pinning the lad's arms to the ground and holding a knife at his throat.

Carlos's laugh was derisive as Pinot and Cerf stood motionless. 'See what I mean'. Carlos tightened his grip on Hérisson. The other soldiers laughed.

'We're here to join you', Hérisson repeated defiantly.

'Can you keep your mouth shut when you have a knife at your throat? When the Nazis crush your balls and pull your fingernails out? When they slash your body with a whip with glass sewn into the tails?'

Carlos threw Hérisson to the ground so he was lying beside Loup.

'Go back home! We can't risk having you here.'

Hérisson struggled to his feet, eyes bulging with rage. 'We came here to fight.' Loup, who had been released, moved beside Hérisson, glaring at Carlos defiantly. Pinot and Cerf moved to support their friends. They were all in this together. The leader laughed as he surveyed the unit. 'We're communists here. You look like nice Catholic boys. Go find another group if you want to fight.'

'We're communists too. Here, look.' Hérisson fumbled amongst his jacket pockets, finally producing a grubby copy of the Communist Manifesto.

Carlos leafed through the tattered pages of Hérisson's worn booklet.

He looked up. His expression had changed. 'Well, we shall see. We shall see.'

Loup stepped forward, 'We're all communists. That's why we're here.' Cerf and Pinot nodded as if their lives depended on it.

Carlos paused. His gaze moving from one to the other. Finally he said, 'Okay. I am Carlos. You answer to me and me alone. We have no past here. If you reveal anything about yourselves or your background, I will cut off your balls myself. All you need to know about me is that I'm in charge. I'm going to let you stay for a few weeks. If you can't keep up or can't cope with the training, you are out, no questions. Here we train hard for an easy war. Understand.'

The friends nodded. The next step of their adventure had begun.

Chapter 10

LA BARDE, SAINT-ANTOINE-DE-DOUBLE

A creaking noise interrupted Sabine's thoughts as she wandered down the lane towards her home. She peered round the hawthorn hedge, once neatly trimmed, now overgrown. The shutters of Madame Dumas's house were open. Sabine stopped, wondering what could have prompted the return of their neighbour. The old lady had gone to live with her daughter in the village after her husband died several years before and the cottage had been shut up ever since.

A woman, very pretty, with hair so dark it was almost black, appeared at the window. *'Bonjour'*, she called, her smile wide. Sabine smiled in response and walked towards the stranger.

'Are you a relative of Madame Dumas?'

'No, we're from the north. I've arranged to rent the place until we're able to go home. Would you like a drink of lemonade? Come in.' Sabine agreed, curious to find out more about their new neighbour.

Inside, the cottage was as she remembered it. Constructed in typical Perigourdine style, the layout very similar to her own home. Traditional *colombage* made from local oak were planted in the ground at intervals of around half a meter. The space between was filled in some parts with wattle and in others with *bricos*. The narrow, local bricks had been lovingly laid out in intricate patterns of diagonals and arches. The main room of the house was the kitchen, with an imposing fireplace, where originally all the cooking was carried out, whether in a cauldron, on a spit, or by *fisele,* when a joint of ham, mutton, or wild boar was hung from a ring at the top of the fireplace. The meat then turned itself over the fire, fat dripping and sizzling onto the dancing flames. Like her own home, although the fire was still used for cooking and heating, there was also a wood-burning *cuisiniere.*

Sabine knew one doorway from this room led to the main bedroom and the other to the *chai* which ran behind the full length of the cottage. This area was reserved for winemaking and more serious food production. A ladder led to the attic, which was usually where the children slept. In Sabine's home, their father had constructed a staircase. As they had grown, he partitioned the attic to make a room for herself and Josette and another for Tomas.

The new neighbour, having introduced herself as Miriam, chatted in a friendly manner as she poured Sabine a drink of lemonade. 'It's not sweet, really' she said apologetically. Sabine shrugged. No one could make lemonade the way they used to, not with rationing. Miriam took off her apron and sat down. Sabine looked enviously at the woman's neat fitting dress. With its white collar and cuffs, and a neatly fitted waist, it was similar to a style she remembered from a magazine.

'Have you family in this area', she asked casually.

'Absolutely not.' Miriam laughed. 'We used to live in Moselle, but we left when the Germans annexed the area. We couldn't stay.' Sabine expected her new friend to explain that they were Jewish, but she didn't. Instead she fell into an awkward silence. Sabine felt embarrassed. Miriam did not look like the cartoons of Jews that appeared so regularly in the press. Two children appeared from the garden. 'Have you finished exploring?' Miriam asked them, pouring the youngsters a glass each of lemonade. "This is Isaac, and that's Sarah.'

Sabine grinned at the children who appeared to be twins. 'How old are you'.

'Ten and three-quarters', they answered in unison.

'You're welcome to come and visit us. We live in the *fermette* at the end of the track. My youngest brother isn't much older than you. He's going into his last year at *college*. He'll be glad to have other children nearby.'

Miriam seemed to appreciate the offer.

'Thank you, that'll help them when they start at *college*. Now off you go, both of you. And don't get up to any mischief.' Miriam sat down again after watching the children run out into the garden.

'We've never lived in the country before. I'd hoped to find somewhere in a town, but it was so difficult. . . there are so many refugees. I was lucky to learn about this place. Madame Dumas's son was delivering wood to the boarding house where we were staying and Isaac got chatting to him. I took it immediately of course. I thought it might be easier to find food.' Once she started talking, Miriam seemed to find it difficult to stop, as if Sabine's easy conversation had opened the floodgates to months of stored up fears and anxieties. Sabine began to notice the strain in her voice and the nervous way in which her new friend's eyes would twitch in first one direction, then another. How her fingers twisted over an elaborate golden ring.

'My husband was called-up into the army. I haven't had any news about him for months. He was at Dunkirk. Missing since then. I'm sure he's still alive, though.' She wrung her hands, and for a moment the brightness in her eyes was replaced with a look of abject desolation. "I'd feel it in my heart if he was dead. I'm sure of it. I'm hoping he got to England and wasn't one of the soldiers left on the beaches. . . to surrender to the Germans. I can't bear to think of him in a camp.' She looked sorrowfully at her ring as her fingers rubbed across it.

Feeling a little self-conscious, Sabine reached across the table and squeezed Miriam's hand.

'I'm sure you're right. He'll be home soon. My fiancé is in a prisoner-of-war camp. In Germany.'

'You understand then'. Tears began to form in Miriam's eyes. But

Sabine didn't think she understood at all. She was worried about René, of course she was. But those few hurried words, that moment she had said 'Yes' when she'd really wanted to say 'No', had trapped her in a situation from which she had no idea how to extricate herself. Agreeing that she understood Miriam's suffering was like telling a lie. But it would have seemed even more strange to Miriam if she heard from one of the neighbours, or Sabine's parents, that she had a *fiancé* in a German camp and hadn't mentioned it. Sabine knew only too well that Miriam would soon know the complete history, perhaps going back several generations, of all the other residents in their tiny hamlet. In such a close-knit community, where watching one's neighbours was considered an acceptable pastime, secrets were almost impossible to keep. Sabine resolved to deal with her situation. Tonight. She would write to René, tonight.

Miriam prattled on, completely unaware of Sabine's discomfort. 'We lived above our draper's shop in town. I've never lived in the country before. I should get some chickens, I suppose. At least we'd always have eggs. And I can plant some vegetables.' Then a rather shy, sideways glance towards her new acquaintance, 'would you be able to help me with some advice?'

'Of course', Sabine squeezed her hand.

'I can sew and make clothing, if you need anything like that done.'

'Thank you very much. I appreciate that. I'd better get back home, now. I have to make today's cheese. We keep goats.'

'Oh, how delicious. I'd love to see how you do that.'

' You're welcome to come and watch. Bring the children.'

As Sabine walked home, she rehearsed, as she'd done so many times since, the bitter memory of those few final moments with René at the train station in Mussidan. If only it hadn't been so public. She could have found the words to say a gentle 'no'. But with him kneeling before her, presenting the ring which had once been his grandmother's, fearing he was being sent to his death, she had whispered the only word she could. She had said 'Yes'. But when he had picked her up and twirled her in his arms, the leaden feeling in the pit of her stomach had told her, as loud as a wailing siren, that she'd given the wrong answer. Even as she stood waving as the train puffed out of the station, she'd been formulating the wording of the letter that would tell him the engagement was off. How many times since had she sat down to write it and had never been able to finish it? Black images of René fighting to protect her had forced her to put down the pen. *This can wait*, she'd thought. After all, there was no prospect of her meeting anyone else. All the young men had gone.

When she got home she didn't reply when her mother called. She ran up to her bedroom, took out the sheet of paper she'd been saving, and began to write. Except she knew there was no way of getting a letter to him. She rummaged about to find the regulation postcard René's mother had presented her with. She stared at the prepared sentences and the little boxes to be ticked to convey acceptable news to the imprisoned recipient. There wasn't a box for, 'the engagement's off. Sorry. It's not you, it's me.' Sabine flung the postcard down and lay sobbing on her bed.

Chapter 11

THE FOREST

The lads formed a row, shoulders pulled back so much they ached. Spines arched and stretched for maximum height. Arms rigid as fence posts by their sides. Carlos walked down the line issuing beige berets to each recruit.

'You are soldiers now', he barked. 'Your *noms de guerre* are the only names you have now. You have no past – only a future. The only family you have now is here, around you. The army. This unit is run with discipline and obeys the rules of war. Except for one.' Carlos paused, studying each one intently as he walked back down the line, as if searching for signs of weakness. 'We do not fight like gentleman.' He laughed. 'This is a guerrilla unit. Here, you'll learn to fight from the shadows.' He paused again, regarding his recruits one by one before continuing in a more menacing tone.

'To fight from the shadows, you must first learn to live in the shadows. Emerging only to strike and then to vanish. Like phantoms. Like snakes. Like the enemy's worst nightmare. Here, only the fittest survive. If you're not up to it, you need to get out now. While you still can.'

No one moved. Carlos nodded and might even have smiled before he continued his briefing in a more relaxed tone.

'To fight effectively we have basic needs which must be met. Food and shelter. For shelter, we have a series of safe houses, caves, and campsites, which we use in irregular rotation. But we're always searching for new suitable sites. Ideally, we never stay in one place for more than three nights. Five nights in one place is the absolute maximum. This is for our own security. The enemy must never know where we are. They must fear to set foot in the forest. Every shadow must seem dangerous to them.'

Carlos paused for a moment, allowing his words to hang in the air. 'These woods, although they appear isolated and empty, are populated by many other groups of Resistance fighters. Each has its own agenda. We fight for equality for all men.' Carlos paused. The men cheered. Hérisson felt his heart pump with pride. Equality. A goal worth fighting for. Worth dying for.

Carlos continued. 'The risk of betrayal cannot be underestimated. In addition to the other groups, the forest is home to refugees, hunters, gypsies, and travellers. Locals who supply food one day may betray us the next. We risk being infiltrated by informers. Anyone guilty of betraying us will be treated as a traitor and punished accordingly.' Carlos's voice grew so cold that Hérisson felt an icy chill run down his spine. Carlos's eyes locked on to his so intently he believed they were searching his soul for any sign of weakness. He nodded, as did his friends. He understood. The tension lifted and Carlos turned sweeping his arm to the area around them, a gesture suggesting it was his kingdom. 'Food is really only a problem during the harshest of the winter months. We're fortunate that the forest is full of meat that can be hunted. We can choose from rabbits and hares to deer and wild boar. And there are fruits, berries, nuts, and mushrooms in abundance. The lakes are replete with fish, and we need never be short of water. Once our basic needs have been met, we concentrate on the real work.'

Once more, Carlos paused and his eyes gleamed as he continued. 'This terrain is perfect for guerrilla warfare. We train and carry out reconnaissance missions. We liaise with other groups. One of our most important tasks is to gather weapons and ammunition.

As long as you're here you'll be under my command. Once you have achieved the fitness and discipline necessary for members of this unit, I can teach you the more important tasks.'

Carlos gestured the lads to gather round. They broke ranks and joined him. Carlos leaned forward. In a conspiratorial whisper he continued.

'You'll learn to construct bombs, to derail trains, and to blow up bridges. You'll learn how to throw grenades, fire guns, and kill with your bare hands. In short, men, you'll become soldiers.'

Hérisson felt the tingle of energy through his whole body. He'd found what he'd been searching for. Purpose, and if Carlos, was to be believed, soon he and his friends would have power. Power to help force the Nazis out of France. He resolved to be the best recruit. At last he'd found where he belonged. This would be his home, here with these men until France was free. Hérisson saluted. His friends followed suit. Loup, then Cerf, then Pinot, although Pinot's expression suggested he felt obliged to follow the example of the others. Carlos, clearly amused by their demonstration, said, 'Sit down. We are all equal here', and then, his tone becoming darker, 'as long as you remember it is my orders you follow.'

More relaxed, Carlos put down his rifle before continuing. 'Your new life begins today. You have no past. Only a future. You'll only be able to assume your former identities when the war is won.'

The four lads emerged from their briefing to be greeted by the other members of the brigade, some twenty men in all. They were shown the tent which they would share billeted and the latrine area by a fellow soldier answering to the unlikely name of 'Lola'. In broken French, he explained the works of the camp. Already hungry, the lads were relieved to see a large cauldron being placed above a fire. A man of similar age to Carlos was in the process of skinning a hare nearby. The man turned to regard them, showing them a tanned face marked by a livid scar down his left check. Hérisson was conscious of the man's appraising stare as they walked past, and of the deft way he handled the course knife in his blood-soaked hand. It was very apparent the four lads were being accepted for a trial period. Little imagination was required regarding their fate if they failed to make the grade. Hérisson whispered a silent 'thank you' to his Spanish grandmother for her insistence that he learn and use Spanish. If not for that, his and his friends' situation could already be very different.

That night, two of the regulars were posted to sentry duty. The hungry recruits took their place around the fire with their fellow *Maquisards*. Soon they were gulping down the soup of hare, beans, and potato. The evening was warm and as the sun slipped below the horizon, a waning moon appeared in the sky.

Around the campfire, faces were illuminated then shadowed by flickering flames, voices talked and dreamed. Although the men were careful to keep their backgrounds secret, it was clear that Carlos and his men were veterans of the Spanish Civil War. They had fled Spain only to be interned in France. Having escaped, they soon found themselves armed by sympathisers in the French army, who were anxious to find a use for the weapons in their possession when the armistice was signed. Carlos and his men had then resolved to fight for France. Once France was free, their brothers-in-arms would join with them to fight for the liberation of Spain. One by one the men spoke. Hours passed as they hypothesised and deliberated the socialist dream, as they imagined the world they would create once the Nazis had been defeated. France would be free first, then Spain, then all of Europe, and finally the world. All men equal. All men free.

Hérisson felt his heart swell. Never before in his life had he experienced such a profound feeling of belonging. He knew he'd come to the place where he would fulfill his destiny.

Chapter 12

LA BARDE, SAINT-ANTOINE-DE-DOUBLE, OCTOBER 1941

The chill winds of autumn transformed the leaves on the trees into a kaleidoscope of reds and golden browns. The vines turned a coppery yellow. Sabine wore fingerless, knitted gloves when she milked the goats, but it was so cold in the mornings that her hands became red and swollen with chilblains. One morning, early, she was disturbed by the coughing of a *gazogene* engine. She put down the churn of milk and cautiously opened the shed door. As soon as she saw the colourful vehicle puff and cough into the courtyard, she pulled off her apron and ran to greet their visitors. Monsieur Saint-Lô, a rotund gentleman, with twinkling green eyes, waved a calloused hand cheerfully as he descended from the vehicle. His cheeks and nose were as red as hers, although in his case the cause was more related to his drinking habits than the inclement weather.

Papa and *Maman* were already emerging from the cottage, *Grand-mere* and her aunt Delphine from their cottage, and other neighbours were gathering, following behind the vehicle to greet the new arrivals. *Monsieur* and Madame Saint-Lô's annual visit was a signal as reliable as the cranes passing overhead that Autumn was drawing to a close and soon winter would be upon them. The harvest had been gathered. Now it was time to make the brandy.

Sabine greeted the perpetually cheerful *Monsieur* Saint-Lô with a kiss on each cheek. He insisted on a further two, as he was originally from the Châtelleraut region where four kisses were traditional. At least that was his excuse. In Sabine's eyes, he had not aged since she was a child. Even his clothing didn't seem to have changed. He still wore a tweed jacket in subdued greens and browns with faded corduroy trousers. Madame Saint-Lô, a small wiry woman with an ageless face, appeared from where she must have been dozing in the passenger seat.

After everyone had welcomed their annual visitors, the serious business began. Each household stipulated their requirements. Monsieur Saint-Lô meticulously pencilled the orders in his notebook, whether it be to distill wine into brandy or another concoction. Madame Saume was the first. Tomas brought wood from their own store and a fire was lit. Within an hour, the century-old copper still was fired into action. And the first barrel of wine was rolled out, in preparation for the transformation into a spirit which would be at least ten times more potent. Sabine lingered, watching the process. It was a comforting ritual from her childhood. A sign that normality could return. That everything was not broken.

Monsieur Saint-Lô, observing her interest, puffed out his chest and began to explain the distilling process, his melodic voice and presence as captivating as the Gypsy troubadours who usually appeared in the spring. Sabine listened, as she did every year, never tiring of the performance.

'It's as much art as science', he explained , as he patted a hand on the copper of the boiler to gauge the temperature. 'The chemistry is simple. The wine is converted into steam, then cooled to form brandy. The reality of the process is more complex.'

He glanced at Sabine, ensuring she was still paying attention, before continuing in his strange Northern accent. 'It's the heat from the wood fire which causes the transformation. But you must heat it just enough, but not too much.' He shook his finger as he spoke. 'And you must make sure too, that enough wine is going in, but not too much.' To Sabine's amusement, Madame Saint-Lô by this time was carefully checking the pipe where liquid was already beginning to drip.

Monsieur Saint-Lô continued, determined to share the love for his trade. 'Even the weather can play a part. My family have been distillers for four generations. Brandy is unique because it is a continuous distillation. That means the wine has to enter the still continuously, and the brandy has to exit the still continuously as well. So it needs to be monitored continuously, twenty-four hours a day.'

Madame Saint-Lô, in continuous motion behind her husband, began to prepare further wood to stack on the fire. Sabine knew it would be *Monsieur* Saint-Lô who would monitor the pipes and stoke the fire through the night, warmed by the alcohol and the company of his customers. Meanwhile, his wife would sleep, ready to take over when dawn signalled the beginning of her shift.

'After distillation', *Monsieur* Saint-Lô continued, 'the taste depends on the oak barrel where it is stored. Some prefer flavours of prune, hazelnut, orange, or apricot. And, of course, the length of time the brandy is stored also plays a part. I recommend at least two years.' He paused, chuckling to himself before continuing. 'But I know not many people are that patient.' He winked. 'The brandy will continue to mature while it's in the barrel. Once it's bottled, the flavour stops developing.'

As usual, *Monsieur* Saint-Lô set up his tent next to their cottage and everyone set about preparing a communal meal. The arrival of the distiller and his wife was always an excellent excuse for a celebration and an opportunity for neighbours to put to bed any petty disagreements and irritations which may have arisen in the period since their last gathering. In the company of the jolly and charismatic Saint-Lô and his wife, it was impossible to let a grudge intrude on the evening.

Sabine ran to fetch Miriam and her children. The visit was an excellent opportunity for her to socialise with the other occupants of the hamlet and an opportunity for them all to try to forget their troubles for a few hours. By the time they returned, a trestle table had been set up in the courtyard and covered with white linen.

Each household produced their offerings for the impromptu communal feast. Soon the table groaned beneath plates of pigeon and grilled chestnuts, bottles of wine, baskets of homemade bread, and platters of neatly arranged cheese and sliced *saucisson*. Madame Boursin had even taken off her apron, which demonstrated the importance of the event. Madame Saint-Lô served a portion of their signature brandy as an aperitif to everyone. Then they all sat down to eat and exchange news.

The hours passed as they moved from one course to another. Even Miriam seemed to relax while her children ran around the camp fire leaping and jumping in the shadows of the flames like pagans celebrating an ancient festival. Sabine found herself relaxing too. It was easy to forget that such a gathering was prohibited, inno-cent though it was.

Monsieur Boursin fetched his accordion and began to play the Jean Gabin song *Quand on se Promene au bird de l'eau*. Madame Saint-Lô, who had an unusually husky voice, began to sing and soon everyone joined in. A few couples danced. Sabine, from her place opposite to the Saint-Lô couple, asked about the process of converting their vehicle so that it could be run on charcoal, and then cautiously began to ask about their travels. On their annual rounds from October to January they criss-crossed France in a pattern set generations before. Who knew what information they could relay?

Even though Saint-Lô had, like his still, imbibed a continuous flow of wine since taking his place at the table, Sabine wondered if his eyes had hardened and steeled when she enquired about his crossings of the demarcation line. She found it hard to believe that the gentle couple could support the *Boche*. Before she could reach a decision, she noticed Tomas stagger to his feet, gripping his throat. *Maman*, who was sitting beside him, began to slap his back while screaming to Papa for help. Tomas's choking became more extreme. His face had turned blue as he gasped for air. His frantic mother beat a regular tattoo on his back but it seemed to have no effect. Sabine raced towards Tomas, shoving aside the dancing couples, unaware of her brother's distress. Then she saw Miriam behind Tomas, gripping him round the stomach with such force he bent over. Something flew from his mouth and he took-in a huge breath. Miriam gingerly picked up the object. 'There. A pigeon bone. Your throat will be sore for a day or two, I expect.'

'Thank you'. *Maman* hugged her son, then Miriam. Papa shook her hand.

'Thank you, thank you. If there is anything we can do for you. I'll never forget this.'

'My mother was a nurse', Miriam explained modestly, embarrassed by the outpouring of gratitude.

Sabine was lost in admiration for her new friend. 'Thank you so much. You must show me how to do that.'

'Yes, of course, but another time. We must go home now. It's time to get the children to bed. They have school tomorrow.'

'*Bonne nuit*', Sabine called to the departing family. As Miriam walked away from the rest of them, holding each child by the hand, she seemed a very lonely figure. The remaining neighbours, who had not even noticed the drama with Tomas, continued dancing and singing. Unsettled by what she saw as the Saint-Lô's attitude to her casual questioning, Sabine did not rejoin them but positioned herself by the edge of the circle, watching the merriment.

She was becoming increasingly conscious of her distance from all of them. Her deliveries to the café in Saint-André, usually of messages, had become more frequent. While she had come to find it more routine than frightening, she could feel how much her beliefs widened the distance between herself and those around her. Little things, barely tangible, like how *Monsieur* and Madame Martin seemed to fall silent when she approached, although as a child she had run in and out of their home as if it were her own. Jean, whose father was a *gendarme,* no longer visited. When she asked if anyone had news of the gypsy family who usually arrived selling wicker baskets in the weeks before the Saint-Lô's arrival, heads bowed and no-one answered. She felt she was becoming an outcast even though there'd been no outward change in her lifestyle or relationships. She knew now, though, that if any of those present here, people she'd known and trusted since her childhood, discovered what she was doing, she'd be in grave danger. She couldn't, and mustn't, trust anyone. It was like wearing a corset pulled so tight she could not even breathe.

Chapter 13

THE FOREST

'Move,' Carlos bellowed. Hérisson jogged along the pathway, heart pounding, legs aching, shoulders screaming in pain from the weight of the backpack, filled with stones from the river, which he carried. Day after day of torture. Since they'd joined, or at least been temporarily accepted into Carlos's brigade, the time had passed in a haze of pounding, relentless, and rigorous activity.

Carlos was determined to make what he called 'proper soldiers' of them. 'Train hard for an easy war,' he barked, if one of the team stumbled or fell. Loup, fired with the same determination as Hérisson, rarely fell behind. Cerf and Pinot struggled. Though a runner himself, Cerf lacked Loup and Hérisson's force of will. True to form, Pinot constantly complained about the unnecessary rigor of the exercises. The others tried to lift his spirits as best they could. Whatever they each thought about Carlos's exacting training methods, if they weren't prepared to comply, they were 'out'. It hadn't been made clear just what 'out' meant, but Hérisson couldn't risk failing. Carlos was ambitious for his brigade and determined they should play a significant role in the liberation of France, even if that was only a stepping stone to the liberation of Spain. Carlos had hinted he had a special role for the best recruit. Hérisson was determined to be chosen.

In the weeks that had passed since their recruitment, his body had transformed. He'd been fit before. The physical work his former lifestyle demanded had made sure of that, but now he could run for kilometers without stopping. His limbs, even with the restricted diet, felt wiry with sinew, built of solid muscle. His face had become leaner and more tanned. He wore a uniform that had been liberated from a rival camp, and even he struggled to recognise himself when he stared at his reflection in one of the lakes they camped beside or when he posed in front of a forgotten dusty mirror, abandoned in one of the barns they used as a hideout.

The training had not been restricted to physical endurance. They'd learned how to mould *plastique,* recognise and set the different detonator fuses used to delay explosions. He'd had possessed basic map-reading skills when he'd joined the unit, but now he could chart his way through the forest without difficulty, even at night, guided by the stars alone. They'd learned how to track animals and men. Crawled through undergrowth and carried out reconnaissance missions to practise sabotage. Trained in hand-to-hand combat and silent killing. In the clearing where they were currently camping for his test mission, Hérisson had crawled up behind the sentry, put his arm around his neck to disable him and held a knife against his throat. 'I'm ready for action,' he insisted afterwards. But Carlos had laughed.

'Can you do it in real life? He had stood right in front of Hérisson, eyes locked on his. 'Can you slit a man's throat in cold blood?'

' Yes,' Hérisson insisted, but even as the words left his mouth, he wasn't sure.

Under Carlos's command they'd learned survival skills and now all four could construct a hide-out rapidly, from fallen branches and leaves. Once inside, they were undetectable to untrained eyes. They learned to snare rabbit and hare, to trap pigeons in high abandoned *palombieres*. And they could gut, skin, and cook their spoils as competently as the rest of the seasoned brigade. They'd dined on mushrooms, *cèpes* and *trompettes de la mort,* roasted walnuts and chestnuts, gathered brambles and wild strawberries. They'd fished the many lakes in their territory, dining afterwards like kings when they roasted trout over campfires set on pebbled shores.

More than survival, Hérisson had learned a respect for the forest which had become his sanctuary. He could distinguish the trees at a glance, from the mighty oaks, chestnuts, and elms that ruled the forest, to the acacias and birch so favoured for firewood. He could hunt the mighty beasts that roamed his territory, the stag, deer and wild boar. He could recognise and imitate the cry of the owl and pewit. And he had learned to live with the forest, moving silently and unseen through it. He and the forest breathed together; he'd become part of the forest and it, part of him.

Once darkness fell, on moonlit nights, selected members of the team would leave on secret missions. If it was too dark for manoeuvres, the men would sit around the camp fire, imaging the future they would create once the war was over. If they were lucky, they'd be drinking Ricard or wine. Their communal dream was for a world with equality for all, where communism would flourish and the suppression of the working-class by the *Bourgeoisie* would be a nightmare from the past. If, after a few drinks, tongues loosened and a soldier revealed some detail of his past, there would be an abrupt end to the conviviality of the evening. Carlos would leap to his feet, raging a stream of expletives in Spanish, kicking the fire until not even the ashes glowed.

'You have no past,' he would bark after them as they headed for their bivouacs. 'Never forget it.'

For all their training, physical and mental, the most important of all, Carlos insisted, was secrecy. To ensure their safety, the operating procedures for interacting with any agent outside of their group was that any one external agent would only ever know two others in the hierarchy of their group. That meant the event of capture and torture there would be only two people the captured agent could betray.

Carlos would spell-out in grim detail the torture methods used by the Nazis and their Vichy collaborators, always reminding them it was better to die fighting than to be captured and talk. 'If you talk, you may save yourself some pain, but you will cause the death of others.'

Nor did he ever tire of running through the security measures necessary to protect the group. No matter how inclement the weather or how unnecessary it seemed, they moved camp every three days. Complacency was as much an enemy as the *Boche*, Carlos insisted.

In any event it was good for reconnaissance. Hérisson now knew the forest like the back of his hand. Every disused barn and empty cabin.

'We know the best hide-outs,' Carlos reminded them frequently. 'The remotest hamlets, the most sympathetic farmers. We know the tracks too narrow for a lorry to turn. We know the ideal sites for ambush. The disused wells where we can dump bodies. The fields suitable for parachute drops. We can cross the forest, in darkness, by tracks unmapped and unknown to the enemy. It is here in the forest, with our knowledge, we will use guerrilla tactics to defeat the *Boche*.

Hérisson was inspired by Carlos and followed his instructions to the letter. A rivalry developed between himself and Loup who was equally determined to excel. Hérisson wondered how much of Loup's desire to best him originated from their positions before. Whatever resentment Loup might have nursed in the past was buried now. They were on equal terms, and he, Hérisson was still going to come out on top. After a slow start, Cerf had become a competent recruit. Pinot still lagged behind the others, but in spite of his grumbling he had shown a determination to justify his place in the brigade. When Carlos reminded them that a role existed for the best recruit, Hérrison became more determined to be selected for the duty, whatever it might be.

Chapter 14

LA BARDE, SAINT-ANTOINE-DE-DOUBLE

Miriam gave an embarrassed laugh as she squeezed the goat's teat again and again. Nothing happened. 'Don't worry,' Sabine reassured her. 'It takes practise to get the movement right.'

'You can tell I'm not from the country, I'm so out of place here.'

'You're not at all out of place. I've always wanted to live in a town,' Sabine explained. 'Sometimes I feel trapped here.'

'It's so beautiful. Peaceful. I found that hard to get used to at first, but now I enjoy it.'

'Quiet, you say?' Sabine laughed. 'With the cock crowing every morning at dawn and the frogs starting as soon as it gets dark. The last thing this place is, is quiet.'

'You know what I mean. I'm sorry I can't go on doing this now, I have to collect the children from school. Thank you for trying to teach me. Come round later if you wish.'

After Sabine had completed her chores, she collected a basket she had prepared and walked down the lane to Miriam's. They had become close friends, with Miriam dropping by to help with the goats, and Sabine regularly visiting her when she had some spare time. She had been tempted to confide in Miriam about her involvement in the Resistance, but the risk was still too great.

'I wondered if you could help me alter this dress,' Sabine asked, producing the garment from her basket.

'Yes, of course.' Miriam laid out the dress on the dining table. 'What is it you want done?' Sabine produced the picture cut out of the magazine of the style she wanted to copy. Her friend studied the image and then the dress. She nodded. 'Not quite exactly the same, there isn't enough material. But I can achieve a very similar effect. Is there something special happening?'

'Some of my friends are organising a *bal clandestine*. I don't know the exact date yet. It depends on when the barn is cleared'.

'Oh, just to dance again,' Miriam said, swirling around the table holding out the dress like a partner.

'Why don't you come? The children would be fine here.'

' Oh, I couldn't,' Miriam's face lost all its radiance, and her eyes filled with tears. "I couldn't go to anything like that now. Not when I don't know what's happened to my husband.'

'I'm sorry. That was insensitive of me'

'No, don't feel you need to apologise. I appreciate the invitation. Don't you feel guilty about your *fiancé*?'

'Yes, of course...' Sabine paused, and sat down at the table, clasping her hands, afraid to speak but unable to hold back. 'To be honest, the whole thing was a mistake. I realised as soon as he left, we should never marry. I don't know how to write and tell him.' Miriam sat down next to her and gripped her hands as she began to cry. 'Now he's in a prison camp. How can I write and tell him? As soon as he gets back, I can break it off. It's not as though I'm going to meet anyone else, is it?' But even as the words left her mouth, Sabine recalled the youths she had met that day, on the hill. The day of her first mission for the Resistance. She wondered where they were now, and if the kind one, Hérisson, with his unruly dark hair and soulful eyes, would remember her. Then her thoughts flicked to Loup and his dark charisma. Then she chided herself for dreaming. Even if they did remember her, what hope did she have of getting a message to them, wherever they might be, of the forthcoming festivity?

Chapter 15

THE FOREST

'Congratulations, men.' Carlos strolled down the inspection line, handing each of them an armband with the Free French flag sewn onto the side with the letters F.T.P. (*Francs-Tireurs et Partisans Français*) beneath. 'You are soldiers now. Welcome to Brigade Rojo.' The other soldiers clapped and then shook hands with each of their new members.

Carlos poured everyone a measure of Ricard, and the men toasted to victory and freedom.

'Now for duties. Pinot – kitchen; Cerf – acquisitions; Hérisson and Loup – sabotage.' Each looked relieved as their duties were announced. Carlos had chosen well.

'Now, Hérisson, come with me.'

Hérisson swelled with pride. Loup glowered and anger flashed across his face as he watched Hérisson follow Carlos to the edge of the lake where they had been camping.

They sat on the bank as if they were enjoying some fishing and Carlos continued in low tones.

'I've been contacted by other brigades, who want to arrange coordination between our efforts. Jean Moulin has been sent by the

British to unify the Resistance under the leadership of De Gaulle. If we demonstrate that we can act together, the British will supply us with weapons and equipment. We need more supplies.' Carlos thumped a fist into his hand. 'We must act. Our brigade must demonstrate our strength. It's how we shall free Spain, then the world. I want you to liaise on behalf of our group. You can move about more easily than I, because you're French.'

Carlos paused, watching Hérisson's face as though still looking for a sign that he could be trusted. Seemingly satisfied, he continued.

'You must report everything to me, Hérisson. This is vitally important. We need to know if we can trust the non-communist groups. We must make them trust us. That's the only way they'll supply us."

Hérisson nodded, excited at the opportunity to have such a prestigious position within the brigade.

Carlos continued, 'You will meet and participate in operations with other units. This will be the Free French Army, but we refuse to compromise our principles. My men will remain under my command. We need to identify a suitable drop point for messages. If you accept this position, you will be responsible for choosing couriers from the local community. Do you accept?'

'Yes, Sir,' Hérisson said, saluting before he could stop himself.

'Well done, man.' Carlos slapped Hérisson on the back. Then, in a darker tone, he emphasised, 'make absolutely sure you are never captured. You know too much.'

Chapter 16

LA BARDE, SAINT-ANTOINE-DE-DOUBLE

As she worked, Sabine's breath formed clouds in the frosty air. She laid the rounds of cheese onto the wooden trays. With their high sides her produce was protected on the journey to market. She covered each tray with muslin, then placed another tray on top, then loaded them all into the custom-made wicker basket attached to the front of her bicycle. She still refused to wear her *sabbots* anywhere other than on the farm, so she laced on her shoes dampening the toes to cover the scuffs. If she walked carefully, it wouldn't be noticeable that the once leather soles were now wooden. She slipped on her coat, now lined with newspaper to make it warmer. A chill wind sliced her hands as she climbed onto the bicycle so she returned to the house to collect her scarf and gloves. What did it matter if they were a bit frayed? The days when she could prioritise appearance above warmth were long gone.

She arrived in Saint-Antoine-de-Double before the church bell had chimed 8:00 am, but most of the market traders had already dressed their stalls. Sabine leaned her bicycle against the wall and removed the cloth to reveal her rounds of cheese, taking her usual place beside Madame Bourac, who sold jars of honey. The once jolly villager had large shadows under her eyes and looked worn out. Nonetheless, she greeted Sabine cheerfully and asked after her family. Sabine gave the usual reply that all was as well as could be expected.

She watched as the villagers emerged, moving along the street from one stall to another. How the market had changed, she thought, remembering the days before the war. Then, even on the coldest days of winter, the market had worn the air of a village festival. In the warmer months, the terrace of the village bar was always full with people exchanging news and watching the life of the village pass by. Today, some of the few remaining village men warmed themselves by the stove, sipping a Ricard while exchanging information. But the watching had assumed an altogether more sinister nature. A *Maquisard* boldly patrolled the market, checking prices, politely suggesting a reduction if a stall-holder's price was deemed too high. If the advice was ignored, the stall holder could expect to have his or her produce either 'liberated' or requisitioned later by the Resistance.

Superficially, people watched as they'd always done, but now this was not innocent curiosity. Today, watching had a purpose. Everyone watched. The observation that a neighbour was buying more food than you might expect could indicate they were hiding someone – a relative wanted by the authorities, maybe a Jew, or a Communist, or any one of the people on the endless lists of the proscribed or suspected – such information could lead to a generous reward, or life-saving privileges. As long as their informer status was not discovered by the Resistance, that is. Then, the charge of treason could result in a field trial, execution, and an unmarked grave.

Members of the Resistance, too, watched. For any sign of betrayal. Those who just wanted to see out the war as quietly and safely as possible watched for any sign of trouble. As a child, before the war, Sabine had perceived her village as a safe place where everyone helped and supported each other, as if they had a common purpose in surviving. If a child ran across the street in front of a horse and cart, or strayed too close to the village well, the nearest person would reach out to prevent a tragedy. Each had a duty of care towards their fellow villagers. Now all this was gone. The war had robbed the village of its heart. The desire to survive had robbed them all of their humanity.

The produce stalls, which had once boasted bushels of goods, now bore only small mounds of shriveled vegetables, or a few scrawny hens. The rabbits for sale had once filled the cages. Now they were thin and wide eyed. Sometimes people from Perigueux appeared at their tiny market, in the hope of finding some food not available in the heavily policed capital of the Dordogne.

Sabine's cheeses were popular, and she soon sold out. Then she replaced the empty trays in her basket and prepared to return home.

Hérisson sauntered into the village, shoulders back and chest puffed out. He had the bearing of a soldier, but still wore the clothing of a farm boy. This was his first mission, and his selection over Loup had served as a formal declaration of rivalry between the two. On political grounds, Carlos disapproved of the proposed unification of the Resistance groups, and was dismissive of the discipline and training of the other groups with whom they shared the forest. But the urgings of Jean Moulin, and the promise of arms and ammunition from Britain, had served as a powerful incentive for the ambitious leader of Brigade Rojo. Hérisson was determined to become the vital link between the brigades.

He wandered through the village, pausing for a cigarette as he watched the stallholders begin to fold away their stalls. It was then he saw the girl he'd last seen flying down the hill from Saint-André-de-Double on her bicycle. Sabine, she'd said her name was. She was pushing her bike out of the market square. He threw down the cigarette and ran across the square, leaping over some woven wicker baskets to reach her. 'Wait!', he yelled, as she climbed onto her bicycle. She turned, her face slipping into a smile as she recognised him.

'*Bonjour*, he greeted her. She blushed as he kissed her on the cheeks, and he was pleased as he felt the frisson of attraction between them. She'd felt it too. He could see her eyes travel over his body and was grateful for the training that had toned him and dispatched the last vestiges of boyhood. He was a man now.

' You found what you were looking for ?'she asked.

Hérisson grinned and nodded. He'd been right when he suspected she knew more than she let on at their first meeting.

'Here,' he said, taking her arm, 'I've a proposition for you.'

She raised her eyebrows in an unmistakably flirtatious way, and again he felt the attraction spark between them.

'Come with me.' He led her down to the communal open laundry at the edge of the village. There was no one there, and they sat on the steps, where they were hidden from view by the walls.

'I've been sent to find a post drop for messages between my Brigade and the others. But I wonder,' looking intently at Sabine, 'Would you be able to do it? That would work because you travel all around with your deliveries.'

'Yes, but what do you want me to do?'

'You live near here don't you? Well, we could set up a drop box near your home for the Resistance to use. If a message was more urgent, you could carry it. Of course it has its dangers,' he sounded serious. 'But there are few patrols in this area.'

Sabine considered it. She couldn't tell him she already delivered messages regularly. She wondered if she should check with Mariette, whether she'd be allowed to take on duties with another organisation. Surely it'd be permitted. They were all working towards the same goal after all, weren't they? And it meant she would see Hérisson again, regularly. She thought guiltily of her *fiancé* and the letter that needed to be written, then dismissed those thoughts. They were at war and she had a role to play.

She pulled herself up straight. 'Yes, I'll do it.'

'Wonderful,' Hérisson leapt to his feet. 'Come on, let's get started.' Hérisson jogged effortlessly beside her as she cycled towards home. As they neared *La Barde*, Sabine pointed to a deserted tobacco barn beside the road, and diverted them towards it.

Leaning her bicycle against the wall, she explained, 'This is my father's barn, but he doesn't use it at the moment.' She went to the door and pushed down the catch. The weathered door swung open. Hérisson followed her inside. She moved to the back of the barn, then pulled one of the wires that caused the wooden slats to lift and open.

'Look,' she said, pointing to a knot hole in the sill. 'A message could be rolled up and slotted here. For anything larger,' she moved over to a stack of roof tiles in the corner. Lifting one, she produced a rusted coffee tin hidden underneath, 'Papa used to keep the keys for the pigsty here. You could use it as a post box.'

'Excellent.' Hérisson expressed his delight that his first real mission had been such an easy success, and also that he'd had an excuse to see the beautiful and enigmatic Sabine again. He bent to kiss her. She sprung back at the contact, surprised by his audacity.

'I need to go.' And she pushed past him and left the barn.

Hérisson followed, a bit crestfallen at her response.

'I need to get home now. Our cottage is the first on the left after you turn the corner.' She pointed. 'You can find me there if you need to.' She made a shrill whistle. 'call me like this if you need to. I'm usually at the market on a Wednesday.'

Hérisson gave her a mock salute, and grinned. She might be acting as if he had overstepped the mark, but she couldn't disguise she had been pleased by his attempt to kiss her.

Chapter 17

THE FOREST, NOVEMBER 1941

An eerie roar reverberated through the forest. Hérisson stopped immediately. A shiver ran down his spine. A sound like no other. There it was again. Human or animal? He had no way of telling. The only certainty was that it frightened him. The sound seemed to come from all around. First from the north, or maybe the west then east. In the dim light of dusk, the sound threaded its way through the trees and wrapped itself around him.

A ghostly fog floated above the lake, spreading outwards, swirling and twisting to envelop the land around the water. Hérisson instinctively moved further away from the water's edge, so he was less exposed. He returned his improvised fishing rod to its hiding place and tucked his catch, a trout and a small pike, into his bag. Under cover of the bracken, he crouched low. Unless he was mistaken, the sound was coming closer.

Clacking noises accompanied the bellowing, almost but not quite drowning the sound of branches being broken and bracken being crushed. A great beast was surely approaching. Hérisson was paralysed by fear. All he could do was pull himself deeper into the shade of the oak tree that sheltered him.

The largest stag he had ever seen burst from the cover of the forest, moving into the clearing by the lake right in front of him. The animal was magnificent, its antlers spreading like the branches of a tree. He tried to count the number of points, but the beast moved too quickly. Suddenly, the animal pulled its head back and roared. That was the noise that had so unnerved him. That strange call erupting from the very core of the animal's being. Then he heard an answering roar from further along the lake, and, as suddenly as the first, a second stag appeared from the woods. The first, and larger, stag lowered its head and charged at the other. Hérisson held his breath, waiting for the other animal to run. It didn't. Head down it took the other's charge. There was an almighty crash as the antlers impacted. He felt the ground beneath him quake.

Heads pinned to the ground by their locked antlers, the animals revolved in a deadly carousel. A few females edged cautiously from the forest. All but one seemed curiously indifferent to what must be the fight for the right to lead and mate. Hérisson watched, barely able to breathe as the battle unfolded before him. He could see the larger male's muscles ripple. He was surely the more mature, but which animal would be victorious? The younger seemed to have more power and Hérisson attempted to shrink even further back against the trunk as the larger beast was forced backwards toward him.

Suddenly the older stag broke the lock of the antlers, raised its head and belled again, creating the most unnerving sound Hérisson had ever heard. The animal's call reverberated through the mysterious mist above the lake, through Hérisson's bones, through time itself. The sound unsettled not only him, but the young contender. The older beast, with new-found strength, began pushing the other into the water. Finally the young stag bowed its head and slunk off into the bracken. The winner stood on the shore and let out another soul-shuddering bellow. The defeated animal cast back a defiant gaze before disappearing into the undergrowth. Next year, they would fight again. Next year he would win. A message for the Resistance, Hérisson thought. Hitler's armies might parade through Paris, crowing at his victory over the French, but that didn't mean the French were defeated.

Chapter 18

LA BARDE, SAINT-ANTOINE-DE-DOUBLE

For the second time that morning, the owl hooted, its call echoing through the quiet air. Sabine paused from mucking-out the stalls. It was too early for any real bird to be making so much noise, which could mean only one thing. Hérisson.

With raised heartbeat, Sabine ran to the door of the shed. The call came again. Glancing furtively at her family's cottage, she skipped across the clearing and into the forest. There was no sign of anyone. But she hadn't imagined the call, had she? Her vision went dark as a hand was wrapped across her eyes. Strong arms held her. Laughing, she pulled his hands away and spun to face him. 'How did you do that? I'd no idea you were there.'

Hérisson gave her a cheeky grin. 'There are certain advantages in my training, and capturing you was certainly one.'

'Ha, but I'm free now,' she teased, backing away. Hérisson darted towards her, arms out to catch her. She turned, running deeper into the forest. Moments later she felt his arms around her and they fell to the forest floor tangled in each other's limbs. Hérisson kissed her and Sabine responded. How good he felt. Hard limbs, soft hair. The smell of the wood fire and roasted meat. So long since she'd been touched.

Since she'd felt a man next to her. Deep longings fired through her body. But what was she doing? 'Stop,' she pushed him away and struggled to her feet. 'I can't do this now.'

Hérisson, not in the least discouraged, got to his feet as well. He raised his eyebrows. 'Later?' he asked, through a grin.

She couldn't help but smile back. Something about his manner made her glow inside.

'I have to milk the goats. They're waiting.'

'I've got a present for you.' He swung open a back pack placed beside a young oak tree, and lifted out a fresh trout. 'I caught it myself.' Her eyes widened. This was a gift that would make even her mother smile. 'Thank you,' she said, wondering how she would explain this valuable present. Hérisson handed her the fish, letting his fingers brush against hers as she accepted it, sending more shivers through her body.

'I've left a message at the drop box but I wanted to see you.'

Sabine blushed. She was no innocent, but it had been so long since she'd felt like anything other than a work-horse. 'I have to get back,' she muttered. Hérisson fell into step beside her as she set off in the direction of the *chai*. 'When can I see you again?'

'There's a *bal clandestine* next weekend. Why don't you come?'

Hérisson looked discouraged for a moment, then his cheekiness and charm returned.

'I'll come if I can.'

Her angry frown betrayed her disappointment. Aware of it, he quickly explained, 'I'm a soldier now. I'll have to get permission.'

'Oh,' Sabine murmured, realising how disappointed she would be if he were not there.

'Don't worry,' Hérisson winked as he merged with the forest, leaving only his voice lingering in the air. 'Nothing will stop me.'

Chapter 19

A DISUSED BARN NEAR SAINT-FRONT-DE-PRADOUX, 22ND
DECEMBER 1941

The strains of the accordion drifted across the fields. Sabine giggled with excitement. 'Hurry up,' she called to Mariette. The girls hoisted their bicycles over the wire fence and carefully hid them in the thick of a hawthorn bush. Fearing even in their isolated location someone might be tempted to borrow their means of transport. Bicycles were as precious as gold or real coffee and cost a fortune on the black market. A new one would be impossible to obtain. Assured both bicycles were well concealed, the girls began to hop and swing in time to the music as they hurried towards the barn.

The gathering had taken weeks of planning. With dances banned, she and her friends had refused to allow the traditional *fetes* for Christmas and the New Year to pass uncelebrated. They had conspired to create a memorable evening in defiance of the regulation and austerity imposed upon them. The days had passed too slowly as the evening of celebration approached, on the darkest night of the year. Sabine had excitedly told Mariette she couldn't wait to dance again, but there was another reason that the days had dragged like Papa's plough through heavy clay soil. It was because, like it or not, she could not wait to see Hérisson again.

They paused for a moment outside the door to fix their hair and check their stockings. That is to say, they checked the line drawn with a pen down the backs of their legs. The fakes required the same attention as a real pair. While there was no risk of unsightly ladders, it was essential to avoid obvious falseness. Finally, satisfied with their appearance, they slipped through the sackcloth hung over the doorway to prevent light escaping as each clandestine invitee arrived. No one wanted a visit from an overly zealous *gendarme*. Sabine paused for a moment, stunned by the barn's transformation. Kerosene lamps fueled with nut oil lined the walls, converting the normally dusty barn into a magical venue for an evening of fun and forgetfulness.

Claude and Stephan beckoned them over, and the girls joined the lads sitting down on benches made from lengths of wood. The farm workers had brought bread and some red wine. Sabine produced some cheese and apples, she had taken from their store in the barn. Mariette had managed to procure a few slices of ham from one of her contacts. As their friends gathered round the makeshift table formed with three planks of wood and two rickety trestles, a veritable feast materialised before them. Christophe produced some *l'eau d'abricot* in an impossibly large glass bottle, together with an eclectic selection of glasses. The friends each took a measure, and raised their glasses, toasting American's entry into the war and the promise of liberty.

'Let's dance before we eat,' Lillette called. Fred jumped onto a robust, oak barrel placed near the door, Claude passed him his accordion and he began to play. Couples formed, swaying gingerly around the cobbled dance floor in time to the music. Faster and faster the musician played, his fingers nimbly flashing, like lightening, across the keyboard. The music grew wilder and more uncontrolled. The dancing became more furious. Stephan pulled Sabine around with such speed that she felt like a spinning top.

'Enough,' she gasped, as the accordionist burst into a grand finale, then bowed and leapt down from his makeshift stage.

The dancers collapsed around the table and thirstily drank another toast to freedom.

Sabine picked up one of the *baguette's* and was about to cut it into tranches when, as if pulled by an invisible thread, she turned to see Hérisson slip through the door, followed by Loup. Sabine took a deep breath when she saw him. Hérisson had been transformed since their first meeting, but so too had Loup in equal measure. Even fully clothed she could tell his body was nothing but powerful, toned muscle.

She found herself wondering what it would feel like to be wrapped in Loup's arms, then blushed, ashamed of her thoughts. Her choice, if she had one, would be to fulfil her promise to René. Only her body was telling her, over and over again, in so many different ways, more and more insistently each time, that it didn't agree. Sabine forced these thoughts from her mind. On this night, she and her friends had gathered together to enjoy each other's company. They wanted to forget about the war and everything connected with it. To be young and free. Her conscience was having a night off. She was going to enjoy herself, and consequences be damned. She would deal with them tomorrow.

She grabbed Mariette's hand. 'Come on, you've got to meet these two.'

'You've not said anything to them about me,' Mariette hissed.

'No, of course not.'

'*Ma belle*,' Hérisson said, whisking her into his arms and whirling her around like they were an item.

'Shh,' Sabine scolded, her face flushing as she glanced to see if any of the others had noticed Hérisson's familiarity. 'This is Mariette,, and here are...', then she stopped as she realised she could not use the lads' names. 'Come on, I want you to meet the rest of my friends,' she said, putting her arm around each of them as she led them to the table. What a stupid mistake she'd nearly made. She couldn't use the names she knew them by as they were obviously *Maquisard* names. But she didn't know their real names. She knew nothing about them. As she stepped across the barn, it felt like she didn't know anything anymore. When she'd jumped up from the table to greet the arrivals, she'd been a young woman meeting a prospective *beau*. As she stepped back towards the group, between Hérisson and Loup, she'd dived back into the covert world she had thought to escape from, even if only for this one night.

'This is Pierre... and this is Jacques,' she said to her friends, introducing Hérisson and Loup by the first names that came into her head. Lying to her friends felt wrong, but it was all part of the game. But still, it reinforced that she knew nothing about her guests, not their background, not their family, not even their real names. René she had known since childhood. She probably knew more about him than he did himself. Was that important? Only time would tell.

From his sack, Hérisson produced some slices of wild boar which he presented to Mariette. Christophe sniffed disapprovingly, 'Are you sure it's fresh?' Sabine's eyes twinkled as she smiled at Hérisson. The meat was seared black round the edges and a delicate pink in the centre, cooked to perfection. Claude spiked one of the slices with his fork, 'all the more for me. Thanks, mate. He just wants the girls to himself.'

Loup broke in. 'Look, I don't want to step on anyone's toes; you guys have done a great job of organising this dance, but we should really have a look-out. Just in case.' Hérisson nodded.

Fred couldn't see what the fuss was about. 'We've never had a problem before'.

Christophe was already on his way to the door. 'I'll go first. We can each take turns.'

'An hour each.' Hérisson called after him.

The banquet began in earnest as the friends relaxed, enjoying the food and alcohol, chatting and teasing. Fred started up the music again, this time on gramophone records, which he carefully unwrapped and handled as if they were fine china, gingerly slipping them into place on the turntable. The air became hazy from carefully smoked cigarettes. Loup pulled Sabine to her feet and they moved onto the floor. He moved closer. Lips brushed against her ear. Sabine became increasingly conscious of his masculinity. She could feel the bulge of his muscles beneath his shirt. She knew if she pressed a fraction closer she would feel the beginnings of an erection between his legs. Did she want that? How could she choose? René made her feel safe, but trapped. Hérisson made her glow. Loup made her feel wild and dangerous, capable of good and evil in equal measure.

Midnight came and went. Still they tangoed and shimmied. Determined to forget all about the war. The lads took turns at lookout. Mariette bristled that she was not expected to take part, but none of the other girls complained. It was too much fun to dance through the night, intoxicated by the sheer pleasure of youth.

'Quick. Put everything out,' Claude hissed. 'There's someone coming. I went to take a piss and I didn't see him at first.' The gramophone was stopped and the lamps extinguished. Everyone stood still and silent. Horizon directed them all towards the *creches* that lined one end of the barn. The oak cow stalls being the only available cover.

Sabine saw Hérisson's hand move to the back of his trouser belt. He pulled a revolver from there and placed it in his jacket pocket.

Sabine felt fear grip her. Her eyes fixed on the door. The handle moved and rattled as it was shaken from the outside.

Hérisson tensed. She heard the gun click as he removed the safety catch. The door swung open. Gréron, the local *gendarme,* appeared in the entrance. His torch swung round the walls, then he walked towards where they were hiding, the beam picking their faces from the gloom one by one.

He spoke with the authority of the law in the area. 'For all of you, this dance is over. Now get out of here before I take your names and contact your parents.'

At once, as if of one body, they silently gathered their possessions and filed, heads bowed, past the official.

Sabine smiled with relief as she climbed onto her bike, even while her limbs shook with fright.

Hérisson winked at her and waved before he slipped away across the field in the direction of the forest. She watched until his form was swallowed in the bloody rays of the rising sun.

Chapter 20

THE OCCUPIED ZONE NEAR RIBERAC – SPRING, 1942

They pushed their bikes along the track which dissolved into shadows each time clouds drifted across the full moon. On a signal from their leader, Yvette, a swarthy man who had taken the name of his willful wife as his *nom de guerre*, they dived into the ditch dragging their bikes with them. The roar of an approaching lorry in low gear ruptured the silence. Having pressed himself hard into the soil as the vehicle passed, Hérisson then raised his head for a second and glimpsed the relief guards seated in the back of the vehicle on their way to the factory. Adrenalin surged through him, making his heart beat faster. This was his first operation with Brigade Yvette and he was determined to show his worth. They were close to their target now. Moving through the scrub, they followed the track until they reached the service gate, selected as the access point because of its distance from the building where the guards spent most of their time.

Yvette had allocated exactly five minutes to breach the fence, snake round the boundary wall, plant the explosives, and escape. Yvette crept to the fence line and cut a hole in the wire beside the gate. Then with a wave of his arm, he signalled the advance. Hérisson took up a look-out position while Yvette and his companion attached the explosives to the oil tanks. An owl hooted. Hérisson froze, wondering if it was a warning signal. A rush of air just above his head, followed by a dull thud and the death squeal from the bird's prey, told him it was not.

Yvette raised a fist, signalling that the explosives had been planted. Hérisson crouched low, head down, moving as fast as he dared. Then he followed the others back to where they had left their bicycles. They ran softly, pushing the bikes, counting under their breaths. One, two, three. A flash of light. A thundering noise filled the air all around them, making their ear drums vibrate and the earth shudder beneath their feet. The night flared brightly, as if daylight had returned for a second. Then all went dark again, only to flash and thunder again as one by one the oil tanks exploded. The faint glow from electric lights in the workshops faded as the power supply failed, leaving the factory in complete darkness except for flames shooting from the tanks. Sirens, powered by an emergency generator, wailed through the darkness followed by the roar of engines as lorries and motor cycles were sparked into life. Orders barked in German filled the night, along with yells for help. Hérisson and the others in the group pedalled faster, panting from exertion, their hearts pounding. They had to get to the protection of the forest or they were done for.

'Come on,' Yvette yelled frantically. Hérisson glanced backwards. He gulped as he observed the shaded beam of a single headlight as a motorcycle rounded the bend. A second adrenalin rush surged through him. One final push and he skidded in a tumble of bike and limbs into the ditch that bordered the forest. He recovered rapidly, peering over the protective bank to see if the escape route had been observed. Vehicles sped past turning left in the direction of the village. They were safe, at least for the time being.

'We must get to the meeting point before they realise they've lost us,' Yvette urged them on.

Keeping to the shadows, they returned by the same route they had come. Once through the trees they climbed back onto their bicycles and sped along the forest track. Minutes later, they saw the lorry, its headlights covered with blackout shades. Yvette signalled to the driver with a thumbs up, the others crowded to the back, throwing the bicycles in before climbing up themselves.

In the distance, amplified by the night, they heard the barking of dogs. The lorry travelled slowly at first, then picked up speed as it navigated the intricate network of roads and tracks through the forest.

'Don't worry,' the driver called. 'These tracks aren't marked on any map. The *Boche* will never find us now.'

After many more twists and turns, the lorry pulled up at Yvette's camp inside the Free Zone. The men unloaded their bicycles and climbed down. Hérisson felt elation. The first co-operative mission had been a success. Carlos would be pleased.

The waiting *Maquisards,* all new faces for Hérisson, congratulated them, slapping them on the back and pressing *eau de vie* into their hands.

'Come on, let's celebrate,' Yvette yelled, waving his arm in the direction of a long table laid for a feast and lined with chairs. Men were gathering around, laughing and joking. Hérisson's stomach grumbled as he smelt roast meat. Then he noticed a pig cooking on a spit over a fire. Conscious, as always, of Carlos's training, he approached Yvette.

'This can't be safe.'

'Don't worry my friend,' he was assured. 'We're all on the same side here. I 've some people I want you to meet.'

Hérisson found himself positioned between two fellow soldiers from the evening's operation. He explained he had been assigned to their unit on an experimental basis. His new comrades, still high from the evening's activities, confided that the next operation was to involve the sabotage of a train from Riberac to Bordeaux. Apparently one of the *cheminots* who worked at the station in Riberac was with the Resistance and regularly provided vital information. Hérisson nodded and mumbled appropriate responses, but the whole situation filled him with foreboding.

As the slices of pork were distributed, Yvette passed round his men, slapping each of them on the back. 'Well done. A successful mission.'

Later on, firemen arrived to join the celebrations, their faces and hands still black from their efforts to extinguish the blazes their fellow diners had ignited. As they ate, the firemen explained that the guards were still hunting for the perpetrators. Hérisson watched and listened, becoming increasingly anxious. Carlos's training was now second nature to him. The secrecy. The constant alertness. The rigorous attention to detail. This gathering, in which he increasingly felt himself to be a reluctant participant, broke every one of Carlos's rules. He was sure their celebrations could be seen from the road that ran nearby. All these people. The careless talk. How would Carlos evaluate the security of a group like this?

Chapter 21

THE FOREST

The long walk back through the forest to return to his base with Carlos's group, gave Hérisson plenty of time to reflect on his recent experience. So preoccupied was he that he didn't notice the ducks that flew up as he approached, or even the squirrel that hurled a pine cone at him from its hideaway high above.

He'd met with Sabine before setting off back to his unit. Sobbing, she told him that the grapevine reported that the *Boche* had taken a terrible revenge for the outrage perpetrated on what they regarded as their territory. The adjacent village had been fined a colossal half-million Francs, and thirty-five local people had been seized and had disappeared – presumably sent to be slave laborers in the Reich. There were posters in towns and villages on either side of the demarcation line offering rewards for anyone able to give information about the raid.

Her news had unsettled him. Although he'd got used to the idea that he'd evolved from hunter to hunted, the information that there was a price on his head, on all their heads, made him resolve to take even greater care. He was embarrassed to think how naïve he'd been when he'd embarked on this adventure. They'd been lucky when

Carlos found them that he'd been considering how to integrate his unit with others. Otherwise, he'd probably have shot them to avoid any risks to his group's security.

By now, Hérisson was hardened to the dangers of the lifestyle he'd chosen. If he entered a restaurant, he was careful to identify an exit and to sit with his back to the wall, so he could watch everyone that entered. Even when camping in the forest, he slept furthest from the fire, furthest from the location most vulnerable to attack. If anything happened, he would have the best chance of escape.

His caution extended to his relationship with Sabine. Even though he believed he could trust her with his life, he supplied her with only the minimum of information. She expressed hurt and offence at his attitude , but he insisted the secrecy was a necessary precaution which protected them both.

In his heart he knew he'd closed off part of himself. He might love her as best he could in the circumstances, but it was not a love for which he was prepared to either sacrifice himself or risk the lives of his comrades. There was too much at stake. His thoughts returned to the celebratory meal, the roast pork, that he could still taste on his lips when he felt hungry. Their raid had been a success, but the price for it had been paid by thirty-five innocent people.

Carlos was cleaning his gun when Hérisson eventually got back. He approached him immediately to inform him about the abductions and the posters.

'What can we do?'

Carlos shrugged. 'We have other plans, other raids.'

'But what about the people who've been taken away?'

'There'll always be consequences. We're fighting a war'. Carlos stood up and his eyes grew steely and cold.

Hérisson was determined not to be intimidated. 'Can't we try to rescue them?'

Carlos spat on the ground. 'This isn't a *camp de jeunesse*. We're not playing a game. Anyway, we don't know where these people are now. They're probably on a train to Germany. We cannot possibly rescue them.'

'Shouldn't we stop the raids then? The locals will turn against us if they see it's our actions that are causing the roundups. They'll turn us in.'

'That's what the Germans think will happen. We can't let them stop us, no matter how brutal things become.'

'But every time we carry out a successful raid, we know innocent people are going to be sent for forced labour, or killed.'

Carlos slapped his hand on Hérisson's shoulder. 'Welcome to the real world, my friend.'

He softened for a moment. 'And those who drop bombs on London, do they think their bombs hit only the targets they aim for? They're killing innocent people, just as the British who drop bombs on Germany. What we're doing is no different. The raid has shut down the factory for now. And reprisals involving roundups of innocents is strengthening the Resistance. Because it shows the French people that the Germans are not their friends. Not their allies. People will know in their hearts that they are evil. I promise you, our acts of resistance give hope. People know they must wait and prepare to rise up when the time is right. We are the ticking bomb that will blow the Nazi scum out of France. It is important.' He touched his nose with a finger in a sign that revealed he knew a secret. 'Our position here will be very important when the time comes. It's vital that we prepare, that we train, that we continue our attacks on well-considered targets. We cannot stop. There's too much at stake.'

Chapter 22

MUSSIDAN

Sabine knocked sharply on the door. Then again. Mariette should be home from work by now. She felt her heart pounding. Surely nothing had happened to her. She knocked again, and this time the door swung open. Mariette gestured her in saying, 'Hurry.' She closed the door and ran up the stairs to her room.

Mariette looked more excited than Sabine had seen her for a long time. 'What's happened?'

'I can't say too much, but everything is going to plan.' Mariette hugged her friend, then slipped to the hiding place and took out a rolled-up piece of paper. 'This has to be taken to the restaurant tomorrow. You can manage, can't you?'

'Of course.' Sabine took the message and slipped it carefully into a pocket she'd made in the inside of her dress.

'I can't wait. The boys could be home soon.' Her eyes sparkled and she looked as happy as the day she'd got married. Sabine's thoughts turned to René. On their last outing, he'd borrowed his father's car and driven them to a popular romantic location by the banks of the river Isle. He said he was frightened he wouldn't come home. That he was risking his life for her. That he didn't want to die a virgin. She hadn't been able to refuse him. Their coupling in the back of his father's Citroen had been memorable only for its awkwardness. Mariette had married, with a special permit, immediately her *beau* had been called-up. The couple had only enjoyed a few days together before his departure. But on that day when she and Sabine had both said goodbye to their men, Mariette and her husband gripped together for the last time on the station platform, Sabine had been left in no doubt that their bond was of an altogether different nature to the one she shared with René.

Even before the train had pulled out of the station, she'd regretted her hasty engagement.

Following his capture at Dunkirk and transfer to a German prisoner of war camp, her engagement to René had become an increasing burden. Her parents were delighted she was promised to such an eligible young man. As her relationship with Hérisson developed, she felt more and more guilty . Their liaisons had to be secret. No one could ever know. She sighed, the weight of her obligations bearing down on her. Even when she was free of René, she knew her father would never accept a son-in-law who was a communist.

Chapter 23

THE FOREST

Hérisson watched Loup saunter along the pathway as it twisted towards the camp, the snared and already gutted rabbits slung over his shoulder. He waved, and his friend held up the bounty. It was almost time for Hérisson's period of sentry duty to end. He climbed down from the *palombière* and made his way towards his friend.

'We'll eat well tonight,' Loup boasted. Hérisson laughed. Except for the harshest winter months, they had lived like kings. Kings of the forest. Even on the hottest days of summer their shaded forest world was cool. Their exercise and training were conducted for the most part under cover. And in the afternoon they could usually find a few hours to swim in one of the many lakes or they could relax in the sun. The nights spent under a blanket of the stars were to be prized like a night in a luxurious hotel. The night sorties were adventures they vied with each other to take part in. Hérisson had enjoyed learning how to identify the constellations and could competently navigate by the stars alone. These skills were particularly useful when the group's nocturnal activities came into play.

And it was just such a nocturnal activity that he needed to discuss with Loup. He'd received a request to smuggle a family of Jews from the Occupied to the Free Zone.

While Carlos did not want to involve the Brigade in the activity because of the security risk involved, he did not object to any individuals carrying this out if they so wished. His sole condition being that none of the core members of the brigade were seen by the 'parcels', as they were called.

As they came together, Hérisson showed Loup a map of the proposed route, one they had used several times already, in the area around Saint-Barthelemy-de-Bellegarde. 'I think there'll be enough light for us to do it in the next few days. Are you up for it?'

'Yes, count me in. But I don't want to go on doing this kind of thing for nothing.'

'What do you mean?'

'People like that'll have money, won't they?'

'I don't know.'

'Come on, they're Jews. Don't tell me they won't have jewels sewn into their clothes and bank notes wrapped in belts round their waists. The way I see it, *we* should be making some money out of this.'

'I'm not going to charge people for saving their lives.'

'Yeah, but while we're saving their lives, we're risking our own. Don't you think they'd be happy to pay us?'

Hérisson hesitated. What his friend was saying was true. People fleeing from the attentions of the Gestapo and the S.S. were likely to be carrying as much liquid wealth as they could. But to demand they hand over some of it to the them didn't seem right.

Loup emphasised his point, smacking his fist into the other hand. 'It's not like it's a soldier or a pilot we're helping reach a neutral country – or to a boat to escape back to England. I wouldn't expect them to pay me. Soldier to soldier, I don't have a problem. But look at it this way. That couple we took across last week, *Monsieur* and Madame Steinman. I bet they had a few francs tucked away in that bag he was carrying. When the war's over, they'll be able to make a fresh start. Able to set up their business again and make more money.

And what they do is trade things that are rare or expensive. And us? What'll we have to show for risking our lives to save people like them?' Loup made a hand signal for zero. '*Que dalle! If* we make it to the end of the war, it's only fair we have something to set us up. We could end up on the street – or worse. We don't *have* to help them. Carlos won't, why should we? And if we don't help them? What then? Why shouldn't they pay? And pay well.'

Unconvinced, Hérisson shook his head.

'Just listen. It's business, commerce if you like. Trade. They're capitalists, those Jews, they understand. We provide a service which is taking people across the line, and it's dangerous. Not many people are prepared to do it. And it's a service that lots of people need these days. How many people are desperate to get into Free France? Hundreds – if not thousands. So it's simply a question of payment for a necessary service. What's a fair price to pay for having your – and your family's life saved?"

Hérisson continued to stare at his friend, having difficulty digesting Loup's words.

'Well,' Loup went on, 'I reckon anyone we take across the line would be grateful, and able to spare a jewel or a ring, or some money, maybe five hundred francs.'

'That's ridiculous. It doesn't cost us anything to do it.'

'Except maybe our lives. Don't you think they pay others? When we get them to Madame Conti, do you think she doesn't charge them?'

'I don't know. I've never asked.'

Loup laughed, but there was no humour in it. 'You're no business-man. That's why I need to take control of this operation.'

'No,' Hérisson insisted. 'I won't have that, and I won't charge either.'

Any pretence at humour long gone, Loup sneered, 'You'll be alright when this is over, me, I want to something to show for what I've done.' He pointed to his chest, 'I'm not doing it unless I'm paid.'

'But I can't ask anyone else in the unit. Carlos won't permit it.'

Loup shrugged. 'You decide.'

Hérisson drew himself up. No hesitation. 'I'll do it on my own then.' The pair stared at each other in silence. Finally Loup broke Hérisson's gaze and sauntered off towards the camp, whistling. As Hérisson watched his friend walk away, sadness engulfed him.

Chapter 24

AN ABANDONED HOUSE CLOSE TO THE OCCUPIED ZONE

Forman unfolded the map and laid it on the table, carefully pushing out the creases with his powerful hands. Hérisson watched intently, in awe of the man's composure. He spoke competently in French, to hear him, it was as though they planned to take sweets from a child, not to blow up the heavily guarded transformer base at Pessac. Carlos had briefed him about the special agents sent from Britain. Men of steel. Elite soldiers respected around the world. That Carlos would skin him alive if he let the Brigade down. But even those words, drummed into him as forcibly as bullets into flesh, had not prepared him. Forman and the men under him in his cell were more like the super-heroes from outer space, he'd read about in comic books a lifetime ago. Being in their presence made him feel like he'd been playing at boy scouts. 'You,' Forman said, focusing his icy blue eyes on Hérisson 'are only on this mission because of your local knowledge. My preference would be to go it alone, with my men. However, it's a joint mission between the British and Free French, and they insist you add value. You fall behind, you get left behind. All that matters is the mission. Understand?' Hérisson nodded. He was frightened but exhilarated at the same time. He wasn't going to let his Brigade down. This mission, codename Josephine B, if successful would knock the submarine base in Bordeaux out of service for months. The men stood round the table as Forman bent over it, marking the route they would follow to the target.

'The attempts to bomb the base from the air have been unsuccessful, so we're going to give it a go ourselves. The supplies have arrived. As soon as there's a clear night, we go. The guards tour the perimeter fence every hour. The guard changes when the morning shift begins at seven. Normally, there are four guards at the base at night, two permanently at the entrance, here,' Forman pointed to a cross on the map, 'And the other two generally patrol the boundary wall together. Our reconnaissance shows they all stop and have a break together about three in the morning. That's when we strike. We arrive by truck then bike.' Forman paused and turned to Hérisson. 'You arrange the transport. Then,' he picked up his previous thread, 'We approach by this route here. The path is passable by bicycle.' He paused and his steely eyes focused on Hérisson. 'You know the route and will guide us if required.' While Hérisson nodded acquiescence, he could not help feeling a chilling finger of fear run down his spine. He had no doubt he would meet a swift end if the locality turned out to be not as he had described. 'The truck will wait here. We cycle to this point, then we will leave and conceal the bicycles. The rear part of the building isn't guarded, except for the perimeter patrol. They expect any attack to come from the air. Our intelligence reports that there's a door at this section of the wall.' Forman pointed to another cross on the map. 'It's bolted from the inside. I will scale the wall, then open the door to the rest of you. Once we're in the transformer grounds, we divide into groups. Each group will be responsible for attaching the explosives to two transformers. We will have no more than ten minutes to make our getaway.

"After the explosion, the guards' communications should be disabled. They won't be able to give an alert. The flames will attract attention. In the worst case scenario, the guards will manage to contact the nearest base, but even then it will take at least twenty minutes for a rescue team to arrive. Any search will focus, first of all, on the area around the access road as this is the only vehicle route to the transformer. When the *Boche* arrive with men in trucks, it'll be impossible for them to follow our escape route. If they've motorcycles, which could use the path we came in by, we'll be more vulnerable. In any event, in the darkness, unless the search party have extensive local knowledge, they won't be able to find the path or know that it links to the road here on the other side.'

The briefing over, Forman issued kit to each man, an automatic pistol, spare ammunition and magazines, a fighting knife, torch, field dressings, grenades, wire cutters, rubber gloves, two days of emergency rations, charges, and incendiary bombs. He retained the rope ladder, compass, watch and whistle.

~

The men set out in a truck Hérisson had liberated from a suspected collaborator. It was normally garaged in his storage yard, and would not be missed until the following day.

They travelled slowly, with the lights off, following the route Hérisson had carefully plotted after a number of reconnaissance outings on his bicycle. He'd marked out all the habitations where they did not know if they could trust the occupants, and at those points they slowed even more to minimise the risk of the truck attracting attention.

Not for the first time, they thanked providence for the many farm and forest tracks that made it possible to traverse the forest and countryside without approaching the main centres of habitation. Nonetheless the journey was nerve-wracking, and while Hérisson could feel the excitement mounting, it was leavened with a large amount of apprehension. This was a real mission. What if it did not go to plan?

They were just about to climb the hill towards the transformer, when the truck came to a halt.

Forman jumped down and joined the driver peering underneath the engine. 'Fuel leak,' he heard the driver say.

'This isn't going any further, then?' Forman said as he glanced at his watch. 'Push it off the road. We still have time, if we cycle hard. We weren't going to go much further by truck anyway.'

The men gathered at the back of the vehicle and pushed the lorry into the ditch.

'It'll give the *Boche* an idea of where we came from, but that can't be helped. At least that bastard can spend time answering their questions once they work out who the owner is. Hopefully at the headquarters in Bordeaux. We'll split up afterwards and each take different escape routes.'

The men set off cycling as fast as they dared. Hérisson felt a thrill of excitement as he saw the transformer towers they were about to destroy, looming out of the darkness. He focused his mind on the mission, using his training to push all fear from his mind. They were going to do this. They were really going to do this. As they approached, a strange calmness descended on him as though everything he was doing, and everything he was about to do, was perfectly natural. The destruction they were about to wreak would make a significant dent in the German war effort. That made him happy, and filled him with a purpose that pushed doubt from his mind.

They left their bicycles at the designated point, stopping briefly to study their target. Then, wearing their heavy backpacks, they crawled towards the base, using the ferns and bushes that grew over the abandoned ground as cover.

As they reached the perimeter wall, Forman stood up and went just below it. Hérisson attached the grip to the rope and was about to throw it upwards when Forman grabbed his arm. 'Wait. There's a high-tension line there. I wasn't told about this. I think it's live.' Hérisson picked up a stick and threw it at the line. There was a crack and brief spark as the strands made contact.

'Fuck.'

Forman signalled to Hérisson and they merged back into the undergrowth. They waited in the oppressive silence to see if the noise had attracted any attention. Forman studied the line intently, then whispered, 'It's still do-able'.

'No, sir,' Hérisson's response was automatic. 'The line's too close to the top of the wall.'

Forman turned to him, eyes blazing. 'Just watch.'

He seized the rope roughly away from Hérisson and threw it upwards. It hooked on the lip of the wall. Then Forman peeled off his rucksack and jacket and dropped them on the ground. He scaled upwards as nimbly as any cat. The group held its collective breath as he reached the top and then carefully edged himself under the wire.

They heard a thud as he dropped to the ground and then the scraping of the bolt being forced backwards.

Hérisson started muttering an apology, but Forman just signalled with rapid darts of his hands, directing each group to the transformers they were to disable.

Hérisson ran, bent almost double, darting between shadows on a course to the furthest target. Following the routine they had practised, the men slipped the fuses marked with red into the dynamite, then raced back to the entry point. Forman made one last check before pulling the door shut behind them. They crawled up the hill as fast as they could, weaving through the scrub.

The saboteurs ducked under the brow of the hill, where they sheltered and waited for evidence of their success. Time passed. Surely the fuses should have blown by now. Hérisson glanced at Forman who was staring at his watch. The minutes passed. Still nothing. Hérisson began to feel the pain in his legs, and noticed warm blood trickling down his arm where he had scraped it on a thorn. As the adrenaline rush faded, the too familiar feelings of fear and despair began to return. The whole expedition had been a failure and now they had to cycle all the way back to camp without falling foul of any patrols.

Suddenly the sky exploded into a thunderous display of flame and smoke. One bang followed another. The ground shuddered beneath them. He found himself breathing hot burnt air. The men rose cheering, so overcome with elation that caution was thrown to the wind. All raised triumphant fists to the sky, except for Forman. 'Get out of here,' he yelled, signalling for the team to follow him.

Bent low, they ran down the hill, now suffused with a reddish glow from the burning transformers. Sirens wailed. Yells in German filled the air. They had to be fast now. Leaping on to their bicycles, they sped off down the track.

Hérisson glanced at Forman. They had done it. Their little group, with just basic equipment, had succeeded where bombing raids had failed.

The siren wail fell silent. The unmistakable roar of a Zundzapp KS750 echoed through the night accompanied by the barking of excited dogs.

Forman slammed to a halt. 'We've got to separate. Every man for himself.'

'Wait,' Hérisson shouted, ' I know where we can cross the river safely.'

Forman looked at him. Straight into his eyes. For a second. Carrying out an appraisal which in the real world could take months or years.

'Lead on,' he ordered, slapping Hérisson on the back. He waved his arm in a forward motion as he turned to the other men. 'Go. Go. Go.'

Chapter 25

THE FOREST

Carlos surveyed the men, circled around the camp fire, as he spoke. 'Our intelligence reports that the transformer station will be out of action for at least a year. All electric trains in Southwest France have been withdrawn. The *Boche* have been forced to replace them with steam trains. Work in the Bordeaux submarine base has been delayed as has production work in numerous factories. This is a major success.'

Carlos paused, then swigged a draft from a bottle of Pastis before continuing. 'We'll let them repair it,' he stood up and punched a fist in the air, 'then we'll do it again, ourselves next time, now the Brits are going to supply us.' The men cheered.

Hérisson rose to his feet. 'But the locals. The commune of Pessac has been fined one million francs and a curfew has been imposed between five in the afternoon and nine next morning. That's one thing, but two hundred and fifty local people have been taken from their homes. My uncle is one of them. No one knows what's happened to them. My aunt has been to the Prefecture in Bordeaux. They told her she'd join those missing if she asked any more questions. My uncle lost an arm in the Great War. He'll not last long in a concentration camp. Twelve German soldiers were shot for failing to protect the station.'

'We don't mind letting the *Boche* do our work for us,' Carlos chuckled. The men laughed with him.

Hérisson clenched his fist. 'But if that's how they treat their fellow countrymen what are they going to do to those local people? What's going to happen to my uncle?' He stared into the eyes of each of his comrades. Did no one else care? Even his friends, Loup, Pinot, and Cerf, were celebrating with the others. He pictured his aunt and his two cousins desperate over the safety of his uncle.

Carlos tossed the bottle of Pastis to Sacha and approached Hérisson. He slapped him on the back. 'We're here to do a job. Beat the *Boche*. This is how we do it. Look what we've achieved. Good reports from Forman. He said you did good for a civvy.'

Rage seized Hérisson. He wanted to be credited for the pro he was. He was determined to be the best. Carlos chuckled. 'He didn't mean it like that. He said he'd take you on a mission again. Can't do better than that. Look,' he produced a cigarette and offered one to Hérisson. 'This is war. If we take action, the other side will take reprisals.' Carlos lit his cigarette and shrugged. 'We're fighting for the greater good. Don't forget that. We can't just roll over and let Hitler kick us in the balls.'

'But any action we take is going to cause the deaths of innocent French people.'

'We know their policy is to punish the local population for any acts of resistance, on the basis that the nearest village must be hiding the perpetrators. The Germans believe this leads to local people informing on anyone they suspect of being a member of, or helping the Resistance. And there are areas where this is working. We have to make sure anything we do is worthwhile. There'll always be a price for victory.'

'But what right have we to put these peoples' lives at risk?' Hérisson threw his tin mug to the ground. 'I can choose to put my own life at risk, but not anyone else's.'

Carlos squared up to him. 'We're at war. Civilian lives are being lost as we speak, through bombings, in concentration camps, through torpedoed ships. We're fighting for a better world. Where people can live freely, without injustice. WE'RE not killing these locals, THE GERMANS are. We're fighting to stop injustice and brutality. If we give up, do nothing, more lives will be lost.'

He looked at Hérisson. It was a challenge. 'Are you telling me you won't fight?'

Hérisson gripped his gun. 'I will fight.'

Carlos continued. "We mustn't look at the lives the sabotage costs. We have to look at the lives that've been saved and will be saved. You and the others on the mission risked your own lives to carry out the attack. We're not throwing lives away. We're saving them. That's the good news. Six of the eight transformers were destroyed. The explosives on two of them must have slipped off. Probably because the surfaces were damp. That's something we need to be conscious of in future missions.

The real importance of the mission is that we're now trusted by the British. The three S.O.E. men made it back to Britain with glowing reports about our assistance and efforts. The British are now trying to identify other targets where we can combine forces to defeat the enemy. They are even now making arrangements to drop further ammunition and supplies. Men, we are one step closer to victory.'

Chapter 26

LA BARDE, SAINT-ANTOINE-DE-DOUBLE, JUNE 1942

The owl hoot was as incongruous as the Nazi flags that draped the buildings in Paris. Sabine smiled. She put down the cheese churn and wiped her brow, smoothed her apron, and wished she was not wearing the breeches she used for work on the farm. She patted her hair and then skipped towards the side door of the *chai,* the one that opened to the edge of the forest. She halted, blinded for a moment by the glaring June sun. After she had adjusted to the sunlight from the cool gloominess of the *chai* she scanned the trees that lined the field, searching for Hérisson. He hadn't emerged from the forest, so it took her a few moments to discern his shadowy outline. She glanced furtively towards the house. *Maman* and Papa certainly wouldn't approve of her liaisons with Hérisson.

Satisfied that no one was watching her, Sabine slipped across the grass. Hérisson pulled her into the forest as soon as she was close enough. He pushed her against a tree trunk and enveloped her in a deep and sensuous kiss. Sabine responded with equal passion burying her hands into his thick dark hair. He smelt of wood and earth and carbonite. She'd not seem him for almost a week and with there being no certainty of when their next meeting would take place, opportunities had to be seized and maximised.

He withdrew his tongue from her mouth and pushed her from him. Sabine groaned, running her hands over his stomach, tugging at his clothes. 'No, there's no time,' he said. He stood back from her, shaking her shoulders in what seemed to her an excess of glee.

'It's happening. It's going to be soon. The message came this morning. We have to get ready. You must take this letter to Mussidan. Today. As soon as possible.' He pressed a tiny scroll of paper into her hand, kissed her, and turned away.

Excited, she urged him. 'Wait, tell me.'

'No time now,' he called back, and with a wave set off into the forest.

She watched him melt into the trees before she slipped back into the *chai*. The cheese would have to wait. She stored the curds in the cool cellar and then made her way past the barrels of wine to the door that led into the cottage.

Maman was kneading bread on the oak table in the kitchen. She looked tired but that was usual. Papa sat by the stove, filing one of the pieces for the plough, which he was trying to adapt in order to make a repair.

'I'm going into Mussidan, do you need anything?'

Maman looked up, fixing her daughter with a beady stare. 'Have you finished the cheese?'

'No, but it needs to rest. The churn handle is broken. I'll be able to get another one from Mariette, they have one they don't use. I won't be long.'

'Well, don't stay and chat. I know what you girls are like. And be careful.'

'I'll be back before you know I've gone.'

Maman grunted. Her father did not lift his head from his task.

Sabine climbed the attic to the room she shared with her sister. She changed into a dress and grabbed her shoes, then climbed down carefully. Outside, she mounted her bicycle and set off down the winding track that led to and from her parents' farm.

She drank in the sounds of the forest as she bumped along the track. It was so easy to forget everything when you were surrounded by nature.

Once the track merged onto the road leading into the village of Saint-Antoine-ur-Double, she was able to travel more quickly. The road was quiet and she passed only one car and a couple of village boys pulling a milk cart.

When she arrived she went straight to the café. Arnaud, her contact, had not arrived, so she took a newspaper from the counter and ordered a lemonade. She sat down at one of the small tables on the terrace and tried to look and act exactly as one might expect a girl waiting for a friend.

The café owner passed, leaving the drink. She sipped it, trying not to feel self-conscious. She glanced at the church clock. Twenty minutes had passed. Had she misunderstood. Arnaud was not usually late. Another ten minutes passed and her sense of disquiet increased. She became more and more conscious of the note. It felt like it was burning her skin.

It was easy to laugh off her courier work, rolling a piece of paper into her bicycle handlebar and travelling with it had always seemed more exciting than dangerous. But such a message committed to paper in full view in the town square left her feeling exposed. If she were caught with the message in her possession it would be her death warrant. Worse would happen if she was captured. She would be tortured, brutally, until she revealed the names of the others she worked with. Only then would she be granted the mercy of being shot.

She shivered as she glanced again at the clock. Her drink was finished. She really had no excuse to stay any longer. After one last look around the square she began to pick up her handbag and gas-mask. It was then she saw Arnaud walking towards her. He was old, to her eyes, with grey hair and a slight stoop. He nodded politely at her as he sat down at a nearby table with his back to her. The café owner approached and took his order.

'Thank goodness you made it,' Sabine whispered under her breath.

'It's good news,' she said, brushing past Arnaud, dropping the note beside his cigarette packet as she moved. He picked up the note as he pulled out one of his cigarettes. By then, Sabine had already left the café and was walking across the square.

Cycling home she felt a sense of exhilaration. Her stomach might be complaining bitterly of hunger, but she'd delivered her message successfully. She was fighting back, not sitting by the fireside, head down, hoping that the war would pass her by unscathed and unnoticed. Like her parents.

It was hard not being able to tell them anything. Even now they did not show the faintest sign of being interested in the Resistance movement. They had followed Petunia's lead as mindlessly as her goats followed their hunger to patches of grass where they could graze. They even seemed to fear the Communists more than the Nazis. That her parents might prefer to live under Nazi than under Communist control terrified Sabine. Still, she refused to be disheartened. Not on such a beautiful day.

The sun beat down, and as she left the village behind and entered the forest she reveled in the beauty of nature. A pine martin caught unawares darted across the track in front of her. A heron stood on the lake, intently watching the water like the villagers who roamed the forest in search of food. Buzzards and kites swooped and dipped in the cloudless sky. She could hear a wood-pecker tap tap tapping against a tree. The sounds of the forest soothed her. Entering the forest was like entering another world. A world free of National Socialism and war. Just people living with the land, as their ancestors had done for centuries. Wasn't that all people really wanted?

As she returned her bike to the shed her mother appeared at the door way. "You were gone a long time."

"Mariette needed some company. She has not had any communication at all from Robert for several months and she is worried sick. I've got the churn handle though."

Maman's face flushed. "Of course. You're so lucky René is safe. You must do what you can.

Sabine nodded, and smiled, steeling her face to conceal her true feelings, as she went inside.

.

Chapter 27

LA BARDE, SAINT-ANTOINE-DE-DOUBLE 8th NOVEMBER 1942

The cry of the starling trilled through the early dawn mist. Sabine put down the milk churn and, after glancing towards the cottage, ran towards the forest, towards the origin of the sound. Hérisson pulled her towards him. Her skin shuddered at the touch of his lips and he laughed as she pulled sharply away. "You're as cold as ice," she scolded.

He grabbed her hands, his frozen grasp penetrating her woolen mittens as surely as rain. "The Allies have landed in North Africa," he shouted as he danced her around. "It's the beginning of the end. Soon France will be free."

Sabine's heart filled with joy as she followed Hérisson's steps in a freestyle waltz. This was the news they had been waiting for. That they had been working towards. The French Colonies in North Africa would welcome the Allies and join forces with them to expel the Nazis first from Colonial France, and then France metropole herself. The time when they would be free to live their lives openly without fear of reprisals was now an approaching reality, not the impossible dream it seemed to be in her worst moments.

She glanced at Hérisson, who for the first time in a long while looked as innocent and carefree as the first day she had met him. If the war's end was really approaching, there would come a time when they could get to know each other properly. She would finally learn his true name. He would be able to tell her where he came from and about his family. Their time together would no longer be moments stolen in secret from both their duties. She could walk through the streets of Mussidan proudly holding her lover's hand with no reason to feel shame or guilt.

Chapter 28

MUSSIDAN, 11th NOVEMBER 1942

Sabine removed her headscarf and genuflected as she entered the church. A few others were present, mostly elderly women queuing at confessional. The priest, a small, busy, man in his late fifties appeared briefly before assuming his place in the box. Mass would not be for another hour. She had arrived early, as she had a message to deliver. Briefly, she wondered if any of the persons present were the destined recipient. Just as briefly, she closed her mind to such questions. It was better not to know.

Sabine took a seat in the seventh pew from the back of the church. She secreted the minuscule scroll of paper in a space cut out of the prayer book there before standing up and making her way to the candles. Sabine dropped a coin in the wooden box, took a candle and lit it. She knelt briefly, praying, or at least pretending to. Finally, she stood and performed the necessary genuflection before leaving.

Initially the secrecy had irritated her. Now, it comforted her. The less she knew, the better. The more disruptive the Resistance became, the more insecure she felt. As the Allied victories became more frequent so had the tolerance of the Germans reduced. Their radios blasted out victory after victory, while the whispered news from the underground press told a different story.

No matter how powerful the *Boche* claimed to be, they could not stop the radio waves echoing their intelligence through the very air she breathed. The American, British, and the Free French had landed in North Africa. This was the beginning of the advance which would beat the Germans out of France and back to Berlin. Soon there would be landings in France. And when that happened, the Resistance, the army in which she served, would be ready to play their part.

She was excited, but frightened too. Proud that she was involved, but scared that she would not be able to live up to her comrades' expectations. She pushed these thoughts to the back or her mind. She had done something at least, and would not be ashamed when the war was over. She walked head high with a smile on her face as she left the church. But as she stepped into the light, she stopped. Her body began to tremble. She could not breathe. One, two, three lorries pulled into the far end of the street. As the lorries turned to advance towards the church she could see they were filled with German soldiers.

Recovering from the initial shock, she dipped her head, assuming a defeated air, as with bowed shoulders she walked down the steps from the church. On the street, she blended into the weary shoppers who had been queuing at the butcher's, and who were now melting into side streets. The prospect of pig's feet, sheep's brains, or a tiny cut of offal or *saucission* was no incentive to remain in the square and be exposed to whatever nightmare was about to unfold. Heart in her mouth, Sabine tried to watch from an alley as the lorries pulled ominously to a halt outside the church. Like clockwork toys, the men descended in regimented order. Their Verdigris uniforms told her they were Wehrmacht -less frightening than the S.S. or the Gestapo. Sabine sidled away and skirted the town centre to reach her friend's. With the view from Mariette's window there was at least some possibility of safely observing what was about to unfold.

The mayor arrived with his clerk, summoned by a soldier. After much waving of arms the mayor and clerk left in the direction of the school with a German officer. The other soldiers fell out of formation and made their way to the water pump, where they helped themselves to drinks. Once they had removed their helmets and put down their guns, they began laughing and joking with each other. They no longer looked threatening. Mariette pointed to one of the tallest blond soldiers. "They're handsome devils aren't they?"

Sabine was horrified at her friend's frank appraisal. At the same time she could not disagree. Were not these men evidence of the Aryan dream, the vision that had fueled Hitler's march across Europe? Pictures of such men bombarded Sabine and Marietta at every visit to the cinema. Perfection. The master race.

"They might be handsome devils," Sabine muttered coldly. "But that doesn't mean we can't beat them."

The town bell began to toll. Mariette stirred beside her, then backed away from the window. "I'll have to go and see what is happening. You wait here?"

Mariette pulled on her coat and hat while Sabine watched anxiously. She followed her friend's progress as she joined the other members of the town gathering in the square. Once several hundred people had assembled the bells stopped their clamour. Sabine tried to catch the words as first the mayor spoke over a loudspeaker, and then the Wehrmacht officer stepped up to address the crowd. First slowly, and then with more purpose, the crowd dispersed. The soldiers began moving purposefully, now directed by their commanding officer.

"What's happening?" Sabine demanded, as soon as Mariette closed the door behind her.

"They're occupying the town. They're going to be billeted in the school. The whole of France is now under occupation. No more Free France. No more demarcation line."

Chapter 29

THE FOREST

The mysterious light of pre-dusk wandered amongst the trees, creating a forest of shadows inhabited by creatures both real and imagined. Hérisson tried to close his mind to everything except his target. The sights were perfectly aligned. His finger curled around the trigger, yet he hesitated, unable to deny his feelings for the boar. Admiration, empathy. Wasn't he now, too, the hunted? Forced to become an itinerant forest dweller like his ancestors from the dawn of time, surviving from one day to the next.

Prey to the benevolence of nature.

Hunger growled in his stomach. There was no room in his life for empty gestures. Not any more. Not since the *Boche* garrison stationed in Mussidan had begun to actively seek out the Resistance groups hiding in the forest.

Hérisson squeezed the trigger. The beast fell to the ground with a soft *thump* as it collapsed on the leafy forest floor. The legs twitched and its hoofs pawed the oak leaves before it finally stilled. Hérisson waited, listening. An owl hooted. Leaves rustled then fell silent. Had it been a hare? Or something more dangerous?

His stomach rumbled louder this time, yet still he waited. Darkness wrapped round him. Finally he was satisfied. It was safe. He approached the animal already shrunken by death. He reached to stroke a finger along its tusks, the once dangerous weapons that could gore a man.

Hérisson bent, loosening the serrated knife from his belt. With a practised hand, he slit the animal the length of its stomach. He pulled the warm entrails from the body and tossed them amongst the vegetation. He tied the animal's feet together and then retrieved the mule, Marguerite, who would carry the bounty to camp.

He glanced at the waning moon, which was beginning to slide across the sky. They were about an hour from base. Provided he encountered no patrols, he would be enjoying roast pork before the dawn light began to wake the forest.

Man and beast picked their way through the ancient forest tracks, Hérisson leading, the mule following though she knew the route better than he. He was walking in the steps of his ancestors in one sense. Life in the forest had not changed in hundreds of years. Yet, in another, everything was different. Their life, the life of rural France, had been ripped apart. The old rules and traditions and values were gone. In their place had risen something worse than anarchy.

Lost in his thoughts, it seemed no time before he arrived at the outskirts of the camp. Bird whistles echoed around him as the lookouts signalled and welcomed his arrival. Men gathered to assist with the beast. Tired eyes sparkled and gaunt faces smiled. Knives glinted in the firelight as hands were put to work, butchering the animal. Wild boar was roasted on sticks over the fire. Men told stories, real and imagined, as they chewed on chunks of the roasted meat. Fat dripped into the fire, making it flare than dull.

Finally, sated and still wearing the blood-stained clothes of his hunting expedition, Hérisson crawled under the tent constructed of parachute silk, where he fell into a deep sleep. When he woke there would be many problems to deal with, but hunger would not be one of them.

Chapter 30

LA BARDE, SAINT-ANTOINE-DE-DOUBLE

Sabine climbed off her bicycle and wheeled it up to the cottage. She could hear raised voices which became louder and angrier as she approached. Sabine hesitated as she reached the door. The words were clearer now. Her father was shouting, his voice harsh and angry.

"... ashamed ... disgrace!"

Sabine reached for the doorknob. It would be easy to slip away. The cheese could wait. Better that than face her father's rage. Except it wasn't being directed at her this time. Josette was virtually screaming, "What do you expect me to do? I won't be an old maid. I won't live in this madness. One day you tell us we have to accept the Occupation. That it will work out in the end. That there mustn't be any more lives wasted. And I listened to you." Josette paused. "Now you tell me that I mustn't dress up, that I mustn't look nice. That I shouldn't have smiled at the soldier in Mussidan. How do you expect me to live? Do you think I am going to stay here for the rest of my life, milking goats and sewing? Josette shrilled, "Sabine might be happy to be a peasant, but I won't be. I can't live like this for the rest of my life!"

"You listen to me, girl," her father responded, even more infuriated, as though that were possible. Sabine paused, taking a certain amount of pleasure that her sister, usually her father's favourite, seemed to have fallen from grace. Finally her curiosity prevailed over good sense and she turned the door handle, entering the kitchen.

Josette was dressed as if for a dance. Her hair was carefully rolled and she was wearing her best dress, the one with the tapered waist in a silky blue, which Sabine rather envied. Her sister was even wearing stockings, though goodness knows where she had acquired them. Her lips were a luscious red and there were traces of kohl around her eyes. Streaked into comical lines by the tears running down her cheeks. She would have turned a few heads at Mussidan market if that was where they had been, before the crying had ravaged her appearance.

"Look at your sister," her father exclaimed. Sabine obeyed. "Going out like a trollop. Bringing shame on the family." Josette paled with shock at her father's words. Sabine even felt sorry for her. *Maman* moved between her and Papa as if trying to calm the situation but Papa side-stepped her and moved closer to Josette. Sabine gasped fearing he might strike her sister but Josette stood her ground defiantly.

"Papa," she said trying to soothe him. "What on earth is the matter? Josette looks beautiful. You know she does. And that is how we dress if we are going somewhere special."

"Only tramps go out dressed like that these days. I've never been so ashamed."

"Have it your way," Josette yelled as she fled up the stairway, to their shared bedroom. "Don't think I am going to stay here and be treated like this."

Her father made to follow her, but Sabine grabbed his arm. "Leave her Papa. Tell me what happened. She'll come and apologise once she's calmed down."

"She'd better," muttered her father.

"Come and sit down," *Maman* soothed. "Tell us what happened."

Her father took his chair by the stove. The red rage colouring his face gradually fading to a rosy pink. "I arrived in town, and just as I was crossing the street to get to the mayor's office, I saw her sauntering along the road with a German soldier. Arm in arm, they were. Laughing. I could have died of shame. She'll get a name for herself if she carries on like that. I won't have it. Not under my roof."

Sabine stood in silence sickened by the implications of her father's words. If Josette was fraternising with the enemy, that made everything she did even more dangerous. But she knew her sister. They might not always be the best of friends, but she was no traitor. Or was she?

"I'll speak to her, Papa," she said, squeezing his hand before making her way up the stairs. She looked down, studying her father in his chair by the fire. How much older he had become. Weary of war, weary of life.

Josette was lying on the bed, sobbing. Sabine sat down beside her and stroked her hand. "What is it?"

"It is impossible here. You have someone. You don't know what like it is to be alone."

"But you're not alone. Never."

"Remember when we used to dream of visiting Paris, of a life that wasn't like this, here on this dreadful farm. I won't be a peasant for the rest of my life. I won't." Josette sat up and folded her arms across her chest like a petulant child. Sabine laughed. Her sister could be quite childish at times.

"You haven't been with a German have you?" Sabine asked.

Josette looked at her sister appraisingly. "And what if I had," she asked slyly. "What would you do about it?"

"Nothing, it's not my business," snapped Sabine. But it was. What if her sister was seeing a soldier, a *Boche*. What would the implications of that be? Would she have to report it? Would her sister be accused of being a traitor? Sabine felt sick to the very core of her being, but she had to go on.

"What's he like?" she asked, trying to keep her voice light and even.

"He's tall and blond." Josette answered defiantly. Leaning back on the bed, her eyes assumed a dreamy appearance. "And he gave me this," she boasted as she reached into her handbag. With a triumphant flutter, she produced a beautifully wrapped box complete with a ribbon tied in an elaborate bow. Its frivolity was so at odds with the sparseness of their surroundings that Sabine gasped.

With the finesse of a magician undertaking a complex trick before an enthralled audience, Josette lifted the lid, revealing a large bottle of Chanel No. 5 cocooned in tissue.

"He bought this in Paris, for *ME*. He has just come back from leave there. Imagine," Josette continued eyes wide. "He walked into a shop in the Champs-Elyées and bought this. For *ME*." Awkwardly she proceeded to lift the stopper. "Here, just sniff this. It's exquisite. I can put some on your wrist for you to try." Josette reached forward flicking a drop of the liquid on her sister's skin. Sabine flinched whipping back her wrist as if she had been burned.

"How could you?" Sabine cried, completely losing her *sang froid* as the implications of her sister's revelations took hold.

Josette's expression changed and her face hardened. "I might have known you wouldn't understand. You and your high and mighty ideals."

"I'm sorry Josette. I didn't mean to upset you," Sabine replied soothingly. The shock was real, but she played it off. She had to discover the extent of her sister's involvement with the enemy soldier.

"Here, I would like to try it." She stretched out her wrist, smiling. Josette stared at her for a moment and then, finally deciding the request was genuine, placed a trace on her sister's skin.

Sabine still felt as if the liquid was scorching into her flesh, but instead of recoiling, she smiled gratefully and delicately sniffed the aroma. "It's perfection. You are lucky."

She patted the comforter, just as their mother had done when they were children. "Now tell me everything. Have you kissed him?"

Josette blushed and giggled. Sabine felt her stomach lurch, but, determined to hide her anxiety, she continued. "I promise not to tell anyone."

Josette laughed and her eyes sparkled as she confided that she had kissed the soldier when she had met him in Mussidan. It was shortly afterwards that her father had seen her and all hell had broken loose.

"I don't care what he thinks," Josette muttered. "One day we have to accept the Germans are here, and the next we aren't supposed to have anything to do with them. I love him." Josette stared into her sister's eyes defiantly. "I don't care what Papa or anyone else thinks."

"It's not as simple as that, Josette."

"He's promised to take me back to Germany when the war is over. He's going to be an architect in Berlin. We'll get married as soon as I can. I won't give him up."

"No, of course not," Sabine squeezed her sister's hand. "But what about how they behave?" "Conrad is a good man," Josette insisted. "He didn't want to be a soldier. He was at university in the last year of his studies when he was drafted. He hates Hitler, but he loves his country. Is that so terrible?" Josette grabbed her sister's arm. "He's not a bad man. If you meet him, if Papa meets him, you would see.

"Will you try to speak to Papa for me?" Josette pleaded.

"Of course. But not now. We'll have to wait until he calms down." Sabine wrapped an arm around her sister. Josette smiled clearly reassured by her sister's support but when Sabine turned to stare out the window, she wiped silent tears from her eyes. What was she supposed to do now?

Chapter 31

SIORAC-DE-RIBERAC

"Hurry," Carlos shouted, looking at his watch. The men jogged more quickly, snaking along the pathway towards the road. When they arrived, they burrowed into the undergrowth to await the arrival of the lorry that would take them to the drop site.

It was almost an hour before the *gazogene* arrived putting and spluttering.

"What the hell," exclaimed Carlos angrily, gesturing at the vehicle in disgust.

"What could I do?" the driver begged. "There wasn't enough fuel for the other lorry. It's already stopped once. It took us the best part of half an hour to get it going again."

"We'll get there if we have to push the damn thing," Carlos said. He signalled the men to board and they climbed into the back. The vehicle spluttered on along the track, guided by the light of the full moon. When they reached the incline leading up towards the village of Saint-Andre-de-Double the vehicle slowed and the puffs of black smoke from its chimney intensified. "Off men, everyone except the driver," Carlos ordered. They descended and began pushing the struggling vehicle up the steep incline into the village.

The men boarded the vehicle again outside the bar they had first visited with Sabine and which Hérisson now knew was, in fact, a meeting place for many of the local Resistance leaders. They drove past the square then down the hill, following the twisting track that led into the countryside. Their destination was the field in the commune of Siorac-de-Riberac, which had been chosen for the parachute drop. Perfect because it was very isolated and the line of trees on the side nearest the road meant it was very unlikely that their signal lights would be seen. In addition the site was sufficiently far from the garrisons in Mussidan, Riberac, and Montpon that they felt sure the aircraft would be safe from flak.

The men settled down to wait in the tree line, tucking into a midnight picnic of bread, cheese and wine. Time ticked by. Still the aircraft did not arrive. The men grew restless. The excitement turned to anxiety and disappointment. The expected weapons and equipment were earmarked for a large scale operation in their area. Without the drop their plans could not be realised.

Claude Benoit, the baker from Riberac whose rounded form was unmistakable, muttered, "I need to light the ovens at six o'clock. If I'm not there, there will be hell to pay."

"If the drop's been called off, maybe we've been betrayed," Pinot interjected, trying not to sound like his nerves were frayed to ribbons. Carlos shook his head. No one was going anywhere. Not until it was certain the airplane would not arrive.

Finally, at just before 3:00 a.m., they heard the distant grumble of a single-engine aircraft approaching from the north. The men followed a practised routine. Guards posted around the perimeter of the landing zone. Then men with torches formed a line to mark the route of the aircraft.

The silhouette of an aircraft crossed in front of the moon. Wings swept slightly forward Hérisson recognises immediately the silhouette of a Lysander. Carlos signalled by the means of an owl's hoot for the torches to be lit. The feeble electric beams seemed insignificant in the wide night sky, but the aircraft was flying low and turned towards them.

It came closer, flying overhead. Then the canisters began to fall. One by one, they thudded into the ground. The men rushed towards them, quickly taking an end each and running them back to the lorry. The sooner they were away from the landing site, the safer they would be. Hérisson cast a backwards glance as they departed from the drop spot. It was his job to ensure no evidence remained of the drop. In the morning, he would return and survey the site in daylight.

The lorry set off along the road, turning into a forestry track at the first opportunity. The men followed behind the lorry, trading quiet words of excitement until Carlos ordered them to keep silent. Soon they reached the barn that had been selected for unloading and distribution of the equipment. They unloaded the canisters, checking the contents of each one. The dynamite and fuses, together with two Sten guns and twenty grenades, were placed back onto the lorry, hidden under some cut wood. The driver would deliver that load to Brigade Yvette at first light. A pre-agreed allocation of guns were placed behind a hidden wall in the barn earmarked for Brigades Cézard and Roland. The spare guns were distributed amongst the men who had not been armed. Ammunition was handed round, with the usual proviso from Carlos about how sparingly it must be used.

Chapter 32

MUSSIDAN

The three woman walked along the road towards the cinema, arm in arm, as they had done every Saturday for the last twenty-three years. Sabine could hear their laughter and from the back they could easily have passed for girls of her own age. When they turned to cross the road she could see their hair neatly coiled into the most fashionable style. Red lipstick. Kohled eyes. She knew that if she were closer, she would see that her aunt Delphine's lipstick would be smudged around her lips, that Helene's eyes always looked sad, even when she laughed and that it was a long time since the cut of Denise's coat was fashionable.

The three were bound by friendship certainly, but it was their shared loss that had bound them together, inseparably, across the decades. They had all lost their loves in the Great War. To Sabine they held a particular fascination, because when she saw them together, the three of them, now middle aged women, trapped forever in another time, dressed for their regular outing to the pictures, she also saw the ghosts of their loved ones. Linked between them, boy, girl, boy, girl, boy, girl. Three premature deaths in the trenches at Verdun had left a hole in the lives of these women, as large as the men they had once been paired with. The women had not grown old, neither had their bodies been distorted by childbirth. They seemed perpetually waiting, hoping against all odds for their loved ones return.

Sabine felt herself more affected now, by her aunt and her friends, than she had ever been before. With Mariette worrying constantly about the lack of news from Robert, and the increasing danger she was sure attached to Hérisson's exploits, she found herself wondering what fate held in store for her. Would she also one day walk the streets of Mussidan dressed for an outing with a man who wasn't there?

Chapter 33

THE FOREST

Loup tossed the red and white tube to Hérisson. "Let's give it a try." Hérisson leapt, catching the object easily. He sat down beneath the large oak tree, which so often served as their private meeting place, and studied the blue lettering on the label. The tube held twelve tablets of Pervitin. He had heard the others discuss it. The drug was standard issue for many of the Wehrmacht soldiers, and had been captured along with some arms from their last raid.

The men had enjoyed some raucous speculation as to the effects of the round white tablets, but none had been inclined to sample them. Carlos had forbidden experimentation, so the pills had been stored, in case they should come in useful along with the other spoils, including German uniforms, guns, and ammunition.

Hérisson hadn't been the least bit curious about the Pervitin, but Loup had been unable to let the subject go. He frequently raised questions about the possibility of experimenting with the wonder drug to ascertain whether it did provide the rumoured attributes.

"What if it really does increase your strength and endurance? If they're giving it to all the *Boche* soldiers, it can't be dangerous. I've heard they can march non-stop for days. What if it's because they're taking this stuff?" Loup bent, and with a swift movement grabbed the tube back from Hérisson. "It's our duty to test it. What do you say?"

Hérisson laughed. Loup had an ability to make even the most mundane of tasks seem like an adventure. And his enthusiasm was infectious. Hérisson had not been curious before, but now he couldn't deny wanting to join Loup in his experiment. What if these pills could enhance their abilities, making them better, and more effective soldiers?

"All right, then. Test it we will."

Hérisson reclaimed the canister and removed the cork stopper. He slid out a sheet of basic instruction that was rolled around the stack of tablets.

"Looks like one should be enough to test," he said, handing his friend a tablet.

"Three, two, one. Here we go," he said, putting the pill in his mouth and washing it down with some wine.

The two stood looking at each other expectantly. Nothing happened. "Maybe the instructions are for girls," Loup said. "Let's take another." Simultaneously they each took another pill. Again they stood looking at each other. Again nothing happened. Hérisson shrugged. "Must be a dud lot." Loup shook his head and took another pill. "I just want to know what it does. They wouldn't be using it if it has no effects."

"Let's get back," Hérisson said. "It'll be dark soon." He hoisted his bag and they set off down the hill. He began to feel a burning sensation inside his body. He was hot. And cold. Then an incredible feeling of well-being swept over him. All the fear and anxiety which had become part of his daily life flowed out of his body, like a waterfall washing over him then dissolving into the earth. He felt as he had done as a child, like nothing could go wrong, ever. He began to laugh and his pace quickened as he descended the hill. Everything was going to be just fine. He imagined Sabine running towards him. She was wearing a pretty blue dress with white flowers scattered around the hemline, and she was laughing. He ran as if he would collide with her, scooping her up and tumbling into the brush with her. Then he heard a cry from Loup.

"Get down. It's a trap."

Hérisson turned round just in time to see Loup signalling before he ducked behind a tree. Hérisson dived to the ground. When he looked up, Sabine was gone. It had become very dark, and the forest filled with sinister shadows. The sun dipped behind heavy clouds, which had appeared without warning. The euphoria throbbing in his veins evaporated as mysteriously as it had arrived.

The forest he had come to regard as his sanctuary was now filled with chasms of darkness. Black shadows seemed to reach from the trees. He turned, stumbling, desperately seeking a path back to safety. His head buzzed and a cloying fear occupied his body.

A blood curling scream shattered the vibrations in his head. He recognised the voice as Loup's. Trying to focus his jumbled thoughts, Hérisson retreated to where he had last seen his comrade. Shapes moved and shifted before him in the waning light. One moment he stood amongst quiet, sheltering trees, the next he was surrounded by *Boche*. His feet caught in a patch of wetland, which had suddenly appeared in the murky, shadowed world he had become trapped in. He pulled his feet from the mire, trying to get free. Panic surged through his body as he realised he was being pulled down, dragged into the cold mud. He reached for his feet, trying to pull them free. A sharp pain in his hand cut though the panic, pulling him to his senses.

Hérisson stopped struggling and started breathing. Slowly. First one breath, then another. This forest was his sanctuary. It hid no Germans. No swamps, at least not here, in the area he knew like the back of his hand. He felt his heartbeat slow. The fear that had engulfed him began to subside.

He reached out a hand, with his eyes closed. He could feel the bark of the tree. A tree was safe. Slowly, he opened his eyes. Terror returned. Hérisson closed his eyes and concentrated.

Another scream broke his concentration. It was closer this time.

"Loup," he called. "It's all right. I'm here. Close your eyes.

Breathe." As his senses returned to normal, Hérisson could hear his friend's breathing. Carefully he opened his eyes. This time the world wavered and shuddered but otherwise was as he expected it to look at dawn. He saw Loup crouched under some bracken. His face was streaked with blood and his jacket was torn. Hérisson moved towards him, coaxing him from his hiding place. Loup emerged and Hérisson put his arm around his friend. "You all right?"

Loup gripped his hand. "Have they gone,"he stuttered.

"We're alone, Loup. Everything is good," Hérisson comforted him, looking at his own bloody hands. Hours passed as they huddled together, waiting for the earth to stop moving, for their hearts to settle, and for the shadows to hide nothing more than the promise of safety should a *Boche* patrol appear.

Hérisson dressed. They looked better after a dip in the lake, but there was no disguising their scratched and torn faces and hands.

"We'll have to tell Carlos we came across a patrol and had to hide out."

"But then he will want to know how many, what weapons they had, all of that. What do we tell him?"

Loup seemed to consider this, scratching the back of his neck. "You're right. I know. He dreams about obtaining an Enigma coding machine. How about we tell him we saw a unit using one and that we tried to follow them to see if there was a way of capturing it"

"Great. He'll accept just about anything is justified to get hold of a machine." Hérisson agreed. It wasn't the best plan, telling a lie to Carlos like that. But they had to account for the time they had spent away from the camp. He wasn't even sure how much time they had lost. It seemed like one day, but what if it was two or more? He shuddered. Whatever they told Carlos, they sure couldn't report the truth.

Chapter 34

MUSSIDAN

"Damn," Sabine whispered under her breath, "Damn." She should have known things were going too well when the *Boche* guards patrolling the market hadn't stopped her. She glanced backwards. The soldiers were too intent on engaging Genevieve, one of her friends in conversation to pay any attention to her, but she didn't want to have to walk past them again unnecessarily. She ducked down the cobbled lane leading from the market square to the river, hoping, amongst the bustle of the market, that Madame Deloitte hadn't noticed her. She touched her head scarf subconsciously. She could just feel the raised edge of the message she had scrolled up and tucked into the pattered cotton. She quickly dropped her hand to her side again. She had made it this far, and didn't need any attention drawn to herself. Not until she had divested herself of the incriminating evidence anyway.

She risked a glance over her shoulder, casually turning her head to the side so she could glance out the corner of her eye. The soldiers had not taken the slightest interest in her movements. She returned to watching her steps, observing her bare legs and threadbare clothing. How she had changed. Once she would have sauntered down the street, lipstick bright red, hips swaying, and wearing her very own self-styled version of the latest Paris fashion. Her hair would be styled in elegant rolls, clean and shiny. Now she aimed only at drab, unnoticeable, grey.

Each time she entered the town she became a shadow, sliding along walls and edging across the pavement. Unnoticed. Unchallenged. Undeterred. Her pace quickened, but though she wanted to run she dared not risk it.

"Sabine," a woman's voice called, shrill and sharp.

She pretended not to hear, determined to avoid any conversation with the caller. She bent her head down, and nipped a sharp left, descending the narrow lane. If she slipped into the baker's, she might avoid the confrontation that she dreaded. After a few minutes of chatter with the shop assistant, whom she knew from her school days, Sabine took her leave and began to make her way along the riverside towards the road home.

Madame Deloitte emerged from a the drapper's and almost crashed into her. "Sabine, didn't you hear me call you?" The woman looked at her disapprovingly. Sabine shook her head, and greeted the lady with a feigned smile.

"I have some exciting news my dear," Mme Deloitte said.

Sabine studied her *fiancé's* mother. The war had aged Madame Deloitte. Her hair was ribboned with grey and her once smart appearance had become faded, though unlike Sabine, she had put no effort whatsoever into the lapse. It was the natural and indeed expected progression for a good mother who worried, endlessly, for her beloved son.

"René is coming home," Madame Deloitte announced, and fluttered an official looking letter before Sabine's face. "It may not be for a few months but he has been accepted for the exchange program. I will have to make preparations. A welcome. And you, my dear, will be there. I know how anxious you will be to see him." Madame Deloitte's' eyes assumed a flinty appearance as they roved Sabine's features, as if searching for a flaw in the perfection.

"You two lovebirds will be able to finalise your arrangements at last."

Sabine blanched, forgetting for a moment the message she was required to deliver. Years had passed since their torrid encounter on the river bank. The feelings she had for René, in that moment, had been those of an innocent girl who had no idea about life or anything else. A girl who had not known what she wanted. And even had she known, she would have had no idea how to express her desires, far less obtain them.

She had changed. She was no longer the innocent girl that René had asked to marry. That girl who had accepted his proposal because she did not know how to say no. He too must have changed. He had experienced war, then incarceration in a German prison camp. It was inconceivable that René now was the same man who had proposed to her on the train platform.

It seemed unlikely that they would now have anything in common, except a hatred for their oppressors. The war, for all its terrors, had opened a world to her that she had not known existed before. She now had choices and prospects. When she and Mariette dreamed about the world and what it would be like when the war was won, they dreamed of a world where they as women could have a bank account in their own name. Where they would have the right to vote alongside the men. They had fought with the men now they wanted equality. Had they not earned the right?

Madame Deloitte beamed at her.

Sabine replied, "I'm so happy he will be home soon. We'll talk about these things once he get's back, but with the war, the way things are now, I don't think anyone can think about the future anymore."

"Nonsense my dear. Life goes on, and we must all make the best of things. René went to fight for our safety. Yours and mine," she said, pointedly. "I think we need to remember that."

Sabine bowed her head. This bloody woman. What did she know? No-one was going to tie her to a lost dream, not with guilt, not with disapproval.

"I'll wait to hear from you," Sabine answered neutrally. "Now I really must go. They're waiting for me at the farm."

" I'm sure they are, my dear. I'll look forward to seeing you soon, as will René."

As Sabine cycled home, the exhilaration she usually experienced after successful delivery of a message dissipated almost immediately. With each turn of her pedals, she became more preoccupied with René's return. She wondered, as she had so many times before, how she would feel to actually see him again. The future she now dreamed of, if it were to involve any man, would be spent with Hérisson.

How she longed for the war to end. Finally, her thoughts of René and his mother faded, and she felt a renewed sense of pride. She was fighting back, unlike the rest of her family. With that thought, as quickly as the pride filled her it abated.

Every act she carried out in support of the Resistance put the lives of the whole of her family in danger. If one person was suspected of Resistance activities, that person would be picked up by the Gestapo for interrogation. Automatically their closest relatives would be earmarked for the same treatment. She had no right to endanger the innocent members of her family, but she did not know how to tell Mariette and Hérisson that she was too terrified to continue. And now René would return home, and expect her to marry him.

These thoughts carouselled in her head almost continuously. Nightmares plagued her sleep. She could feel the energy sap from her body as each day the façade she was obliged to maintain became more burdensome. René's imminent return would be yet another grenade to juggle whilst tightrope walking the division between the *paysanne* life she lived openly and the shadowy life she occupied in the Resistance.

René's return would force the issue of her engagement. But even if she managed to escape that obligation, she would still not be able to meet openly with Hérisson. His life was lived entirely in the shadows. Even worse, she could not be certain that her parents would not denounce Hérisson if they discovered his political allegiance, such was their fear of Communism.

Sabine pedalled on, longing with all her heart for an end to the war.

Chapter 35

LA BARDE, SAINT-ANTOINE-DE-DOUBLE

"No, I won't let you." Papa roared.

"I'm going. You can't stop me!"

Josette was wearing her best coat. A small brown suitcase, which Sabine had never seen before, was positioned by her side. She was waving a sheet of paper defiantly before Papa's eyes. He snatched the authorisation from her hand. Smoothing it out carefully on the kitchen table as he read the content. Sabine had just returned from a delivery and joined her father to study the document. Her body shuddered as she understood the words. Papa ran his fingers through his hair, and looked anxiously at his wife, who stood by the range, expressionless, eyes shadowed and heavy with worry.

"I'm sorry Papa. I warned you."

A motorcycle roared into the courtyard.

A tall, handsome German solder climbed off the motor bike and bowed to the assembled family, who had followed Josette out of the kitchen when the visitor arrived.

"Are you ready?"

Josette smiled and went to stand beside the motorcycle.

Papa started towards the soldier. "She's too young. I won't allow this."

"Sir," the soldier bowed. "You have no choice. Your daughter has applied for and been accepted to the program."

"I love you all," Josette said. Then she climbed onto the motorcycle behind the soldier. The family watched in stunned silence as the motorcycle roared away carrying its passengers.

Papa turned and wandered back into the cottage.

He sat at the table and put his head in his hands.

Sabine watched anxiously as her father rocked back and forth. Her father relapsing into a catatonic state was the last thing they needed.

"Has she really signed up?" *Maman* whispered.

Sabine nodded, trying to look upset although secretly she was relieved. Josette might be going to Germany on the S.T.O.(compulsory work service) but it was bound to be safer for everyone than having her stay here. If she was suspected of being a collaborator, her life would be at risk. And if she already was a collaborator, she could put the whole family at risk.

Her father banged his fist on the table.

"She's not eighteen. I'm going to the *Commisariat*. I'm going to stop this."

"No, Papa. She's made her own decision. You saw that."

"Get the *livre de famille*."

Her father glared at *Maman*, who walked to the sideboard and took out the document that served as a record of her parent's marriage and recorded the births of their three children.

Tears welling in her eyes she handed it to her husband.

"I'll come with you," Sabine insisted, although the thought of entering the building terrified her.

They set off, cycling side by side in silence.

Once in Mussidan they cycled to the building that was now drapped in Nazi flags. After they had chained their bikes to a drainpipe, Papa set off purposefully up the stairway to the entrance. Sabine felt her heart break for her father as she watched him. With his small stature, farmer's clothing, and beret sloped across his head, he did not present any kind of threat to the tall Aryan soldiers who guarded the entrance.

They inspected him dismissively before allowing him access. Sabine followed her father into the building. Accompanying him broke every rule that Mariette had drummed into her. She had to avoid drawing attention to herself at all costs, but she couldn't let her father go inside alone.

Papa explained that he objected to his daughter enrolling for the voluntary workers scheme, and that she was too young to go to Germany alone. He opened the *livre de famille,* pointing to Josette's name. The receptionist, a polite young soldier, nodded sympathetically and said he understood. He directed them to wait and explained that he would try and speak to the Commandant. They each took a place on the wooden seats that were placed along one wall of the reception hall. Sabine shivered as she looked up at the portrait of Hitler glaring down at her from its place on the central stairwell. Just being in the building made her tremble.

Her father seemed unaffected by his surroundings and sat in silence staring straight ahead. There were three other persons who also appeared to be waiting. They too looked neither right nor left and made no attempt to interact with their fellow attendees. Sabine did not recognise them and pretended to read a book in an effort to calm her nerves.

They were kept waiting for three hours and fifteen minutes, if the wall clock was correct. Finally, they were ushered into the commandant's office. He was a tall man, with cold grey eyes. Her father removed his beret and stood with it between his hands as he said good afternoon. Sabine burned with shame as she witnessed her father's submissiveness, then shivered when she felt the commandant's eyes rove over her body. With a polite gesture, as if he regarded them as equals, the commandant bade them sit down.

"I understand your concerns about your daughter," he said politely. "But you must understand, this is a voluntary scheme, which has been negotiated with your government. It is an excellent opportunity for your daughter to obtain valuable training and experience in Germany. I'm sure you agree there are no similar opportunities here."

Papa met the commandant's gaze.

"It's a question of age. She's not old enough to join the scheme. There's been a mistake."

The commandant stood up. "*Monsieur*, there has been no mistake. Your daughter will be well looked after. You have no need to worry."

"But she's too young."

"The place has been allocated. A calculation made. A prisoner of war notified of immanent release. We cannot upset the balance. We would require a replacement to release your daughter." The Commandant smiled thinly. "However if you can suggest someone?" His gaze turned upon Sabine.

Papa hesitated.

Sabine felt dizzy. My God, she thought. Would her father really sacrifice her, to guarantee Josette's safety. She'd never been more conscious of being the least favourite child than at that moment. Her life and the happiest moments she had shared with Hérisson whirlpooled in her mind.

Her father shook his head in one sharp movement.

"In that case, *Monsieur*, there is nothing I can do. If you are quick, you might even be in time to wave goodbye." He glanced at his watch. "The train to Bordeaux is due to leave in three minutes."

Papa stared at the clock on the wall. Then rising to his feet he put on his beret, nodded to Sabine to follow him. They left, running down the stairs and out of the building. Papa's shaking hands fumbled with the padlock key as he tried to unlock the bicycles. Sabine's heartbeat faster and faster until Papa undid the lock and gathered the chain. Then they pedalled furiously to the train station. Bunting was positioned around the entrance and a brass quartet were in the course of packing their instruments. Sabine and her father ran onto the crowded platform just in time to see the train pulling out.

Papa noticed one of his friends, Georges, the tobacconist from Saint-Antoine-de-Double. He bustled through the crowd to reach him. "Did you see Josette here?" he asked.

Georges nodded. "Yes. She was in the same carriage as my son. They'll be looked after. That's what we've been promised."

Papa's eyes filled with tears. "She was too young."

Georges eyes filled with suspicion. "She must have volunteered then. My son was drafted. He didn't have a choice."

Chapter 36

THE FOREST

The track stretched out before Hérisson, twisting through the trees. He heard the roar of the motorcycle as it accelerated up the incline. Cursing his decision to spy on the German patrol, he spurted forward, lungs hammering against his chest, but it was too far. He could never make it to safety in time. Not if he kept on the track.

He leapt off the road, following what looked like a boar run thought the brambles. Thorns dragged his clothes, but he didn't slow down. Head kept low, he treaded through the undergrowth. Even although it was autumn and the leaves had fallen from many of the trees, the forestation was so dense he would not need to travel far before he became invisible to anyone on the road.

He was grateful for his stolen boots, his footfalls squelching through the sodden ground.

Still maintaining a run, he slipped and slid on the wet leaves. The raindrops continued, causing the leaves still hanging to branches to rustle, as if it was the wind that moved them.

The motorcycle stopped, but Hérisson did not dare look back. Instead he crouched lower as he weaved his way through the moss covered trunks. Ivy twisted at his feet and youthful oaks tried to delay his journey. Ahead he could see a ribbon of bracken almost at head height. The rich red ferns were as welcoming as a warm fire and a hearty meal. If he could reach them, there would be no prospect of a lone pursuer finding him. Not without dogs. And one thing he could be certain about was if the soldier was on a motorbike, he would not have a dog.

Once Hérisson reached the protective curtain of ferns, he lay down. He was virtually invisible now. He peered down the hillside and watched the soldier appear over the crest of the incline. It was too far to discern features, but Hérisson could sense the soldier's disquiet. Darkness was beginning to fall, and the forest danced with shadows. The soldier turned around and disappeared from sight as he made his way back to his motorbike. Hérisson considered persuing him, but decided against it. He had had enough close escapes for one day.

Chapter 37

MUSSIDAN

The screech of brakes forced Sabine to glance backwards. The army lorry had rounded the corner and was now surging forward as the driver accelerated to clear the bend. She cycled onto the safety of the pavement and got off her bike. She glimpsed the grey-green uniforms of Wehrmacht soldiers as the canvas at the back of the lorry flapped open. Seeing so many of them was frightening, but did not instill the terror that even the sight of the S.D. or Gestapo invoked.

The lorry crossed the bridge over the L'isle and then slammed to a halt outside the closest house to the road. Some soldiers descended from the lorry, peeling back the canvas covering the bed, to reveal a flak gun mounted inside. Two of the soldiers took position behind the gun, swivelling it in a southerly direction. Others lifted binoculars, scanning the sky for their target.

The streets had cleared as the lorry passed, and Sabine found herself alone on the pavement. A solitary figure was dangerous. She had to get off the street, but she also wanted to find out what was happening. Pushing her bike, she ran down towards the nearest property, then followed the wall hugging in close so that she was not conspicuous. Peering around the corner she could see the soldiers still positioned on the ground around their truck while others were in the vehicle, manning the flak gun and watching the sky.

Sabine's attention was grabbed by a roaring noise from above. Soon she saw the airplane trailing smoke. The flak gun cracked into action and the barrel waved in an arc as the soldiers tried to reach their target.

"Please let them get away," Sabine prayed under her breath. What should she do? If she tried to reach Mariette, her friend might have a contact nearby who could do something to disrupt the soldier's attack. If not, could she reach one of the Resistance groups?

All her thoughts were for nothing, as she saw there was no time. Flames shot from the plane as the flak gun found its mark. Sabine saw parachutists fall from the dying aircraft. The plane continued its noisy descent, heavy black smoke, spiralling from the engine. She climbed back onto her bicycle and pedalled as fast as she could up the hill. She had to reach a vantage point that would grant her some idea of where the parachutists and plane would come down. The plane had already disappeared into the forest whilst the parachutes floated towards earth at a more leisurely pace. The *Boche* soldiers, now that their targets were out of reach, hauled the canvas back over the lorry bed amid frantic yells before setting off at speed towards the forest.

Sabine breathed a sigh of relief. If they did not have a local guide to assist with navigating the labyrinth of roads and tracks traversing the forest, they had little chance of finding the downed airmen or the plane. Not before one of the Resistance groups who riddled the forest.

Sabine was certain the plane had landed somewhere beyond Saint-André-de-Double. The parachutists had seemed to be closer, perhaps by Saint-Etienne-de-Puycorbier or Beauronne. She was sure that Hérisson's group were stationed in the deserted tile factory, near the edge of the village. She decided to seek them out, in case anything she had seen could help with finding the airmen.

She cycled as fast as she could out through Saint-Front-de-Pradoux. The road was quiet. The locals had developed a talent for sliding into the background anytime there was troop activity. It was an important survival technique. Being on the road alone made Sabine conspicuous. Yes, she had her cheeses to deliver, but was that so urgent that she was out and about in the forest when *Boche* troops were hunting enemy airmen?

Her legs were aching by the time she reached the track to the old factory. The route was too overgrown to be cycled with ease, so she hid her bicycle in a copse of blackwood and walked cautiously in the direction of the building, keeping an eye out for the sentries she knew would be watching her.

Just when she had decided the Brigade must have moved on, a youth stepped in front of her. She had expected to be approached, but even so the rifle pointed directly at her heart was terrifying. The young man wore a beret sloped across his forehead, and the armband on his shirt had an F.T.P. insignia. His face was as smooth as her own. Not old enough to shave but old enough to hold a gun. She was relieved she had come to the right place, but the gun pointed directly at her was making her feel faint.

"I need to see Hérisson," she stammered.

"Who are you?" the young man asked coldly.

"I have information about an airplane and airmen. I need to see him urgently." The young man whistled, three shrills, still with his gun pointed directly at her. Another youth appeared, and the first told him, "She's asking for Hérisson."

"You'd better take her to Carlos," the second youth said. "I'll take over here. Go."

She was directed by the first youth at gunpoint, into what had once been the factory office. The room was empty, apart from a desk and one chair. The guard waved her towards the desk, then stood with the gun trained upon her. A man appeared.

This must be Carlos, she thought. She had heard so much about him from Hérisson, and had somehow imagined a much bigger man. And a less handsome one. He seemed to emit energy from every pore. And he was angry. "What the hell are you doing here?" he demanded in heavily accented French. Two further men entered the room, tanned, like Carlos. They studied her expressionless.

"I, I, I wanted to tell Hérisson. I think I know where the airmen came down," she spluttered nervously.

"How did you know we were here?" Carlos demanded, ignoring her explanation.

"I deliver your messages," she explained quickly. "You're Carlos aren't you?"

The commander walked round her.

"Our placements are secret," he said, now standing at her back. "How did you know to come here?"

"I meet Hérisson. I deliver messages; that's the only reason I'm here." She felt more anxious than ever and was regretting her rash decision to visit the camp. Carlos muttered very fast in Spanish, then the two others left. The youth pointing the gun at her remained in position and Sabine prayed fervently that Hérisson would come to her rescue.

It seemed like hours before he marched through the door, with Loup following closely behind him. Both wore a beret and armband. Her eyes focused on Hérisson and she moved instinctively towards him. The rifle clicked. Sabine froze like a statue and looked pleadingly at Hérisson. "What's going on?" he demanded.

"That's what I want to know." Carlos said marching towards them. "How does she know my name, and your name? How has she turned up here, with a wild tale about crashing planes and parachutists?"

"She is the messenger," Hérisson answered. "You can trust her."

"If she's your courier, she just needs to know your name! Not mine! Not where the unit is stationed! This is a serious breach of protocol!"

Hérisson stood to attention. Sabine could see the anger flowing through him. Why didn't he explain. He could trust her with his life.

Carlos looked as if he was too angry to speak. If Hérisson wasn't there, she would have been terrified. However, as always, she felt reassured by his presence. She believed he would protect her no matter what.

Cerf arrived. Also breathless. "I saw a parachutist. Pete and Ava have gone to try and track them down. If they are successful, they'll make their way to the café in Saint-André."

"Right." Carlos snapped. "You," he said, pointing at Hérisson. "If there are any further breaches of security involving her or anyone else, I'll have your balls." Carlos turned to Sabine. "You. You're a courier, right?"

" Yes," she said, standing to attention.

"Right. I've a message for you to deliver to the café in Beaupouyet." He sat down and carefully coded a note. Sabine rolled the piece of paper and slid it into the pocket in her dress.

"Get it delivered urgently. Then forget about this place. Don't ever come here again," Carlos ordered in a voice which held such menace Sabine felt a chill run down her spine. "You," Carlos said, pointing now at Cerf and Loup. "Get back and join the others. The Nazis know there are parachutists down. They will be combing the forest. Hérisson, escort her to her bicycle and get her on her way, then come back here immediately. We need to move further away. The forest isn't going to be safe. Now move, men! There's no time to lose!"

Hérisson complied with his orders and led Sabine to her bicycle. He kissed her briefly on the lips as he said goodbye. "Promise me you'll be careful," he insisted. She nodded. She didn't need any encouragement. She was terrified of meeting that lorry full of soldiers with the flak gun. She cycled furiously down towards Mussidan. When she reached the turning for Saint-Front-de-Pradoux, she would have to decide whether it was too risky to cross the bridge at Mussidan. If she couldn't cross the Isle there, she would have to find a point further down, and that would mean leaving her bicycle behind. She'd look even more suspicious without it. At least with the basket of cheese there was always the explanation that she was making a delivery.

She pulled of the road and into the ditch twice when she heard the rumble of engines coming up the hill. Better to risk a little dirt on her clothes than risk being questioned by the occupants of the trucks. She watched several vehicles filled with soldiers go past. It looked as if the full complement of the Mussidan garrison had been deployed in the search for the airplane and pilots. She hoped Hérisson's group had moved to safety, and that the others had been successful in whisking the airmen out from under their enemies' noses.

When she arrived at the edge of town, a few people began to appear on the streets. She decided to risk cycling through the town. Adopting a leisurely pace, Sabine and did her utmost to appear casual although her heart was pounding.

Once though the town, she put her head down and pedalled furiously. She had over ten kilometers to travel to reach the village, and another hill to climb at the end.

The restaurant was still open. She made a play of bartering with the owner over her remaining cheeses while simultaneously handling delivery of Carlos's message. Once relieved of her duty she set off for home. That meant another traverse of Mussidan, and it was getting dark. She was reluctant to take the risk, but the alternatives were even less appealing.

It was pitch black by the time she arrived home. *Maman* tuttered as she sat down at the table, clearly exhausted. "What on earth dear? You've been gone all day."

"The deliveries took much longer than planned."

Her father took a drag of his cigarette and looked at her suspiciously. "You need to organise yourself better. Your mother never needed to spend the amount of time away that you do."

Sabine nodded her agreement submissively, anxious to avoid an argument. But she could not fail to notice the distasteful manner in which her father seemed to regard her. She felt ashamed for lying, but then more ashamed of him for his refusal to see the Vichy government for what it was.

Chapter 38

LA BARDE, SAINT-ANTOINE-DE-DOUBLE, SEPTEMBER 1943

She carefully put down the basin of whey, listening intently. Had she been mistaken? Again came the sound. The distinctive owl hoot. At this time of the morning it could only mean one thing. She covered the liquid with a dampened linen cloth and slipped out of the door. Hérisson emerged like a shadow from the cover of the forest. "Come on," he urged, beckoning her with his arm. Glancing towards the cottage, she slipped across the grass and joined him.

He kissed her, picking her up and twirling her around. "I have a surprise."

"What is it?" she asked excitedly, wondering if it would be chocolate or silk, maybe even coffee. "I have the loan of a motor bike for a few hours. I'm taking you out."

"Impossible," she said. "I have to finish the cheese. *Maman* and Papa will never allow it."

He looked at her. "Come on, how often do we have an opportunity to do something normal?

I might not get another chance. You have to say yes. Tell your parents you are going for a walk. The cheese can wait, can't it? Just two hours."

Sabine smiled, catching his excitement. He was right. The last few months had been hard. Since the German defeat at Stalingrad in February the *Boche* had become even more brutal. Patrols were increasing. The capture and horrific torture of Resistance hero Jean Moulin had affected them all.

Nodding she said "I will grab something from the kitchen."

She kissed him before running to the cottage, collecting a small sack with apples and some bread and liver pate from the kitchen.

"*Maman*, I am going into the forest to search for mushrooms. There was a beautiful full moon last night and I am sure there will be a magnificent crop around the oak copse."

"Yes, of course. Be careful." *Maman* replied barely looking up from the shirt she was mending.

Sabine hardly heard her mother's words of caution, so excited was she for the chance to escape with Hérisson, even if only for a short time. She grabbed her bicycle and set off.

Once free of the farm, Sabine secreted her bicycle. Hérisson recovered the motorcycle from its hiding place. Sabine climbed behind and hugged him close. The motor surged into action with a jolt as Hérisson kicked down on the starter. She was terrified of falling off as they bumped over the rough track into the depths of the forest. She hugged close to Hérisson and soon began to feel more relaxed, enjoying the freedom as they sped along with the noisy roar of the engine echoing around them. They soon reached a lake and Hérisson pulled to a halt. A heron, disturbed by their arrival, rose gracefully into the sky. Taking her hand, Hérisson walked her to a secluded corner where they laid out their picnic.

Sabine sat down on the grass, savouring for a moment the peacefulness of their surroundings. All was silent except for the rustling of leaves as a barely perceptible breeze wandered through the willow trees lining the edge of the lake.

"I've wanted to take you here for a long time," Hérisson confided.

"It's very beautiful."

"I've hunted here," he said, and pointed. "I've never forgotten it. I promised myself I would take you here. We can swim. The water is fresh. It is fed by the stream that enters over there."

"Someone might come," Sabine giggled.

"No. I've never seen anyone else here."

After gentle lovemaking, they wandered hand in hand to a copse of oaks where Sabine hoped they would find some *cepes*. They kicked amongst the vegetation that covered the forest floor, searching for the nutritious bounty. Hérisson found the first, its base pitted but still worthy of collection. Sabine the next. They moved steadily, scouring the tree bases for the most promising locations. They soon gathered several kilos of mushrooms and the desired alibi for Sabine's absence. They attached the sack to the back of the motorcycle and headed back to the farm. Sabine was flushed with happiness when she proudly placed the sack of *cepes* on the table in the kitchen. Her mother immediately began sorting and chopping the best parts. They would cook some and give the rest to Aunt Delphine. If the *cepes* were not eaten that day, they would be riddled with worms. Still edible, but not nearly so good.

Chapter 39

LA BARDE, SAINT-ANTOINE-DE-DOUBLE JANUARY 1944

A low mist drifted from the lake, its ghostly fingers wandering over the fields, teasing around the farm buildings and their cottage, making the buildings appear as if they were floating on clouds. Sabine's father expected the low winter sun would soon break through the cloying mist, so the family had begun to prune the vines as planned. It was one of the jobs that Sabine hated. The trimming was normally carried out when the winter was at is harshest. The vines would leave her hands scratched and scarred for weeks, as if seeking vengeance for the vicious pruning, that was required to ensure a generous crop in autumn.

They each positioned themselves at regular intervals along the row of vines. She, her mother, Aunt Delphine, and *grand-mere* wore knitted mittens with no fingers, and their heaviest coats lined with newspaper to provide additional insulation. She had wrapped a scarf around her neck and face, covering her mouth, and added an extra layer of socks before she put on her *sabbots*. Despite the layers, the cold wrapped around her like an icy blanket and she could see her breath in the frozen air. Her father as usual had not worn gloves, although his beret was pulled down over his ears. He seemed to find the cold invigorating. She smiled as she noticed her brother had not worn his gloves either as he tried to emulate his father. Already his hands were white and she could see he tried to hide his need to shiver.

They worked rhythmically, gathering the pruned shoots and placing them in bundles. Later, the women would tie the bundled *sarments* and store them in the barn to be used as fuel for the grill when they cooked meat. This work, done together as a family, was when she felt her sister's absence most acutely. In previous years, Josette had always been positioned between her and Tomas. With one person less, they progressed more slowly. They had not even finished half the pruning by the time they stopped for lunch.

Seated around the kitchen table, they tucked into a thick broth. They ate quickly, then washed the bowls with red wine and mopped the residue with heavy chunks of bread. If anyone gave a thought about stopping for *sieste*, they kept quiet about it. With the vines to be pruned and the pressing early darkness of the winter months, sleep would have to wait. Warmed by the wine and reinvigorated by their lunch, the family returned to the work in hand.

Sabine's hands moved automatically as she snipped and pruned, as if she had been born knowing the best shoots to leave to ensure fruit in the next season. Her mind wandered as she worked. They had received virtually no news from Josette since she had left. Two regulation postcards had arrived, both with a box ticked to indicate all was well. Papa had taken the cards, glanced at them, then thrown them into the fire, ignoring *Maman's* pleas to keep them. Sabine had found Papa's attitude difficult to understand. He had insisted that they accept French surrender, which, as Josette had so poignantly insisted, meant accepting the German soldiers and all that came with it.

His daughter's relationship with a *Boche* and her departure to Germany without his permission had been a humiliation he refused to accept. He would not permit any reference to Josette within their home and all of her remaining belongings had been redistributed around the village. The only evidence that she had ever existed was her name in the family bible and her record in the *livre de famille*.

Tomas had pretended to follow his father's lead, but he could not conceal that he was becoming older and more aware. Gone were the days when he catapulted stones at the geese and hens with his friend Gustave. The pair rolling with laughter at the birds squawks when their weapons hit home. The requisition of half the herd of goats had hit the family hard and now Sabine often her brother and his friend pair falling silent when she approached and conversing in whispers. She observed the anger on his face as the shortages pinched harder, as tales of reprisal and requisitioning intensified. She feared for her brother. She did not want him to become involved in the Resistance. It was too dangerous.

She pruned more fiercely, working to finish before darkness fell. Always the war hung above them, the question of when it would all end. How much longer could Germany sustain its stranglehold on their country? The more Tomas praised acts of Resistance, the more apparent became the fear in her father's eyes. She could see the clock ticking in his head. Would the war end before Tomas was old enough to become involved, or would the war, in its final, thrashing, death throes steal his only son?

Chapter 40

MUSSIDAN, 16 JANUARY 1944

'Come upstairs,' Mariette gestured frantically. She closed the door immediately behind Sabine and leaned against it.

'I needed to see you.

Ever since Jacques Binger, that bastard collaborator, was shot right outside the Hotel Andanson last week, the Resistance has cleared out. There are rumours that the Gestapo will carry out a search of the town. We have to be extra careful. No leaflet drops, nothing, not for another few weeks anyway.'

Fear suffused Sabine, betrayed by the paleness of her face. Shooting the 'collabo' in plain sight was an action sure to incite reprisals.

'I pray they'll negotiate a settlement soon'.

'Germany's going to have to surrender,' Mariette pressed her friend's hand. 'Don't worry, it's only a matter of time. The power of the Resistance is growing. Now there are parachute drops in the Forest every night there's enough moonlight. The *Boche* don't even dare go there. Once spring comes there'll be landings, here, in France. And a major operation in this area, imagine. We'll be liberated this very year.'

The young women relaxed, chatting about their plans for when the war was over. The end of all the fear and deprivation no longer seemed an impossible dream. Now it was tangible. Freedom would return to France soon, perhaps in the next few months.

'What was that?' Mariette had straightened up and was staring towards the door.

Sabine shrugged and took a cautious peep through the window. 'Can't see a thing, it's so foggy.'

Mariette relaxed again, shaking her head. 'I've become so jumpy. Every little sound has my heart start racing.'

Sabine reached for her friend's hand and gave it a squeeze. 'We'll be okay. Like you said, *Liberté*, soon.'

Mariette nodded and squeezed Sabine's hand in return. 'Are you ready to walk round to the church?'

'Yes, I'll just get my coat.'

Mariette drank back the rest of her coffee, stood up and carefully studied her reflection in the mirror. Her husband might be far away but she hadn't lost any of her vanity. After making some finishing touches to the pins in her hair, she was ready.

They strolled arm-in-arm towards the church. It was very quiet. Several other parishioners walked in the same direction. Others patiently queued at the baker's.

Sabine pulled her coat around her, watching her breath merge into the grey fog, which only made it seem colder. As they began to climb the steps of the church, the bells chimed the hour. Sabine thought she heard shouting and turned before entering. Since there seemed to be nothing untoward she entered the church thinking how odd it was that the dense mist from the river could distort sound and bend distance, making the most mundane of noises sound sinister.

At the end of the service, as usual, neither hung around for confession. As the rest of the congregation filed out of the church, they were halted at the top of the steps. The foot of the steps was surrounded by stern faced German soldiers pointing guns at them. A Gestapo officer in the now all-too-familiar black leather coat and hat was screaming at the parishioners in German- accented French. To his left stood other Gestapo men each with a German Shepherd growling, snarling and jumping against their leads as though they, too couldn't wait to see action. Sabine, Mariette and the others were ordered to form a queue to have their papers checked. Armed soldiers ran past them, apparently to search the building.

Mariette whispered, 'that's Otto Schneider, he's a sadistic bastard.' Sabine could feel the terror rise in her gut. Just the sight of the Gestapo officer with his cold eyes and sinister leather coat was enough, to instill fear in the bravest. And Sabine was not brave at all. She glanced at Mariette who squeezed her hand reassuringly. 'Just keep calm', her friend whispered.

Sabine took a deep breath and tried to stop her hands from shaking, though her heart rate was close to danger level. She tried to surreptitiously observe what was happening. As well as the soldiers guarding those who had come out of the church, there were many more in the streets. All the roads fanning out from the church were blocked. Soldiers were moving from one house to another along each road. If the occupant didn't open rapidly at their knock, the door was kicked open with a splintering crash and the men charged into the property. How many soldiers were there? Too many to count. Even though they were Wehrmacht, that brought no comfort. They were under Gestapo command and that meant no mercy. For anyone!

At last it was their turn to show their papers. Mariette managed a coquettish smile as she handed over her identity papers. After a few brief questions, she was waved-on. As Sabine handed over her papers it was obvious her hand was shaking, but this seemed to amuse the officer who waved her on.

They walked away as rapidly as they could and returned to Mariette's home.

'I daren't walk past them on my own', Sabine admitted, choking back a sob. 'I'll have to wait here until they've gone.'

'Of course. Don't worry, all the Resistance members have left.'

'But I overheard one of the soldiers. They're looking for Arnaud. That means someone has talked. They must have an informant.'

'Listen, no one in our group has been caught. It can't be more than a suspicion. And he's got safely away. Once they realise they're too late, I'm sure they'll leave.'

They waited, anxiously, peering out of the window from time to time hoping to discover what was happening. After what must have been several hours they heard a pounding noise nearby. Mariette stuck her head out of the window as far as she dared but still could see nothing. She turned to Sabine.

'I'm going to slip out, I've got to find out what's going on.'

Sabine's voice shook and she seized her friend's arm. 'Please, no, don't. It's too dangerous.'

Just then an army truck pulled into the square and halted. Through the slats in the shutters, they saw Madame Dumas being dragged like a sack of flour between two soldiers and flung into the truck. As the canvas lifted, there was a glimpse of rows of frightened faces inside.

Mariette spoke between clenched teeth. 'My God, Madame Dumas hasn't put a foot out of line. And she's got two young children. This is terrible.'

'Did you recognise anyone else?' Sabine asked her.

'I got a glimpse of Monsieur Escoffier, the coal man. He's had nothing to do with the Resistance either.'

The vehicle pulled away and an eerie silence fell over the town.

'Wait here, Sabine. I'm going to find out what's happened.' This time, there was no dissuading Mariette. She left with the assurance, 'Don't worry. I'll be careful.'

When she returned a little later her usual confident expression had been entirely wiped from her ashen face.

'They didn't find the Resistance people they were looking for, not any of them. But they had a quota of thirty-five people to fill, so they took people off the street just as they found them and they took the wives or family of anyone they suspected of being in the Resistance – or of helping it. No one knows what's going to happen to them. But they know who's involved in the Resistance. They knew who to look for.'

Sabine couldn't help noticing her friend's hands. They were shaking. Gone was the confident person who'd recruited her. For the first time, Mariette was evidencing real fear.

Mariette shook her head as though to rid it of the thoughts that were poisoning it. 'This means someone has betrayed us. Only a few people know who's in the movement.'

'But surely that means we're all in danger. Every one of us?'

'No, Arnaud is the only person in Mussidan who knows you and me have been involved. He's always very careful. As long as he's free, we're safe. And you have Hérisson to watch out for you, don't you? He would never give you up.'

'I'm scared.' Sabine blurted. ' I wouldn't be able to keep silent if I was tortured.' And, overcome with emotion, she began to cry.

'Courage'. Mariette, once more playing the comforter, placed a hand on her shoulder. 'We're all frightened, but our liberation will come. We just have to be even more careful. It's not going to be for much longer.'

Chapter 41

THE FOREST, 22nd January 1944

The buttons were stiff and the material coarse from laundering. Hérisson adjusted the belt to cover the hole left by the fatal bullet that had dispatched its former occupant. Once the helmet was placed on his head, he stood up as tall as he could, elongating his spine and adopting the expressionless face of typical member of the *Milice*, Vichy's very own version of the S.S. Once he was satisfied his disguise would pass muster, he glanced across at Christophe, who had been carefully shaving. A three-day stubble was as much the mark of a *Maquisard* as a clean jaw and meticulous appearance was the uniform of a *Milice*. Now they both looked the part.

Christophe ran through the plan again. "All clear?" he asked, regarding each one in turn as he distributed their identity papers. They all nodded. They were about to embark on their most audacious sortie ever.

The cars, two black Citroens borrowed from a local garage, together with sufficient fuel to make the journey, stood polished outside the barn. Two swastika flags were positioned in brilliant chrome holders on the bonnet of the leading car. Hérisson climbed into the front beside the Loup who was driving while Christophe, playing the commanding officer, took his place in the back. They set off at a relaxed pace. Hérisson leaned back into the leather seats, trying to relax, although his heart was beating faster than the engine.

They passed several patrols on the journey towards Bergerac, but their vehicle did not attract any attention. Christophe regularly lifted his hand in reply to raised Nazi salutes from *Boche* soldiers. Hérisson took a deep breath as they entered the town. He had not been there since before the occupation. The town associated with the famous French writer, Cyrano de Bergerac, had drastically changed. Now heavily garrisoned, Bergerac was saturated with German soldiers. With German signposts and Nazi flags draped from every public building, it seemed the spirit of the town had been trapped and imprisoned in the Gestapo headquarters.

Their vehicle wound its way through the narrow streets of the old town, with the second following behind. As the car bumped and rattled down a cobbled alley, Hérisson drew in his breath, as if he might make the vehicle more able to squeeze through the narrowing lane. The high, close walls around them made him feel as if they were travelling back through time, to when the town was new, and its medieval streets stank as open sewers spewed their sludge into the River Dordogne. What had they seen, these towering, shambolic buildings? Quaint in the days before the war, they now stood too close to the seat of local Nazi power to hold any charm. At virtually every café, there were soldiers, *gendarmes* or *Miliciens* sipping French wine, or sampling *fois gras* and *entrecôte* as if the local produce, like everything else, was part of the spoils of war. All these parasites on the body politic of France were fawned over by simpering *restaurateurs* too frightened to refuse their trade, or worse, collaborators who welcomed the stolen money their clients spent so lavishly.

'There,' Hérisson called, pointing to the street name as they passed. Loup reversed at speed causing a cyclist to swerve. The old man neither glowered nor gestured as his cycle skidded into the wall. But his eyes spilled hate. Hérisson stared back, meeting his gaze without flinching. Passers-by bowed their heads and melted into the stone walls. As the cars continued their journey, the lane emptied before them. Gun loaded and ready in his hand, Hérisson felt power. He steeled himself for what lay ahead.

He imagined himself a gangster in one of those Hollywood movies he'd immersed himself in at the cinema, in the days when such things were possible. He felt ready to leap from the vehicle in a glorious blaze of bullets and fire. Respect was his to claim. Fear he owned, and could hold in check, proud to have been chosen for this delicate mission into the lion's den.

The cars drew up at their destination. Hérisson accompanied Loup and Christophe as they knocked officiously on the door. An elderly French woman answered. He watched her expression transform as she opened the ancient door. First, pleasure at the expectation of a welcome guest, changing to one of shock, then of abject fear. When Hérisson asked for the whereabouts of her daughter, the woman immediately began to shake. She retreated, leaving the door open, calling for her husband.

He came to the door, already infected by the woman's fear. 'It's a small celebration for our wedding anniversary. Only a few close family.'

'I asked, where is your daughter.' Christophe gave a perfect, clipped, imitation of the icy manner of an officer in the *Milice*.

Hérisson felt shame at his earlier elation as the man's hands began to shake and his jaw trembled. Their mission was no longer an adventure. This time there would be a human cost to pay. The gentle elderly couple, in whose lounge he now stood, would be the ones paying the price.

'Your daughter, *monsieur*!' Christophe barked impatiently. *Monsieur* Million began to shake and muttered she was attending mass at the church. The men returned to their car. Hérisson checked the location of the church on the map although with its spire towering above the town it wasn't going to be difficult to find.

They arrived to find the eight-o-clock morning mass still underway. The men removed their hats and, having identified the daughter through discreet questioning, waited patiently at the rear of the chapel while the priest concluded the service.

Hérisson ignored the cold gaze of the parishioners as they filed nervously out of the chapel past the men. Each no doubt wondering if it was for them the hour of reckoning had finally arrived. Finally, the nun began to walk down the aisle towards them. Hérisson studied her features, calm and serene as though she had nothing to fear. Doubt entered his mind for the first time. His allegiance lay with communism, but it was impossible not to be affected by the holiness of the location and the serenity of their soon-to-be prisoner. Luce Million, also called *Soeur* Marie-Philomene, did not seem surprised by their approach. She walked between them to the outside of the church. They walked down the steps and then Loup thrust the letters of denunciation in front of her.

'Did you write these?' he demanded. The nun looked at the handwritten documents and nodded.

'In that case, *Sister*, we require you to accompany us to Gestapo headquarter in Perigueux. We have made some arrests and we need you to identify one of the suspects. The sister nodded, evidencing no emotion. She was directed into the first Citroën. The vehicles diverted to enable her to collect some belongings from her parents' home. She was escorted into the house by Loup and Hérisson, who watched as she collected some clothing and hugged and kissed her parents, assuring them that she would return shortly to be present at their celebrations.

The journey passed in silence. The nun did not question either their destination or the length of time for which she would be required to provide assistance. Neither did she ask who had been arrested. The men grew increasingly conscious of the direction their investigation must take, given her frank admission of having written the letters. All remained silent apart from muttered directions.

The journey to Thiviers, along the ill-maintained winding road north of Perigueux, took over an hour. Even then the sister did not enquire why they were not going to the Gestapo headquarters in Perigueux as she had been originally told.

Eventually they arrived at the lonely farmhouse where the suspects were being held. The place was obviously neglected. Weathered shutters hung loosely from the cracked and pitted walls. If Sister Marie-Philimone wondered about the suitability of using the apparently abandoned property as a holding pen for members of the Resistance, she did not ask.

They led her into the kitchen, which was only identifiable as such by the stone sink on the far wall. An icy wind blew through the broken window above it. Though a rusted cauldron hung from the kitchen irons in the fireplace, it did not appear that a fire had been lit recently.

Tallet, leader of Bridgade Violette, having asked her to sit in the only chair available, entered the other room and returned pushing Cézard, chief of the North Dordogne sector in front of him. Cézard's arms were roped behind his back, his hair ruffled and streaked with blood. His face, too, was bloodied and grimy. Yet still his eyes blazed with anger and hatred, and he spat with force in the direction of his captors.

'Is this the man you describe in your letters?' Tallet asked.

Marie-Philimone responded calmly and evenly as though teaching an attentive class of children.

'Yes, this is the Cézard I mention. That's definitely him. I know he arranges parachute drops and plots against our government in Vichy'.

Cézard stepped towards her. Tallet moved forward and loosened his ties. The nun stared at the men as they ripped their hats from their heads and crowded around her.

Cézard charged forward until he stood just before the startled nun. 'Why did you denounce me?' he roared.

For a split-second fear appeared in her eyes and then her features resumed the calmness she had maintained since the first moment she was asked to accompany them.

'I ask you again. Why did you denounce me?' Cézard, almost incoherent with fury, grabbed the letters and waved them in front of her face.

The nun stood up and the men took a step back, surprised by her apparent lack of fear and obvious lack of remorse for what she had done.

Her contempt for him obvious, 'That is my secret', she answered.

Cézard kicked the chair she had been sitting on, splintering it into its sections as it skittered across the floor rattling against the fractured clay tiles.

'What made you do it?' Tallet insisted.

Marie-Philimone smiled enigmatically, shaking her head.

'What do you intend to do now?'

The men looked at each other. The nun was a collaborator by her own admission. She was too dangerous to be allowed her freedom and the *Maquis* did not take prisoners. They had neither the places to keep them, nor the manpower to guard them.

Chapter 42

LA BARDE, SAINT-ANTOINE-DE-DOUBLE

Sabine lined the rows of cheese and stood looking at them, pleased by the order they represented. Here, in the *chai*, her private world, she was able to maintain the routine normality of everyday life. Here, she had complete control, and it was beginning to be the only place where she felt safe. The only place she could successfully exclude the outside world and forget about the realities that forced their way upon her each time she emerged into the sunlight.

The distant rumble of an engine disturbed her tranquillity. Her heart began to beat a little faster and she felt the now familiar fear she experienced every time there was the slightest variation in the routine of the day.

She suppressed the urge to run, persuading herself she had no reason to be frightened. She cleaned her hands and cautiously opened the door just enough to see what was happening outside.

A motorbike rolled into the courtyard. The driver was not in uniform. Already that was a relief. The driver removed his helmet and goggles. Recognition took moments. She pulled back into the shadows, but it was too late. She had been seen.

'Sabine.' René called, and waved. Did he really think she hadn't seen him? She took a deep breath and, pushing open the door, walked into the sunlight. His left eye was covered with a black eyepatch and he limped as he walked towards her. The war was just beginning to take its toll on her. Perhaps for him it had already done its worst.

'I got back this morning. I came to see you as soon as I could.'

She managed a smile. Oh, how she wished she'd been better prepared for this.

She glanced down at her feet knowing now she should have done this by letter. It would have been easier on them both.

'Sabine', he said, taking her hand. She let it rest in his palm for a moment, before snatching it away. Even that had changed. It was calloused and scarred. No longer the hands of a boy.

'I'm sorry. I should've prepared you. For my injury.' He gestured towards his eye and leg. 'But I promise you, Sabine, I'll still make a good husband. The injuries won't stop me working. I'll have a good position in my father's business. It'll all be mine one day. I can provide you with a good home. A good life, like I promised.'

He sounded so sincere. Sabine was overwhelmed by shame. She tried to find the words to answer.

René assumed her silence reflected his changed appearance. 'I know I don't look quite the way I used to, but I promise you, I still love you with all my heart.'

Finally and painfully, the words rose to the surface. Still looking at the ground. 'I'm sorry, I can't, not now.'

His voice rose as anger replaced apology. 'Sabine, remember, we promised each other.'

'I know what we promised, but everything's different now. I can't, I can't promise anything, not when we're in the middle of a war. You've no idea what it's been like here.'

The eruption came. 'Look at me, for God's sake! Where d'you think I've been? If you'd any idea, you wouldn't dare disrespect me like this.' He took a step towards her, his demeanor signalled physical aggression as his next act. She'd never heard him raise his voice before. Frightened she took a step back.

She tried to soothe him. 'I'm not being disrespectful.'

'You're my *fiancée*. We're engaged. You made a promise. Everyone knows.'

'Yes, we got engaged before you went away. But I can't be your wife. It's nothing to do with your injury, I promise you that. It's me. It's my fault. We've not seen each other for so long now. So much has changed. I've changed. I don't want to get married and have children. I want to have my own property. I want to vote. I want to have my own bank account. I want to make my own decisions for me.'

'You're being ridiculous.'

'Why?'

'Because I'll look after you. You'll have everything you need.' René paused, looking at her in genuine puzzlement. 'You want to have your own vote? Really?'

She nodded.

'What does that have to do with our being married?'

'Nothing and everything. You want me to be the same girl you left behind. The girl who dreamed about her wedding day and the children she'd have.

Now these things seem to me to be from another world. They're like the morning mist that creeps up from the river. They're not real any more. I fear being tied down to them as I fear this war, which clings to me like a heavy fog.'

'I can't believe you're talking like this. After everything we said to one another.'

He stepped away abruptly. She caught the pain in his eyes. Gripping his hand more tightly she said, 'Then, I meant everything, but . . .' She held her other hand to her forehead, 'This war.'

'I should never have come. I knew I couldn't expect you to want to honour our engagement because of my face.'

She traced a finger over his cheek. 'I still see you as you were. For me, you haven't changed. But *I have*. I'm not the person you said 'goodbye' to at the station.'

'Don't be silly, of course you are.'

'No, René. I'm not. Those promises were made by someone else, and now they're promises I cannot keep.' She paused and looking straight into his eyes, said, 'I'd hoped you'd understand.'

'Is there someone else?' He flicked finger and thumb together 'That's it. While I was away fighting for our Country, you've been carrying-on with someone else. A conscription- dodger. That's my reward for my sacrifice. My mother told me.

She said you' been seen with a communist.'

Sabine stiffened. She was quite sure he'd see her pallor, her face betraying her lies to him. But not just that, if knowledge of her involvement with the Resistance was as widespread as he'd suggested it was, not only was she in deadly danger but her whole family as well.

'You're being ridiculous. I should've written to you to break off the engagement. It would've been fairer. I'm sorry. I see that now. Please, please, forgive me.'

She stared at the ground again, quite unable to witness the the flood of emotion she knew would be crossing his face. She felt very alone and exposed as they stood opposite each other in the courtyard.

Her father appeared at the door and called over, '

Home at last, René! Join us for a celebratory drink.'

Sabine silently cursed her decision to keep her family ignorant of her intention to end the engagement.

René's lips curled into a snarl. He hissed, 'I don't think that'll be appropriate, do you?' He spat the words out, and this time when she looked into his eyes it was anger and disgust she saw.

She could feel the force of his hatred.

Wilting under it, she mumbled. 'I'd have made a terrible wife.'

'Of that I have no doubt. I went to war to protect you all. A price I'll pay for the rest of my life. And you?

You............. I gave you a chance. You'll regret this, I promise you.'

He turned and walked away, forcing his injured leg to move faster. He climbed awkwardly onto his motorbike, started the engine, and disappeared in a cloud of dust.

Chapter 43

THE FOREST

Cézard and Tallet sat smoking, staring out over the countryside as the sun sank below the hills in a blazing glorious sunset. Standing guard at the edge of the clearing, Hérisson could hear their conversion.

'Damn that woman.'

'We've got to do something. We can't keep her here much longer. She's been reported missing.'

Cézard laughed. 'Yeah, we've been lucky. The Gestapo think the *Milice* have her and the *Milice* think it's the Gestapo that've got her.'

'I've been told she was sharing a bed with that rascal, the priest, Ferry. Someone's denounced *him* for aiding the Resistance, so, in the eyes of the authorities she's probably a member as well.'

'If only they knew.'

Tallet spread his large hands to emphasise his point. 'What she's done is treason. If her letters hadn't been intercepted, who knows how many people would've died.'

'And we all know what the sentence for treason is.' Cézard stubbed out his cigarette and began rolling another.

'Why won't that bloody woman agree to being transferred across the mountains to her sisterhood in Spain. Anything!'

He banged his fist down on the table and took another gulp of *l'eau de vie de amande*.

Tallet leaned forward. 'She's in Holy Orders. I can't just order the men to shoot her. That makes us no better than the Nazi scum.'

'Yes, but we can't just leave things as they are. We're going to have to do something, and soon.'

Tallet scratched his head. 'I know the former Archbishop of Strasbourg. He came as a refugee to Perigueux about the same time as me. He served in the last war and he has some independence and distance from the situation. I can trust him. I'd like to take his advice.'

'Very well. Sounds fine to me.'

'We can go tonight.'

Chapter 44

LA BARDE, SAINT-ANTOINE-DE-DOUBLE

The family were still seated around the table just as they'd been when she'd left to collect a fresh round of cheese from the *chai*. Papa wiped his mouth with his napkin, removing the crumbs of bread from his moustache. *Maman* began to cut some fresh slices from the *baguette*. Tomas stared at his plate as if expecting it to refill magically with food.

'I thought I heard a tap at the door', Sabine said. Papa shook his head. No one else looked at her. 'Hurry up, we're all waiting for that cheese', her father added, breaking what was becoming an uncomfortable silence.

Sabine sat down. Something was wrong. Something had happened in those few minutes she had been outside. She stood up, went to the door and opened it. Two children were running down the road away from their house. She could tell by their clothing, a blue checked dress and a cream shirt with grey shorts, that it was Sarah and Isaac.

A black Citroën screeched into the yard followed by a Kübel-wagen filled with soldiers. Even before the car stopped its door swung open to reveal the hated Otto Schneider of the Gestapo.

Soldiers leapt out of the smaller vehicle and formed a guard. A harsh German voice barked orders. Sabine closed the door and leaned against it, as if that would stop anyone. A rifle butt hammered against the wood. Still she didn't move. Her father leapt to his feet and shoved her to the side. After a warning glance at his family, he opened the door.

The soldier, rifle raised to strike again, lowered his weapon. 'The Steins. Where are they?'

Papa shrugged and shook his head.

'We'll have to search your house then.'

Papa stood back, opening the door wider. The soldier pushed past followed by two colleagues. Ignoring the occupants, they carried out a perfunctory search of the house and buildings while the family sat round the table in silence. Finally the soldiers appeared satisfied and left.

'What happened?' Sabine said under her breath to her mother.

'Nothing. Finish your meal. This does not concern us.'

'They came here, didn't they?'

No one answered

Sabine's voice rose to screaming pitch. 'They came here for help and you closed the door in their faces.

I promised their mother if they needed help, to come to me.'

'You had no right!' Her father's anger matched his daughter's. 'Them coming here has put us all in danger.

Yes they did come. There was a knock at the door. I opened it. I could hear the motors coming. There was no time to do anything. I closed the door.'

'I don't know you anymore!' Sabine screamed at him, bursting into tears. 'I don't know who you are any longer.'

'I'm your father. It's my duty to protect you. To protect my family. I couldn't put you all in danger for no purpose. There was nothing that could be done. I'd do the same thing again.'

Sabine continued to sob, 'I promised if it came to this I'd help them.'

Her mother reiterated her husband. 'There was nothing we could do.'

Full of anger, Papa shouted, 'Listen to me, girl. You've no right to place us all in danger. I've tried to warn you, but I won't let you do it to us.' He pointed a finger directly at her. 'Understand me, I won't have it. This is my house and either you obey my rules or you find somewhere else to live.'

She stared at her father in disbelief. Shocked by his threat to throw her out of the family home. Appalled by his refusal to help innocent children.

She glanced across at Tomas. He bowed his head to avoid her look. When was he going to grow-up, she thought. Her mother was wringing her hands as usual.

'I'm going to look for them,' she said, standing and going to the door.

'If you step out of that door now, do not come back.'

Sabine reached out her hand to the door handle.

With a speed that belied his age and disabilities, her father appeared next to her and seized her outstretched hand. 'I mean it. You will stay here until this is sorted.'

Chapter 45

PERIGUEUX

The Archbishop inclined his head. He held his hands together in the graceful manner of a man of God. 'I have given the circumstances you've described to me some thought. This is a woman who has betrayed her country. If the Resistance is going to survive, it has to defend itself. I do not have to tell you what you have to do. But if she is condemned to death, I will send a priest to hear her confession and to be present at the execution.'

Tallet and Cézard bowed their heads. Hérisson, who'd been drafted-in as driver, closed his eyes. Had they come to this?

Chapter 46

LA BARDE, SAINT-ANTOINE-DE-DOUBLE

As soon as dusk began to fall, Sabine slipped out of the cottage and keeping close to the barn wall skirted the courtyard. She walked cautiously along the lane towards where the Steins lived. Even in the rapidly diminishing half-light, she was shocked by the devastation. The door had been smashed off its hinges and the house thoroughly looted.

She checked every room but there was no sign of any of the family. Murmuring silent prayers, she slipped back out into the night, ears alert for any indication that the soldiers were still in the area. Cautiously, she moved along the lane in the direction of the village.

When she reached the tobacco barn, she edged inside, then slipped the latch over the door. Lifting the kerosene lamp high, she moved over to the pit and brushed away the straw. 'Miriam,' she whispered. Silence was her answer. Hands trembling, she lifted the hatch and peered into the darkness below. The woman was huddled in the corner, eyes wide, like a trapped hare. Her body relaxed as she recognized her friend. 'The children. Have you seen them?'

Sabine couldn't bear to tell her about how her own family had behaved. To reassure the stricken mother, she whispered, 'I saw them

running into the woods. The soldiers didn't have dogs. I don't think
they found them. I hoped they'd have made it back here.' Miriam
began to sob. 'I couldn't reach them. I was at the well when I heard
the soldiers arrive. I couldn't get back to the house. I ran.'

'We'll find them,' Sabine tried to sound positive.

'There's an old *palombière* near where they disappeared into the
forest. I showed it to them once when we were searching for chestnuts. We can check there first.'

The women picked their way carefully through the trees,
following a narrow winding path. The high structure of the *palombière* reappeared and disappeared as clouds drifted across the waxing
moon, as if nature were performing a magical show just for them.
Having arrived at the foot of the structure they gazed upwards,
hoping to discern the children amongst the shadows.

'Isaac, Sarah', Miriam whispered as loud as she dare. Sabine
could sense the other's awful fear, and that started the pricking tears
welling in her own eyes. She'd been sure the children would be here.
If they were lost in the forest there was little chance of finding them
before the soldiers did, especially if they returned at dawn with dogs.

'I'll climb up', Sabine volunteered, although the thought of
climbing twenty meters up the ladder in the dark was making her
knees shake.

Miriam shook her head. 'It has to be me.' She put a foot on the
first rung and began to climb. Sabine stood holding her breath as her
friend disappeared into the darkness, like Jacques climbing the
beanstalk. She heard rustlings and turned in alarm, but it was only a
badger scuffling through the undergrowth. Then her friend hissed
down from the darkness. 'They're here. We're coming down.' The
time they took to descend seemed to go on for ever. Sarah was the
first and froze some fifteen meters from the ground. Sabine had to
climb up to coax her downwards. Finally they were all safe on the
ground together.

'We must all wade down the stream to confuse the dogs, then
there's a barn on the other side of the hamlet where you can hide
until tomorrow night. I know someone who can help you.'

Chapter 47

THE FOREST

Sabine fell into Hèrisson's arms as he emerged from the treeline. 'Thank God you're here', she said, her voice trembling. 'It's been terrible. The Germans tried to round up Miriam and her children. I've managed to hide them but they need help to get away from here.'

"I'll see what Loup can do. Don't worry.'

'Can't you take them?' Sabine pleaded, worried about any delay.

'No, I can't take them myself. I'm being posted with Cerf and Pinot to a camp with Brigade Violette in the north of Dordogne.'

Stunned – and with a note of desperation. 'You're leaving here? But why?'

'I've been ordered to help with training new recruits. Now the Resistance groups are working more closely together, it makes sense to have us train together as well.'

'For how long?' She couldn't keep the concern out of her voice. More than ever now she depended on his presence in her life.

'Look, it'll only be for a few weeks. I'll be back before the cranes fly over.' Hérisson clasped his hands, blowing into them against the cold. 'I don't mind. The winter's been so bitter, it'll be a relief to have a warm place to stay, even if it is far from you.'

'I'll send Loup to meet you here at dusk. He can lead your friends to the next safe house on the route to the south of France. They'll be able to escape over the Pyrenees into Spain. They'll be safe, I promise.'

Chapter 48

PONT-LASVEYRAS, PAYZAC

It was a relief to see the smoke curl upwards from the chimney after the long walk. The air was bitterly cold, and although the snow had almost melted away, the prospect of hot food was invigorating. Hèrisson quickened his step to match Cerf's, leaving Pinot to finish the journey alone.

As they approached the buildings, he could understand why this place generated such excitement. It was very beautiful. The narrow path wound its way through mature woodland, finally revealing the secluded property perched on the river bank. Behind the buildings waters roared and foamed over the weir. The house was of typical Perigourdine style, with a sharply pitched roof covered with orange-coloured clay tiles. The walls were stone, gathered no doubt from the surrounding hills. A wooden balcony lay to the south of the building which appeared to have the living quarters on the first floor with pens for animals on the ground floor. A narrow mill stream ran beside the mill, which was smaller than the house and situated much closer to the river.

As he paused for a moment to appreciate the setting, he wondered how the rescue of the Steins was going. Having persuaded

Loup to help, despite the family's lack of funds he knew his friend would do all in his power to get the fugitives to safety. He was broken from his thoughts when one of the recruits appeared on the balcony and directed them to the stairs. As Hérisson climbed upwards he paused for a moment to consider the location. He wondered what Carlos's opinion would have been. Yes, no-one would stumble across it but could they be certain that no one, collaborationist or German, wasn't aware they were using the empty buildings as a base? It lay at the very end of a narrow track, nestled at the back and to one side among steep, rocky hills. The remaining side was up against the river, swollen with fast-flowing icy water from the winter rains. Getting out of there by river would be impossible during the winter months. He resolved to discuss the suitability of the location, and the placement of guards, with the leaders of Brigade Violette and Rac who had sent recruits for training.

On entry to the large reception hallway, the welcoming smell of hot food greeted him. The recruits clustered around, anxious for the latest news. Hérisson was shown around the two rooms in use, Jean Delgage, the operational leader explaining the owner was a Doctor Dutheil from Limoges who used the property only as a summer second home. Intelligence assured them that he hadn't been there for over two years.

Because of its isolation, the Resistance had requisitioned the property to use as a training base for new recruits, a popular decision because the winter had been so bitter. 'We'll move as soon as spring comes, as soon as the cranes fly over. But for the moment,' the leader shrugged and looked around. 'There's nowhere else to go. If these lads are caught in the forest they'll be shipped off to labour camps in Germany. In any case, trying to shelter this number in the woods at this time of year...'

Hérisson understand only too well why they didn't want to leave. It was a luxury to have a roof over your head, water nearby, and a fire to keep you warm and make hot food. He'd have been unable to imagine such a scene if he weren't seeing it for himself. A return to the forest, and the hardships that entailed, was not a decision to be taken lightly. Yet he was conscious of how insistent Carlos always was that Brigade Rojo move every three days.

'À *table*', the erstwhile cook shouted. The youths pulled up seats and gathered around the table. Hérisson's mouth watered as he watched the cook spoon the steaming stew onto his plate. He seemed to have been hungry since leaving home all those years ago. Never again would he take a meal for granted. The harshness of the winter had taken its toll on them all. Everything had become more difficult.

Whilst the lumpy, brownish-cream coloured mound on his chipped plate did not look appetising, it tasted as good as the best meal he'd ever eaten. Onion and garlic had been mixed in with the potatoes, and the rabbit meat, although modest in portion, was tender. He tore off a piece of bread and used it to wipe every morsel of food off his plate. Afterwards, they drank ersatz coffee made from ground walnuts. Then they crowded around the fire with cups of warmed red wine, anxious to discuss their next mission of sabotage.

Arnauld proudly described their operations, moving from talk of patrols and sabotage to discussing the expeditions to gather food and other essential supplies. Throughout the time they'd been training, the recruits had enjoyed hot meals, usually vegetable soup supplemented with rabbits, hares, and pigeons they'd caught or snared. Occasionally they had dined on large game, like deer or boar supplied by the local *chasse* who wanted to demonstrate their support. Nor had they ever been short of bread. The father of one recruit was the proprietor of a *boulangerie* in the nearby village of Payzac, and ensured they always had a generous supply.

Chapter 49

THE FOREST

Sabine jumped up and down trying to keep warm. If she had to wait much longer, her toes would be frozen numb. Dusk was falling fast. Black clouds covered the sky. Soon night would make the journey to the barn where she'd hidden the Steins virtually impossible. If only Hérisson had been able to help.

Hands flashed across her face, blocking her sight and she felt strong arms around her. She struggled briefly, then smelled the smoky odour of charcoal and tobacco, and felt a kiss on her cheek. It *was* Hérisson after all. She turned her head to return his kiss and saw Loup. Her disappointment vented itself in rage. 'Let go of me ', she jabbed at him with her elbows and stamped on his foot.

Loup only laughed. 'Do you want me to help you or not?' His mouth twisted into a leer. Sabine backed away shocked by the suggestive tone of his voice.

'Hérisson promised me you'd help.'

Loup took a step towards her, now so close his lips were almost touching hers. 'But he isn't here now. It's just you and me. Alone.'

Sabine knew she mustn't let him see how intimidated she felt. 'Please Loup. They need our help.' Time stood still as they stared into each other's eyes. Suddenly Loup's manner changed and he returned to the relaxed joker she was more familiar with.

'Come on, I was only teasing you. We have to move quickly. The miller can only wait for so long.'

Sabine set off weaving through the woodland, with Loup following closely behind.

~

Sabine waved as she watched Miriam and the children disappear into the forest.

Loup would take them to the mill in Saint-Antoine-de-Double. From there they would travel onwards through France to safety. Then Loup would rejoin Hérisson to help with the training of the flood of new recruits.

Chapter 50

PONT-LASVEYRAS, PAYZAC, FEBRUARY 1944

The walls and floor of the room were of bare stone, the small windows half-shuttered. The only light came from a solitary kerosene lamp hanging from a rusty hook secured in an ancient oak beam. The odour of fuel did little to disguise the smell of damp and decay, which seemed to make the venue all the more suitable for what was to happen there.

An oak table that had seen better days was placed in the centre of the room. On the left side of it, a flag of the Free French forces, its colours faded, stood in the brass casing of an ammunition shell. Three wooden chairs lined one side. The best chair in the room had been reserved for a lone placement against the rear wall, facing the table.

Hérisson, having to make a real effort to overcome the desire to vomit, took his place at the chair closest to the flag. Tallet and Cézard, no indication of stress on their stern faces, then took their places beside him at the table. As the nun, wearing her habit, was led into the room and directed to the vacant chair, the tension was as tangible as the damp that clung to everything there.

Strangely, it was she, the prisoner, who seemed most at ease. A calmness and serenity surrounded her like an aura. It would been so much easier to pursue the awful business ahead had she been weeping and begging for mercy. As it was, her presence seemed to transcend the surroundings as though her spirit had already found sanctuary and was at peace.

Cézard, as the presiding judge, was determined to conduct the proceedings in proper form.

The announcement was made in an appropriately solemn tone, his eyes never leaving the woman seated on the opposite side of the table. 'This is a legitimately constituted tribunal of the Free French Forces convened to judge charges made against the prisoner.' Still locked eye-to-eye with her. 'You are Sister Marie-Philomene, born Luce Million?'

'I am.'

'You appear before this tribunal charged with treason against the French state by collaborating with the occupier. It is alleged that you posted a number of letters addressed to the Gestapo Headquarters in Perigueux. It is alleged that in these letters you named members of the Resistance who are fighting for the freedom of France. Further that you gave detailed information about Resistance activities, in the sure and certain knowledge that as a result of the information, which you willingly provided, these men would be sought out and executed by the occupying forces. What do you say to the charge?'

'I have nothing to say.'

A note comprising a few lines on a scrap of paper was produced and shown to the accused. 'Can you confirm this is your handwriting?'

She looked at it. 'That is my writing.'

'And can you confirm these are the letters which you sent?' Several sheafs of paper were produced and shown to the witness.

'I have already told you I wrote the letters.'

Cézard looked up from the paper he was writing on. 'Do you have anything you wish to say in your defence?'

'I have nothing to say.'

For a little more than a minute, the men at the table conferred in whispers, then Cézard said, 'The accused will stand'.

The nun rose, her face as expressionless and devoid of emotion as when she had entered the room.

Cézard cleared his throat. In a clear voice, determinedly devoid of any emotion, he announced the verdict. 'This tribunal finds you guilty of treason.' Silence followed. The nun remained standing, serene.

'Do you have anything you wish to say before the tribunal passes sentence?'

Hérisson stared at the now convicted prisoner willing her to offer some explanation, some excuse, anything. Before this dreadful play reached its otherwise inevitable conclusion.

'I have nothing to say.'

Almost as though unwilling to proceed and desperate not to have to, Cézard repeated himself. 'Do you have any expression of remorse you wish to make or any excuse for your behaviour? Are there any circumstances you wish to draw to the attention of the tribunal before sentence is passed.'

'I have nothing to say.'

And for the third time the hand of mercy is extended.

'I must draw to your attention that the sentence for treason is death.' A pause to allow that to sink-in. 'If there are any circumstances which mitigate your behaviour or if you have any regret, now is the time to say so.'

'I have nothing to say.'

The men round the table looked at each other. Tallet rose and walked round the table to the convicted prisoner. He took up the paper on which she had been asked to identify her handwriting. 'Look, this note you provided to a shopkeeper when he asked you to write something to check that a pen was working. The words you wrote were, "I am mad. I should have been locked away."

'Why did you write that? What did you mean by what you wrote? Tell us woman, we are not barbarians.'

'I have nothing to say.'

'Very well, your response has been recorded', Cézard said, placing his pen on the table. Tallet returned to his chair and sat down.

'This is the last opportunity. I beg you to tell us why you did this.'

'I have nothing to say.'

Following her, by now expected, answer, Cézard looked at the men on either side and spread his hands, palms upward.

'Very well', almost a sigh. Then in a voice deliberately heavy with solemnity, 'in the absence of any explanation for your actions, in the absence of any expression of remorse for your treachery and in the absence of any request for clemency, the tribunal has no alternative but to sentence you to death for treason.'

A heavy silence followed.

The nun's face remained expressionless and calm as if her spirit had already left her earthly body and begun its journey to a better place.

Cézard continued, 'You will be taken from this place and held under guard until dawn tomorrow. Then the sentence will be carried out. May God have mercy on your soul.' He crossed himself and bowed his head.

'I have nothing to fear from death. For me it will be a joy. I go to meet Him to whom I have dedicated my life. To Him whose kingdom surpasses that of any earthly state.' The nun's voice was clear and strong in the longest passage she had spoken since her arrest.

The men regarded her, each regretting her courage had been so badly placed.

'Canon Sharneberger will visit with you in order to pray with you and to perform the last sacrament.'

As she was about to be led away, she turned to them. 'Thank you.'

Although exhausted, Hérisson hardly slept at all that night, and it was with dread that he saw the dawn light edge over the skyline. Having being assigned the duty of waking the prisoner to see her final earthly sunrise, he set about the grim task.

She was already awake and followed him up the steep path to the clearing that had been chosen for her execution. The firing squad comprised seven youths, one of whom had been given a blank bullet.

The calmness *Soeur* Marie-Philomene had exhibited throughout her incarceration and trial continued. On seeing the post to which she would be tied, she requested that she instead be allowed to kneel, untied and without a blindfold.

The youths lined up in an orderly line, each praying he had the gun which held the blank. Hérisson watched them, admiring their resolve and cursing the circumstances which had conspired to bring them together on this bitter dawn.

Hérrison carried out his penultimate duty as the youths readied to complete their grim task. 'Do you have any last words?'

The nun shook her head.

He gave the command, 'Ready.' The squad raised their weapons to the firing position.

'Aim.' The sights of seven rifles were locked on to *Soeur* Marie-Philomene's breast.

'Fire!'

Seven rifle shots shattered the hitherto silent dawn. A flight of birds took off, as though they carried her soul skywards.

The woman's body crumpled to the ground. They buried her nearby.

Chapter 51

The gale howled outside, drowning out the sound of the water roaring over the weir. And inside their hideout, the recruits made even more noise. 'Stay', they implored the messenger, Ravel. 'Eat here tonight. You'll have a good meal and a fresh start in the morning.' Flakes of snow had begun to fall, and travelling by night was already an unpleasant proposition. Although he'd rested only briefly after spending two days walking all the way from Perigueux, Ravel shook his head.

'No, I want to get on my way. My coat is warm and I know a place to shelter within an hour's walk. I'll have a sense of a journey begun if I leave now.'

'Here, then. At least take some bread and cheese', another recruit called.

Hérisson heard the items being shifted off a shelf.

'Thank you', the messenger acknowledged, putting the food into his sack. 'I don't know what it was, but I heard strange sounds in the forest on my way here. It's unsettled me a bit.'

'We'll keep an extra look out.' the first recruit assured him.

'Good luck', said the other.

'And to you all,' Ravel replied, and then he was gone. The door opened into the violent wind for a moment before it was shut tight again. The recruits began to make preparations to bed down for the night.

Hérisson felt unsettled and began to make plans for the next operation, an attack on a railway line near Riberac. Generous supplies of arms and sabotage material from Britain, coupled with information that when the time came for the landings on France's north coast there'd simultaneously be an airborne drop of a force of crack troops into the Dordogne area to attack the Germans from the rear had enthused the Resistance groups. When he heard the news Carlos was triumphant. 'It's because we're the best', he'd shouted, punching his fist in the air. 'We've shown the way. Freedom for Spain too. Soon.' His men had cheered. As had Hérisson, Loup, Cerf and Pinot. They knew they were lucky to have become adoptive Spaniards.

By the time he had completed his route map, the others were already sound asleep, spread over the floor to the extent that he had been unable to find a place to lie down. He crouched, with his back against the wall, and closed his eyes. His thoughts filled with the image of Sabine. He wondered whether she, too, was unable to sleep, and if she was thinking about him. His limbs began to ache and he stood up. Moving gingerly across the floor, he settled on a chair at the table and began absent-mindedly sorting the beans for the following day, removing weevils and chaff.

Gradually, light began to slip through the window. Hérisson stood up from his task. Soon it would be reveille. Once the others resumed their duties, perhaps he would be able to snatch a few hours lying down, even if he couldn't actually sleep. Just as he stretched his legs he heard the crack of a gunshot. The kitchen window shattered and something whizzed past his ear.

He dived to the floor, yelling to the others to wake up and keep low. As he slid along the floor trying to reach his gun, a stream of machine gun bullets rat-a-tatted through the windows. Hérisson climbed to his feet and pressed himself hard against the wall.

Keeping his back to it, he sidled along the wall until by turning his head he could glance out of the window, trying to locate where the attack was coming from. The air around him was full of cries and shrieks of pain from those injured by the hail of bullets as the recruits tried to formulate a defence.

'Bloody Germans', Hérisson yelled at them. 'On the other bank of the river. I can see their helmets.'

'Yeah, and there are shots coming from the path above the mill', someone else said.

Pinot joined in, panic-stricken, 'They're coming up the path, we're surrounded.'

Hérisson looked at his friend whose eyes betrayed his utter terror as the implications of their situation took hold.

'We've almost no ammunition.'

Jean shouted from beneath a broken window where he'd taken shelter, 'We surrender! Stop firing!'

The machine gun stopped. Jean led the men to the door, hands on their heads.

As he emerged he was struck with a rifle butt and staggered.

'Lie down on your bellies, all of you', barked the Wehrmacht captain who was obviously in charge.

The men lay down where directed on the muddy ground.

Their boots slamming into the wooden staircase, Wehrmacht soldiers stormed into the mill, where the injured youths waited. Hérisson moved his head a fraction and immediately saw Pinot who was lying next to him, lift his head. A gun shot cracked through the air. Pinot jerked then lay still. Hérisson could feel the warm life-blood soaking his own clothing as it seeped from his dead friend.

Hérisson fought to keep the shock of this attack from paralysing his thinking. Mind racing, he tried to work out what would give him the best chance of survival. Lying in the dirt waiting to be shot seemed the worst kind of death. If he moved like lightening, could he reach the closest guard and seize his weapon? Could he move at all? He felt the warmth of fresh blood inside his trousers and realized then that he had taken a bullet in the thigh. But could he at least take some of them with him.

What would Carlos do?

He took a long slow breath and tried to lie as still as possible. Breathing slowly, dropping his heart rate. Getting back control over his mind. Quieting every nerve in his body. He concentrated on Sabine and wondered if he'd ever see her again. He thought of all the things he'd wanted to say to her and had never quite managed. He thought about what he'd say if he ever did see her again. He thought about all his plans and dreams. All slipping away, draining into the mud like the blood of his comrade.

'Who commands here?'

Hérisson continued to lie as though dead. He heard Jean claim leadership.

The *Boche* captain yelled, 'Get up', then kicked the eleven youths closest to him.

'On your feet, you communist scum.'

The youths scrambled to their feet. The officer ordered them to pick up equipment and follow a young soldier in single file up the path.

Desperate as he was to know what all this meant, Hérisson dared not move.

He soon found out. A rifle bolt was drawn back followed by a shot. Then another and another. He heard the voices of the condemned, '*Adieu, Maman.*'

Hérisson mouthed the words, '*Adieu,* Sabine.'

He felt a burning pain in his back. Then only cold darkness.

Chapter 52

LA BARDE, SAINT-ANTOINE-DE-DOUBLE

Sperlle Order
Areas of revolt or insubordination must be sealed-off. Civilians arrested. Accomplices eliminated immediately. Houses concealing shooters to be burnt to the ground. Commanders have authority to carry out summary justice without fear of repercussions.

Sabine slid the cheese into plates, the routine so familiar it required no concentration. Her mind drifted, straining for a sound that signalled Hérisson's return. The hoot of an owl, or the whistled rendition of *L'internationale* if he was in particularly good humour. But Hérisson was late. Days late. Time stretched out. Days turned into weeks. Weeks had become a month. Every minute was interminable as she waited and waited and waited.

Yesterday she had gone to search for one of the other groups in the forest, but they'd moved camp and she'd returned home in despair. He'd promised her he'd be back before the cranes passed over on their journey north to their breeding and nesting sites in Russia and Finland.

When the cheeses were done, she returned to the house. Her parents looked up expectantly as she entered, and her father started to mutter about how careful they all had to be.

'I'm going into town', she said, unable to bear spending another minute at the farm. She needed to keep her mind occupied. At least if she went to see Mariette she might be able to glean some news about what was happening, and why Hérisson might not have returned.

As she cycled through the village on her way to Mussidan, everything seemed much the same as usual. She waved to Monsieur Rousou, the beekeeper, and carefully swerved past Mme Beauchamps, who was laundering blankets in the wash-house. How could the world continue to turn when she was in such turmoil? Mariette was at home, and they climbed the stairs to her bedroom. They took up their usual position, perched on the iron bedstead and peering out over the square.

'Look', Mariette said, producing a newspaper article from the Nazi-controlled press and handing it to her. 'Read this.'

'It says, "Dangerous men have been executed in a Nazi attack near Payzac. The men were traitors and had been involved in the execution of a nun."'

She turned to Mariette. 'Do you know who's been killed?'

'I have a few names but not all of them.'

Sabine crossed herself. 'I don't even know Hérisson's real name. He won't tell me. He could be dead. He could be one of these men and I wouldn't even know.'

No longer able to control her emotions she burst into tears. Gently Mariette took the newspaper from her hands and put her arms around her. Her friend rocked her, saying words of soothing and comfort, as the sobs continued.

'We don't know if Hérisson was even with these men, do we?'

Sabine shook her head.

'Then we must pray for his safety. We mustn't give up.'

Sabine wiped her eyes, ashamed of her lack of control. Mariette knew only too well what she was going through. Worse, Sabine had never seen her friend collapse or shown any sign of weakness. The only thing she showed the world was an iron will and steely determination.

Even the Sperrle Order of February, aimed at eradicating all Resistance by terror hadn't affected Mariette, who'd never doubted that the Nazis would be defeated. While Sabine envied her friend's confidence, she was unable to replicate it. The publication of the order applicable to Dordogne, Corrèze and Lot and Garonne increased her dread. She could feel the tension around her as she tried to go about her normal daily business. Everywhere the fear in her neighbours' eyes. Watching the grim-faced German soldiers, their fingers poised on the triggers of their guns as they strode along the street in Mussidan. The Allies might be winning the war but the Nazi stranglehold on her community was becoming tighter and more deadly.

Chapter 53

PAYZAC

He was conscious of sounds – human voices, though not the words they used. Could this be the hell which the Church insisted yawned for all communists? It appeared they baked their own bread, otherwise why was his stomach grumbling, roused by the appetising smells permeating wherever it was he had ended up?

He tried to feel his body, made conscious attempts to move, but the effort was too much and he felt himself drifting away.

A hand stroked his brow. Sabine? No, this hand was wrinkled by weather and age, knuckles gnarled into knots by arthritis. He opened his eyes, trying to think properly, trying to identify his surroundings.

A kindly face stared down at him, eyes bright blue, lively despite the antiquity of the features surrounding them.

'André', she called.

She was joined from the gloom by a man who appeared to be of similar age.

They stared down at him as he tried to form the words

'Where am I?'

'Take it easy, son', the man said.

There was a knock at the door and the couple gave each other a startled look. Another sharp rap and their features relaxed into a smile. The man moved to open the door.

Hérisson looked up at Paul Chatrin.

'You're awake. Good. We have to move you again.'

Hérisson attempted to pull the covers aside and stand up but he reeled back dizzy with the effort.

'Take your time.'

Paul put an arm around him, supporting him and guiding him to the door. The couple fussed, fetching bread and some sausage and *l'eau de vie de poire*. Paul slipped the offerings into his pockets then thanked them.

Hérisson wanted to thank them, too but his efforts just produced an unintelligible mumble.

They hobbled into the light of an early dawn and Paul helped him onto the back of the cart where he covered him with used grain sacks.

'Lie still,' he instructed. 'We're not going far.' As the mule set off, Hérisson slipped into a merciful unconsciousness of his body being rocked and tipped with the cart's motion over the rutted track. The last thing he was aware of was the dusty smell from the sacks bringing back memories of his adolescent work in the *chai*. When he came round, he was lying on a different bench in another house. The smells were the same, and Paul was still there.

'What happened?'

Paul pulled a stool out from beside the fireplace and sat down beside him.

'That's what you're going to have to tell us.'

Hérisson grunted and tried to sit up.

'What's happened to me? Why do I hurt so much? And where am I?' It was as though the shock had taken away his power to remember. He realised he was alive but nothing else made any sense. How could he answer Paul's question?

'We found you lying outside the mill. You'd been shot but there were signs of life. You were carried to the top of the ravine and put in a car. We rushed you to the doctor in Payzac. He didn't think you'd make it, but we took you to the hospital in Pergiueux anyway. Doctor Fontaine operated on you. Immediately he'd finished we took you to the farm where the old folks took you in, then, as you know, we moved you here. We'll have to do it again in a few days. Now they know you didn't die, the Gestapo and the S.S. are combing the countryside for you. We just managed to get you out of the back door of the hospital as they burst in through the front.'

It all felt too much for him to take in.

'You'd got a bullet in the leg and another one in your shoulder – oh, and a broken jaw. The doctor thought you'd probably been struck with a rifle butt.

Hérisson nodded. He remembered the searing pain. The cold ground. The harsh German voices.

'The others?'

Paul shook his head.

'You're the only one. The only witness. What do you remember?'

He sank back in the pillows, wincing as the memories returned. One murderous gunshot after another. The last *adieux* of his comrades.

'All dead?'

'Yes, apart from those they took to load the trucks, eleven of them. They've been sent to Poland as far as we know.'

In spite of his training, he wept as he remembered Pinot, his friend. If it hadn't been for him, Pinot would never have got involved with the Resistance. It was his fault Pinot was dead.

'But how? The lookouts . . . what happened?'

'We found one with his throat cut. They had no time to warn the rest. Loup and André heard the shots from the other side of the river but weren't able to do anything. All the recruits possessions were confiscated or burned. But not the house. That makes us think it was the owner who informed. The ambush was well-planned. Those bastards knew where the lookouts were positioned – and the habits of the unit.

'Hell,' Hérisson moaned. 'Each was shot with a bullet in the back of the neck. They slaughtered them like rabbits.

'The doctor thought whoever shot you must have missed. Though how, at that range, who knows?'

Hérisson leaned back again. 'D'you know, It's almost enough to make me believe in God again.' Fury tightened every sinew and every muscle. 'I want to avenge them. How long do you think before I can join the unit again?'

'Be patient. Your leg may never heal completely. It might be time for you to be pensioned out."

'Never. Not after this. I won't stop fighting. Not until this is over. Not while I have breath in my body.'

Chapter 54

LA BARDE, SAINT-ANTOINE-DE-DOUBLE, MARCH 1944

Formations of cranes crossed the cobalt sky, their squawks echoing through the forest. The migration was fully underway. Sabine gazed upwards. Spring had finally arrived. The winter had been the cruelest in her memory. The coldness that had lodged in her bones over the last few months would never leave. Not ever. But the return of Spring brought her no joy. Hérisson had promised to return before the cranes went north. No message had come. Months had passed. That could only mean he was dead, caught at the massacre at Pont-Lasveyras, or sent east to be worked to death.

She'd read the Resistance newspaper report of the incident. Mariette had managed to get hold of a list of those killed. Sabine ran her fingers over the names, like a blind person reading braille, searching comfort from the pencilled indents on the paper. But there'd been no hidden message there for her. She had raked every corner of her memory for a clue to his real name. In all the words they'd exchanged surely there was some clue as to his origins. No name on the list had brought a flash of memory, or prompted a revelation of his identity. No name on the list had called to her saying, I am he, mourn me, celebrate my life for now I am gone. They were names, only names, of other families' loved ones. Not hers.

But did that mean she could never have truly loved him? Could she really see his true name on a death list and not know deep inside that through it he spoke to her? Through all the obscurity, a whisper she recognised?

She tried to focus on her everyday life, but constantly her ears strained for the hoot of an owl at midday or a jauntily whistled forbidden tune.

But it never came.

~

The last of the cranes had passed when René came to call. Already the buds were forming on the cherry trees and the daffodils were beginning to burst into life. It was the traditional time for renewal, for new beginnings, for spring love.

'I've come to appologise for my behaviour. I hoped we could try again.'

Sabine looked into the battered face, seeking the boy she'd fallen in love with. Her first love. But not her last. She took his hand. Emotion flooded her.

'I'll always love and respect you. But we can't start again.' She looked around the farmyard. Her home. It looked the same. But everything had changed. She had changed. Nothing could ever be the same again. 'This war. I can't decide anything until it's finished.'

'Sabine, I understand how you feel. But I can protect you. My father has co-operated with the Germans. Whoever wins the war, we'll be safe.'

Instinctively, she drew back and took her hand away. A huge gulf. A pit. A grave filled with brave men now lay between them. Her tone reflected it. 'Do you know what you're saying?'

'Think about it. That's all I'm saying', he reached forward, grabbing her hand. 'Listen to me, for God's sake. Hitler has a secret weapon. Once it's operational, maybe in the next month, the war will turn. Germany will win.'

Sabine tore her hand away. Shocked by René's words. Could it be true? What if it was true? After all they had suffered, borne only by the belief their struggle could not be fruitless. No, it couldn't be true. She mustn't believe it. Summoning all her strength she said, 'I think you should leave now.'

René seized her by the wrist and yanked her toward his now contorted face.

'Look, I've heard you've been helping Jews, that you're a courier for the Resistance. Haven't you seen the posters everywhere offering rewards for information. Don't you realise that even being denounced is enough to get you shot!'

'Get out.' Sabine screamed. Disturbed by the noise, Tin-Tin bounded from the barn where, judging by the dust on his coat, he'd been trying to sniff out some rats and began to bark at René, who stepped backwards, climbed onto his bike and kicked down on the pedal. As the bike roared past Sabine, he yelled,

'I'll make sure you regret this.'

Chapter 55

LA BARDE, SAINT-ANTOINE-DE-DOUBLE MARCH 1944

Sabine laid the muslin over the lines of cheese, then leant down to pick up the milk pail. A screech of brakes shattered the peacefulness of the *chai*. She was rigid with terror. It was a sound that could mean only one thing. Discovery. Only the Germans had fuel for trucks these days, and there was only one thing that would take them to the isolated hamlet of La Barde. Denunciation.

Her eyes darted around the *chai*, wondering for a moment if it would be safer to hide, or whether she was brave enough to try and brazen out whatever accusation was to be levied at the inhabitants of their farm.

Her father stood at the door of the cottage. His frame stooped in submission as the jack-booted officer strode towards him.

'*Monsieur* Faure, where is your daughter?'

If there was trouble coming she'd brought it on all of them by her refusal to follow her father's advice. She had to take responsibility. It was her fault. Now she was going to have to be braver than she'd ever imagined she could be. For her family's sake.

She wiped her hands on the cloth. And opened the door, slipping out into the courtyard. Her terror amplified as she saw who the visitor was. Otto Schneider, accompanied by a couple of his henchmen.

Her father still stood silently. Her mother appeared behind him, a characteristically worried expression on her face. Although Sabine could not see her hands she knew her mother would be wringing them.

'Your daughter?' Schneider barked. 'I will not ask you again.'

Sabine's heart went out to her father. He was ready to defend her. He always had been. He just did not know how to.

'Is it me you are looking for?' she called to the German.

Schneider twirled around.

Sabine felt her flesh crawl with disgust as the man's eyes travelled over her body, undressing her. He leered at her.

'*Mademoiselle* Sabine Faure?'

'Yes.'

'Well, well, well.' Schneider walked all round her like the farm cat inspecting a trapped mouse, the devouring eyes brazenly demonstrating how much he would enjoy exercising the rights of the conqueror.

She felt sick but stood straight, eyes forward, determined to hide the trembling in her limbs, forcing her mind to go blank. Whatever terrors lay ahead, she must not betray her friends.

'We have received certain information...', the Schneider said cryptically.

Sabine continued to look straight ahead.

'...that you are hiding Jews.'

A huge internal wave of relief.

Whoever had denounced her did not know the whole truth.

She intended to sound unconcerned. 'You're more than welcome to search here.'

A black leather glove flashed across her face, pain seared her cheekbone; the force of the blow threw her to the ground. From her position on the muddy courtyard, she struggled to her feet. There was a shot and she turned in horror to see her father collapse to the ground grasping his stomach.

Schneider yelled, 'Don't move or we'll shoot you all.'

Her father crouched back against the wall, gripping his side. Her mother tried to tend to his wound.

Sabine was now on her feet, her clothes plastered in mud and farm ordure. Schneider moved close to her. He held a letter in front of her face. 'What does this mean?' he snarled. Sabine struggled, trying to focus on the writing blurring before her.

'Talk, while you still can.'

She shook her head. 'I don't know what this is about.'

As fast as a striking snake, Schneider reached out, grabbed the collar of her blouse and ripped it downward.

She glared at him unmoving as her breast was exposed. His eyes took in her bare flesh. He cocked his head and smiled.

'One last chance, *Mademoiselle.*'

She shook her head, the words came out as little more than a whisper, 'I don't know anything.'

A Wehrmacht soldier roared into the courtyard on a motorcycle. Dismounting, he handed Schneider a message. He flipped open the note then smiled thinly at Sabine. '*Mademoiselle,* I regret I have been called away. More urgent business.'

He crumpled up the letter and threw it at her.

'If I have to question you again, it will not be here. It will be in more appropriate surroundings. The Gestapo headquarters in Perigueux.'

He leapt into the vehicle in which he'd come, followed by his men.

Sabine ran towards her father who was now a grey colour. With her mother's help she dragged him into the kitchen, they placed a blanket under him to protect him from the cold tiled floor. Then her mother lifted his shirt. They examined the wound with relieved sighs. The bullet had only grazed his side. *Maman* doused the wound with alcohol and the pair bound it with bandages made from a bed sheet torn into strips.

After they got him to sip some brandy, Papa seemed to recover a little. After they'd made him comfortable, Sabine realised she was still shaking. 'Here', her mother said gently, handing her a glass of brandy. 'Tidy yourself up and sit down. We've all had a shock.'

'Did you see what happened? There was no reason for him to hit me. No reason for him to shoot father. The letter ...' she jumped up from her chair and ran out into the yard. She grabbed the paper from the ground and went back into to the house. Carefully she wiped it clean and spread it out on the table.

To whom it may concern, Sabine Faure is hiding a Jewish family at her family's farm at La Barde, Saint-Antoine-de-Double
A concerned well wisher

Her parents moved closer to look at the paper. 'Who could have done this?...' Sabine asked, her hand trembling, her emotions no longer under control.

'...Only someone who knows me well enough to know my name and address. But this is a death warrant. I can't believe someone would do this out of spite.'

Her father put an arm around her shoulders and hugged her to him. 'These are the times we live in. Take this as a warning, Sabine, for all our sakes. Someone wants to cause trouble for you. Those bastards have made it quite clear there are no limits on what they will do to us. You can't risk coming to their attention again. Do you understand?' Her father turned her towards him and looked tenderly into her eyes. He put his arm around his wife in a rare sign of affection. 'We can't risk losing you. We won't let those bastards take you away. But you must do what I say, Sabine. No more risks.'

She went up to her bedroom and put on another blouse. The torn one she lay on the bed, running her hands over it, piecing the ripped material together. Her hands began to tremble and finally she broke down and the tears flowed.

Movements downstairs called her back to the present. Her mother was laying the table for their lunch as if nothing out of the ordinary had happened. Sabine went down the stairs wanting to scream and yell at them that they had to do something, that they couldn't just go on as if nothing had happened. The visit had destroyed her. She could feel the nerves in her body dancing as if each had been touched by an electric current. Everything had changed. Until today, the Nazi menace had for her somehow stopped at the gate of their home. The farm had been the only place where she'd felt safe. Even when on her most dangerous of missions, even when she was most fearful of pursuit or betrayal, as soon as she passed through the gate to their farm she'd felt safe. Now even that illusion, for illusion it had truly been, had been brutally shattered and with it her ability to continue.

She knew she would never be able to withstand an interrogation by the S.S. and the Gestapo at their nest of evil in Perigueux. Even when she knew that betrayal meant almost certain death for those she informed upon. Even Hérisson's. The tears began again. Even him. Could she find the strength to keep his name from her tongue?

Her father's fingers trembled as he stoked the stove and his eyes had resumed the haunted look that she recognised so well. Her mother too had changed. The normality she feigned was a performance, for whose benefit Sabine could not be sure, but she could see the agitation behind the calm façade her mother forced herself to present.

Then Tomas arrived carrying logs. He stood framed in the doorway, his presence met by complete silence.

'What's wrong?' he asked.

Maman placed a loaf of bread firmly on the table, then a knife beside it. 'Nothing', she said, giving Sabine a warning glance. 'Come and have some soup. You must be hungry.'

Each took a place around the table. Sabine beside her brother. Could he not see? Hadn't he noticed the tyre tracks in the yard? That her father seemed to have withdrawn into a world only he inhabited. That her mother was unusually talkative. She opened her mouth, ready to tell him about Schneider's visit, but she closed it again. She would not be the one to set him on the path to joining the Resistance. She could not take the blame for that. So she ate her soup, one spoonful after the other. In silence. As her brother explained about a bird's nest he'd found.

Papa emerged from his trance. 'Did you light a fire?' I smell burning.' Tomas shook his head.

Preoccupied as she had been with her own thoughts, Sabine had not noticed the smell. She stood up and walked to the door. As she looked north, towards Saint-André-de-Double, she could see a column of black smoke rising above the trees. Even as she watched she could see it was spreading, blocking the sun. The odour of burning timber grew stronger and fragments of ash began to float down through the air.

Her family joined her at the door.

'I'll go and see', said Tomas. Going outside and getting onto his bicycle.

'I'll come with you', Sabine called.

'Be careful', their mother begged.

The two of them sped down the lane, then followed the road heading in the direction of the smoke. They'd almost reached the village when *Monsieur* Goudet from the post office stood in the road in front of them. He waved them to a standstill. 'Turn back, get home as fast as you can. And stay there.'

'What's going on?'

'There are *Boche* everywhere. They say they're going to burn the Resistance out of the forest. It's not safe for you to be out. Hurry now.'

They turned their bicycles around and headed back home as fast as they could.

When they got home they helped their father gather the agitated livestock into the barn.

'But what if the fire comes this way?' Sabine asked. Papa scratched his head. 'Surely they can't intend to burn the whole forest.'

'How do we know?' Sabine could feel panic rising again. Just when she thought she'd managed to control her fear, something else happened and her terror level intensified.

Chapter 56

PAYZAC

Hérisson plunged the knife into the oak table.

'They didn't find us by bloody accident. Someone told the bastards we were there. We need to find out who – and make sure they don't live to do it again.'

Paul shook his head. 'I've been over it again and again in my mind. The place was so isolated. The *Boche* couldn't have ambushed the lookouts unless they knew where they were positioned. How many people had that information?'

'Well, of course, everyone who was there.'

"There are only four survivors. Loup and Cézard who were out on a mission at the time, Ravel, the messenger who left the evening before. You. And it was a miracle that you survived, so I'm excluding you as a suspect.'

Hérisson snorted. 'Thanks a lot.' But all the while his mind wandered over the names. Cézard, the charismatic Brigade leader surely was beyond suspicion. Loup, his friend and member of their original band of four? The conversation they'd had so many months previously when Loup argued they ought to profit from assisting Jews to cross the line came back to him. How far would he go? He dismissed the idea as fast as it had arisen. Loup, too, must be beyond suspicion. That left Ravel.

'He said he'd heard suspicious noises in the forest. Would he have done that – given us a warning – if he'd sold us out? It wouldn't make sense.'

Paul agreed, ' Anyway, Ravel and Arnaud were like brothers. I don't believe for a minute, even if Ravel would betray the rest of us, that he'd do that to Arnaud.'

Hérisson shrugged. 'That leaves . . . no one.

I trusted everyone in our group implicitly,' he said as an afterthought. But Carlos's words came back to him as though in a douche of cold water. 'Trust no one. To trust is to die.'

Paul stalked up and down the room.

'It must have been one of the villagers, the caretaker of the place maybe. Perhaps one of the local foresters saw what was going on and tipped-off the owner. He's said to be sympathetic to Vichy.'

Hérisson slammed a fist on the table . We shouldn't have stayed so long. It was just so bloody cold this winter.

We can't have any more mistakes like this. Virtually all our recruits wiped out. All our equipment lost.'

He could never rid himself of the voices of his friends as they called to their loved ones with their last breaths. At night it was even worse, when the nightmares came. He didn't know if he'd ever sleep again. Would he ever be free of the fear that now seemed to weigh on him so heavily. The energetic enthusiasm with which he'd begun this odyssey seemed so foolish now. When the images of his friends' corpses became too vivid in his mind, he focused on the mission, the freedom of his homeland. He forced himself to see the retreating German forces, and the tricolour flags of liberation flying over a once-again free France. It was all he saw now. He would avenge his friends. He would see victory. Or he would die.

Chapter 57

THE FOREST

'You okay?' Carlos asked. Hérisson nodded. The doctors allied to the group had pronounced him fit enough to return to the unit and though he'd been left with a slight limp he was able to move almost as fast as before.

'Good man. We''ll see this out together.'

Carlos produced a map. Rapidly, he briefed Hérisson and Loup on their mission.

'This is what I want you to do. The signal came today. Another parachute drop. I want us to operate with the smallest team. To minimise risk. If this goes well, I've been assured this area will be crucial when the landings happen. Think about it, lads. Our unit will be crucial in the liberation of France.'

Chapter 58

MUSSIDAN

Sabine knocked again, louder this time. Still no answer. She turned the door handle and entered. Mariette was sitting in a chair staring at the stove which was cold. Sabine shivered though she was wearing a coat.

'What's wrong?'.

Silently, Mariette passed her a white card that she had held clasped in her hands. Sabine recognised it immediately, the kind that prisoners were allowed to send. Black print of standard phrases with a tick box beside each one and a small area for a more personal message. This section was always heavily censored and frequently arrived completely blacked-out.

This one was different. There were no censored phrases. There were no words at all. And only one of the selected boxes was ticked, the one that said 'dead.'

Initially, for Sabine, the penny did not drop. 'I don't understand'.

'It means he's gone', her friend whispered. She turned her head to stare up at Sabine.

'But surely not. There's nothing. No explanation. Even they wouldn't be so cruel.'

'I felt it. Weeks ago. The day he passed. I knew something bad had happened.'

'But . . .'

'I've been to the *Mairie*. They said it's true. That's what happens. They send out a postcard just like this, to the closest relative. The officer was very polite. He said he'd try and find out more information for me.'

Sabine put her arms round her friend and hugged her. 'I am so sorry, my darling.'

They stayed that way for a while, Mariette quietly crying and Sabine doing what she could to soothe her friend's pain.

'I've got to tell his mother but I can't. I just want to sit here and remember him. I can't go just yet.'

'Would you rather I told her?'

'No, it'll have to be me. I'll have to go soon. Mustn't leave it too late.'

'Let me come with you. I'll walk along with you.'

'It'll only make it more real. Once I've told her, it won't seem possible that it's all a mistake. I keep thinking I'll get another message to say there's been an administrative error. Someone else with the same name. Not him. Maybe if I wait until tomorrow.' Her voice faded and the distant look returned as she went back to staring at the stove.

Sabine had no idea what to do. This was her friend who'd always known the answer. Whose positive and confident beliefs had blunted the edge of her own doubts and fears. She'd never seen her friend so lost. That stimulating energy had just drained from her body. She didn't want to leave her, but she still had the message to deliver and it was clear Mariette wasn't able to help.

Sabine relit the stove. Then put a kettle on to boil. She gripped her friend's hand in hers. 'Darling, I have to go but I will come back in a little while and see how you are. Is there anyone I can ask to come and be with you?'

Mariette shook her head. 'I don't want to disturb my mother, she has enough to deal with. My father's bad at the moment. These last few months, it's brought it all back. His health gets worse every day.'

Sabine made her a cup of coffee and passed it to her. 'Drink this. I'll be back as soon as I can.'

Sabine carried her bicycle down the stairs. Now she'd have to deliver both messages. There was the best part of a day's cycling ahead of her if she was to reach both Beaupouyet and Sioriac. She decided to go to Beaupouyet first as Madame Chevrier at the café would be sure to give her a bowl of soup, and it was starting to rain heavily. She was more frightened than usual of being stopped. It wasn't the sort of day that anyone would be out unless they'd no choice.

She pedalled down the hill and around the town using the lanes running along the river where she was least likely to be seen.

She needed to return to Mariette as soon as possible. She'd stay with her all night as long as she could get back to the farm to tell her parents she'd be away for the night and be in Mussidan before darkness fell.

The following morning, the girls returned to the *Mairie*. Field Officer Kolp dipped his head when he saw them enter. He paused for a moment and then approached them.

'Madame Daigneault, please follow me to my office.

They were led into a modest office, unchanged since before the war except for the Nazi flag behind the desk, Hitler's picture and the heavy blackout curtains. The officer was extremely polite and exuded sympathy.

'Immediately after your visit yesterday I telephoned the camp where your husband was being held. I was informed that he died as a result of a mining accident. It was instantaneous. He didn't suffer.'

Mariette's mouth fell open. She barely managed to stammer, 'A mining accident? But we were told he was working on a farm. In good conditions. I don't understand. I've been sending food parcels to this address.'

The officer shook his head. 'I've checked. Our records are meticulous. I'm sorry. I've asked for his personal effects to be sent to you.'

Mariette clasped her handbag to her body and struggled to her feet, Sabine supporting her. The officer accompanied them to the doorway to the outside. '*Mesdames*', he said, 'if there's anything I can do, please contact me.'

As they went down the steps, Sabine turned and could see he was still watching them.

Chapter 59

LA BARDE, SAINT-ANTOINE-DE-DOUBLE

Sabine scurried past the ruins of Madame Dumas's house. The soldiers who'd come in search of Miriam and her children had set fire to it so they couldn't return. Since the March round-ups and reprisals everyone was frightened. Over fifty buildings in the forest had been destroyed with flamethrowers; twenty people had been shot. One of them, *Monsieur* Dupont, a garage owner from Riberac, an old friend of her father's, had been shot outside his garage, in front of his wife, for giving diesel to the Resistance. No-one knew what was going to happen next. She'd resigned herself to Hérisson's death and she and Mariette comforted each other as best they could. Only the hate she felt for the occupiers kept her alive. Forced her to put one foot in front of the other.

As she reached the tobacco barn she noticed the door was ajar, just sufficient for a person to pass. She was certain it'd been closed when she'd passed earlier. Cautiously she edged into the dimness. A calloused hand gripped her mouth. She struggled trying to scream.

'Don't you know me?' She relaxed and the arms gripping her so tightly fell away, allowing her to turn.

'My God', she breathed. 'You're alive', as she grasped his face between her hands.

'My darling', Hérisson said tenderly, taking a moment to gaze at her and twining a loose strand of hair between his fingers. Then they hugged each other tightly. Rocking in each other's arms as time itself stood still.

Chapter 60

THE FOREST

'Where did you get that?' Sabine reached out and grabbed the ring from its hiding place.

'What the hell d'you think you're playing at?' Loup lunged at her, twisting the ring from her gasp.

Sabine stepped away, holding her wrist where he'd hurt her. 'I've seen it before, I know whose it is ' she yelled at him. He laughed and tossed the ring in the air leaping upward and catching it before she could get close.

'It's mine now.'

Hérisson tossed the cigarette stub to the ground and approached them.

'What's going on?'

'He's got Miriam's ring.'

Hérisson turned towards Loup.

'Is that true?'

Loup took an aggressive stance towards his colleague. 'It's my ring.'

'Examine it!', she said to her lover. 'there's an inscription in

Hebrew on the inside. Miriam told me it means, "Forever in my heart". It was given to her when she got married.'

'Give it here'. Hérisson reached out his hand.

'It's my ring', Loup said between clenched teeth.

Sabine demanded, 'Look at the inside, go on. Look. Prove me right.'

'So what', Loup said, holding out the ring for examination. 'I was given it. It's mine now and that's the end of it.'

Hérisson shrugged. Sabine sat down holding back her tears. The ring was Miriam's. She'd said she'd keep it with her always. Now Loup had got hold of it. What did that mean? What had happened? Miriam had promised to send her a message once she reached her aunt's. But so far there'd been no word. She hadn't given that much thought because there were so many other things to worry about. And she'd been so sure the family were safe. Loup had said the trip had gone to plan. But now he had Miriam's ring and his aggressive reluctance to offer any explanation for how he'd come by it stoked her fears.

She tried to catch Hérisson's eye, but he was already intent on scrolling the message she would carry. Loup, though, returned her stare as if he'd nothing to hide. Maybe she was mistaken. But she didn't think so.

Later, when she and Hérisson were walking along the pathway towards the track that would take her home, she was still troubled.

'I don't understand how Loup has that ring.'

'You don't know if it's the same ring.'

'Don't treat me as if I'm some kind of idiot. I'm telling you, it *is* Miriam's ring. So what's he doing with it? And why won't he tell us how he got it?' Stopping in her tracks, she went on,

'Even if... Even if it isn't Miriam's ring, whose is it and how come he's got it?'

'Look, don't you think we've more important things to worry about? I trust Loup with my life. This message is really important. It's about the next sabotage. We live how we live. We steal uniforms from *Camps de Jeunesse*. We break into post offices to steal ration cards. We liberate bread and anything else we need from collaborators. The *Boche* shoot us on sight. Pinot and all the others are dead. There are posters in the villages offering rewards to people who'll denounce us. One ring. One stupid ring. Why should I care about how he got it?'

Sabine bowed her head. He was right but Miriam was her friend and the sight of the ring had unsettled her.

He went on, 'I'll see what I can find out. I'm sure Miriam's fine. I bet you get the message you're expecting any day now, and then all this suspicion will be forgotten. Anyway, who's to say she didn't give him the ring for saving them? She wouldn't be the first to have rewarded their saviour.'

Sabine smiled, but she was still worried.

Chapter 61

LA BARDE, SAINT-ANTOINE-DE-DOUBLE

Spring had brought dread, and now summer brought instead of the *beau jours,* the thought of which usually sustained the forest-dwellers over the winter months, but yet more fear. And it was an all-pervasive fear that penetrated Sabine to her very bones. It was steeped in the wine she drank, and stirred through the soup she ate. So strong, it suppressed even the taste of turnips, which now seemed to be the staple of every meal.

The fear mingled with the flavour of her cheeses so much that she could no longer distinguish one from the other. Everything tasted the same. Once her home had been her haven, as secure in her mind as any of the majestic chateaux that lined the cliffs above the Dordogne. Now she was frightened to stand still. Frightened to move. Frightened to hide. Frightened to stand in the open courtyard.

The wisteria that twisted round the porch blossomed. Grapes swelled and began to ripen as they absorbed the summer sun, but she could find no joy in this natural act of renewal. All her energy was burned in efforts to keep the fear at bay, to keep the horrors of capture and torture from searing her consciousness. She choked on thoughts of what could happen to her and her family. She could not speak. Her eyes flitted and dived like swallows as they searched for the source of each *crunch* and *click*. Her days passed in a fog of apprehension, ever aware of physical attack, or denunciation, or for the most frightening sight on earth. The deathly black uniform, with its lightning flashes, of a member of the S.S.

Constantly, Sabine's prayers were for victory, for no more orders, for no more danger, for the moment when she could lie in her bed at night and sleep with no dreams, no nightmares, nothing. Just deep and restorative slumber.

When the war was over, when she was safe, that's what she'd do. Sleep, night after night, until the night could pass without her waking bathed in sweat, or trembling, or reliving one horrific event after another, the images cascading before her eyes like those of the flickering newsreel at the cinema.

Chapter 62

SAINT-GEORGES--BLANCANEIX, 10th JUNE 1944

The men crowded around the solid oak table, so large it domi-
nated the cluttered kitchen. Madame Sendrier glanced cautiously out
of the window, then carefully closed and locked the shutters. The
Allies might have landed in the north, but that didn't mean they
could throw caution to the wind. She lit the lanterns and the pungent
smell of walnut oil permeated through the room. She produced
glasses, cups, tankards and jars, which were passed around, until
everyone assembled held a receptacle of one form or another. After a
nod of approval from her husband she reached into the wooden press
by the stove and produced a large dust-covered glass bottle with a
faded but neatly handwritten label gummed on the front. *L'eau de vie,
cerise 1939.* She shared her smile with everyone round the table. 'I've
been saving this', and she patted the bottle affectionately. 'Picked and
bottled before the fall of France.' She passed the brandy to her
husband, who uncorked it with a certain reverence. Then he poured
a generous serving into each of the proffered containers.

'A good day's work, men.'

Everyone raised their glasses. 'To victory.'

The alcohol helped settle their nerves, but they were all still charged with adrenaline after the day's events. Together with other units of the F.T.P. and the A.S. they'd successfully managed to prevent the elite 11th Panzer Division from reaching Bergerac where the German garrison that still held the town was struggling to keep control. More than that, during the two days of combat they had knocked-out two armoured vehicles and prevented the tank division from crossing the Dordogne. The impact of what they had achieved was unquantifiable. Bergerac could be liberated at any moment.

Hérisson glanced round the group. Even in the gloomy darkness of the kitchen, their eyes shone. The freedom they had fought for was at last imminent. Every day brought them closer to victory.

They were all now more men than boys. Even though they weren't all old enough to shave. No-one who had endured what they had could be considered a child. The innocence of youth had been stolen from them.

'À la *Victoire*.'

For the first time, the words did not have a hollow sound. Victory was in their grasp. They could taste it in the very air they breathed. They could see it in the eyes of the German soldiers they faced. Defeated and retreating, their souls were dead. Do I look like that? Hérisson had wondered, before he allowed himself to be caught up in the excitement around him.

Finally, Tallet stood up, arms raised.

'We have won the battle, but not the war. There is more to be done. Tomorrow, we will occupy the town of Mussidan.

Tallet resumed his place at the head of the table. Madame Sandrier cleared away the bread while her husband produced a box of chess pieces. Tallet spoke urgently as he briefed them, using the chess pieces to indicate the position of the important landmarks in the town. The white king represented the station. The white knight, the mayor's office. The black queen marked the German garrison, and the bishops, the bridges into the town. Tallet confided that for days, London had been sending a continuous stream of messages. A large airborne invasion was imminent. The manoeuvre would place elite troops on the ground to sabotage the enemy's communications and prevent them joining other units that might move to reinforce those hard-pressed in the battles in the north. It was imperative to the success of the operation that because of its strategic location the town of Mussidan be under the control of the *Maquis*.

'We're honoured to be entrusted with this operation. The future of France rests in our hands. Tomorrow we must not fail. Once we control the railway station we can prevent supplies reaching the Luftwaffe aircraft factory at Saint-Astier and we can stop the tanks the *Boche* are brigading to send north by rail, to counter the Allied attack.

The men cheered at the news as Tallet continued the briefing.

'Planning is the key to the success of this mission,' he reminded them.

Hérisson listened intently. His cell, comprising himself, Loup and Cerf would attack the train as it arrived. Carlos and his men would occupy the sidings. Hérisson ran over the plan again and again in his mind, remembering Carlos's training. It was the only way he knew to keep panic and fear at bay.

Focus ahead. Focus ahead. Only the mission. Only the mission. It was all that mattered. Not him. Not any individual. Only the mission. And that they succeed.

Morning came quickly. Before the church bells pealed eight, the men climbed into the lorry and set off on the short journey to Mussidan. Swirling mists hung over the river, waiting to be dispersed by the warming rays of the sun. Even in the summer months, morning could come late for the towns and villages that lined the banks of the Isle.

The lorry rattled along the narrow country road towards the town. They stopped briefly, checking that the men were hidden and that the lorry looked no different than any other that might be on the road that morning. The *Boche* still had a garrison in Mussidan, and soldiers would be patrolling the town. When Tallet was satisfied, the lorry set off again.

The finale to the days exploits would be to blow the bridge crossing the Isle, cutting off access to Mussidan from the north. As they travelled through the centre of the town, Hérisson caught the fresh smell of baked bread. For once the enticing odour did not make his stomach growl. He was much too nervous. They all were. He glanced at some of the others, especially the youngest of them, like Hubert. He had never held a gun before. This would be his first experience of combat. He whispered a few words of encouragement to the lad.

The vehicle stopped briefly at the *Mairie* allowing men to descend, then looped backwards towards the railway station. They pulled up outside the entrance and the men descended as planned, forming rapidly into a line. Hérisson directed Cerf and Loup to hide in the hedges that lined the entrance to the station and to wait for the arrival of the train. Tallet took control of the passengers who were waiting to enter the platform.

Their intelligence did not specify the exact time the train would arrive, as the occupying forces kept such information even from the stationmaster until the very last minute. They knew only that it would pass at some point during the day. Hérisson prayed it would be in the morning. The prospect of being on high alert all day was exhausting.

He edged towards his post and crouched in the shadow of the hedge. One man of the group ostensibly was guarding the station personnel, the others stood guard outside the station. Any civilians seemed to melt into the morning mist like shadows. His eyes strained into the greyness, trying to discern the outline of an approaching train along the endless tracks which stretched, empty, along the flat landscape before merging into infinity at the horizon.

It was the noise he heard first. The steady exhaust beat of a steam engine – chough chough. Then the black smoke from the chimney before it merged with the grey mist. Finally, the locomotive came into view. In front of it he could pick out flatbed wagons. He knew these were reinforced with steel plates on the base to protect against mines on the track. Stretching behind the engine, was the tender heaped with reserves of coal and water. Then came two further reinforced flatbed wagons holding bags of sand, then two coal wagons, which were high enough for men to stand up in and were regularly used to transport troops. Bringing up the rear of the train was the guard's van, which would have a French guard and German soldiers

Men emerged from cover and thew a rain of grenades at the train as it squealed to a stop. A second wave of grenades failed to reach the train and exploded just short. Soldiers leapt from the train. An officer yelled instructions in German, and waved his hands furiously at the troops before he ran along the platform, firing with a handgun as he went. The *Maquis* machine gun positioned at the entrance to the station returned fire, felling the *Boche* soldiers like skittles at a fair. After a volley of fire from the cover of the guard's van, Hérisson saw the gunner collapse. An unconscious act, he ducked down in the scrub and began crawling along the edge trying to reach the machine gun.

He was pinned down by fire from a group of Germans taking cover behind the train. His comrades circled to attack from the other side. Cries and moans from the injured and dying filled the air. Closing his mind to the chaos around him, Hérisson half rose and made a run for the machine gun, keeping low and zig-zagging as he raced across the platform. He skidded to a halt as he reached the weapon. Grabbing the handle, he trained it on the soldiers sheltering behind the station sidings.

'Hell. Look.'

Loup had reached him, and was grasping his arm. Cerf white-faced was just behind. Hérisson turned in the direction his friend was pointing. He froze, numbed by what he saw. In slow motion the long grey barrel of a large tank turned and swivelled in his direction. It had been about to cross the railway line, but had stopped and was now turning in their direction. In minutes it would be able to reach the station and it wasn't alone.

As it trundled along the road to the station, it was followed by another, and another. 'A whole fucking regiment. Fall back men!' Tallet cried, signalling frantically. Hérisson sprayed another rain of bullets in the direction of the soldiers near the train, firing as he backed away hoping to provide enough cover for their retreat. Hubert stood up waving his gun and shooting at the train. 'Don't fall back.

Let's fight them', he yelled. Hérisson grabbed the kid and pulled him to the ground. 'You're fucking mad. We can't fight tanks. Fall back! Faster!' he yelled as he saw the tank crossing the track. They gathered the injured and dying, and piled back into the lorry. He climbed in beside the driver and grabbing a Sten gun, emptied the magazine, pinning down the enemy on the station platform. The lorry coughed, then finally started and they sped off down the road, away from the town. As he glanced back a whole line of Panzers was entering the town. 'Fucking Hell', he shouted. 'That's not a regiment – that's a whole fucking armoured division. Where the hell did they come from? Why didn't we know they were there?'

The driver pressed the metal to the floor and with engine roaring they bumped along the track finally disappearing into the countryside.

Chapter 63

LA BARDE, SAINT-ANTOINE-DE-DOUBLE, 11th JUNE 1944

Sabine washed and dried her hands. Glancing skyward she watched a swallow dip and turn before swooping towards the barn. One of the goats bleated, then another. Sabine approached the fence, wondering if a fox had caused the animal's distress. She stopped, ears straining as she too heard a rumbling noise echo up the driveway. Her heart pounded, and her palms turned clammy. For a moment she remembered the arrival of the distiller, *Monsieur* Saint-Lô, and the joy his annual visits had brought. Before the war, the sound of a motorised vehicle arriving brought pleasure. Now it was something to be feared.

She ran towards the house. She was only halfway across the courtyard when a truck swept through the gates and screeched to a halt beside her. She stood immobilised as the commander climbed down from the vehicle and approached her, flanked by several of his men. More soldiers descended from the rear of the truck, rifles cocked as if they were a firing squad. The canvas flipped open, allowing Sabine to see inside. Under guard were several of her neighbours, including *Monsieur* Teabo and his son Michel, who was the same age as Tomas, Jean Perrou, the water diviner, and *Pére* Watteau, his wrinkled face impassive as he kept his head up but his eyes closed, as if he had found a means of transcending from the events around him.

'This is the farm of *Monsieur* Faure', the *Boche* officer demanded.

She nodded.

'Where is he?'

She continued to stare at him, eyes wide like a rabbit caught in the glare of headlights, frantically trying to work out what was going on and how she should react.

Hearing a noise from the house, Sabine turned her head, as did the commander and his soldiers.

Her father appeared at the door.

'Ahh', the officer was smiling. He turned and walked towards her father after signalling to the men to watch Sabine. The German pulled a sheet of paper from his pocket and waved it in front of Papa. With a clipped voice, he read. 'By order of Colonel Wilde, 11th Grenadier Regiment of 11th Panzer division, all men between the ages of sixteen and sixty are to be taken to the town hall in Mussidan so that a check of papers may be carried out.

Follow me.'

Her father nodded obediently and walked to the lorry at gunpoint. *Monsieur* Teabo held the canvas aside for him as he climbed in.

Sabine made to approach the commander, but her guards took aim at her as soon as she moved. Her father pleaded with his eyes for her to not take any risks. At that moment her mother appeared at the door. Her face crumbled at the sight of the soldiers. Tomas ran around the corner of the barn from where he had been sorting the maize. The officer's eyes narrowed and his mouth twisted into a thin smile. 'And who is this? You're not on my list.'

'He's only fifteen', Papa protested. There was a dull crack as a rifle butt made contact with his skull. Sabine started moving towards her father. A soldier cocked his gun and she stopped.

'Get in', the officer yelled at her brother.

Tomas, suddenly pale, approached the truck and climbed in

beside his father, who had sunk down on his seat, blood trickling down the side of his face. Sabine and her mother watched helplessly as the lorry pulled off. Sabine hugged her mother. 'Don't worry', she said, knowing how ridiculous she sounded. 'Stay here, I'll find out what's happening. I'll come back as soon as I can.'

'No', her mother whimpered, 'you mustn't. Don't leave me, I beg you.'

Her mother's shaking hand gripped her arm, but Sabine brushed her away. 'I know what I'm doing.' She ran to the barn, collected her bicycle and set off as fast as she could after the truck.

She'd never made the journey to Mussidan at such speed. As she cycled through the centre of Saint-Front-de-Pradoux she experienced a terrible sense of foreboding. The streets were deserted. Shops were shuttered. Nothing was as it should be. Yet there was no indication of what was so terribly wrong. As she approached the bridge, her heart stopped.

A tank was stationed across the main street of Mussidan, blocking access. From her side of the bridge, she could see another at the *Route de Périgueux* and another further along at the *Route de Montpon*. The town was surrounded, but why? What had happened? Soldiers stood with their rifles readied, on guard, not laughing and joking as they sometimes did. Other units, with German Shepherd dogs, were moving from one house to another. 'Hurry. Move. Faster,' the soldiers called out amidst the barks of the animals. The sounds drifted across the river, sending chills down her spine. Men were being escorted from their homes, some half-dressed, as they were marched in the direction of the Town Hall, hands on their heads.

She was so frightened she wanted to vomit. She wanted to turn round and go home. She could wait there with her mother like they'd been told. Except she couldn't leave her father and Tomas. She had to find out what was happening. She climbed down from her bicycle. She recognised the under-officer who had been so kind to Mariette standing guard on the other side of the bridge and taking a deep breath, walked cautiously towards him.

'I need to find out what's happening to my father and brother.

Papa was bleeding quite badly when they took him away.' The young man looked at her and nodded. 'Be careful', he warned as she passed.

'For God's sake, get off the street.'

She turned, searching for her friend. Mariette was crouched down behind some refuse bins, beckoning frantically.

'Follow me', she hissed.

They crept along the street, then climbed up to her friend's bedroom. The shutters were partially closed as usual to deflect the sun's rays, but it was possible to see the square through the gaps if they angled themselves carefully.

A crowd of men and boys were gathered in the courtyard of the *Mairie*.

'What's all this for?' Sabine asked.

Mariette, her eyes blazing, explained, 'Two hundred *Maquisards* came here this morning. They occupied the police station, the *Mairie*, and the railway station. They attacked the train when it arrived. Then the bloody *Boche* arrived. With tanks. Apparently they were on their way to Limousin to relieve the Das Reich tank division stationed there and just happened to hear the attack. The battle with the *Maquis* must have lasted an hour. It was going on all around us. The *Maquis* pulled out. Now the town's surrounded.

That Gestapo bastard Hambrecht has taken charge here and ordered the roundup of local men. That's why they're being herded together at the *Mairie*.'

'But why have they pulled-in the local civilians', Sabine whispered, though she knew she wouldn't want to hear the answer.

'They think they'll get names of those responsible. Then they'll start looking for them. Don't worry. They're long gone.'

'How many Germans were killed?'

'We don't know. Everyone's trying to stay off the street until we know what's going to happen. You know what they're like. If they don't find out who was responsible, they'll take reprisals and start shooting suspects.'

'My God', Sabine whispered, her mouth dry. 'But these men aren't involved in the *Maquis*. And I can't see any of the ones we know are.'

Mariette squeezed her hand. 'Neither can I.'

They watched in silence as each of the prisoners was led to Hambrecht, who directed where he was to go. There appeared to be three groups. One where the men had to stand with their hands above their heads, and two other separate groups. Sabine could see no obvious rationale for the groupings. She watched in horror as a lorry pulled up and she saw her father and Tomas being pulled from it and made to wait in the queue, then eventually placed in one of the groups. At least they hadn't been separated.

'My father had nothing to do with this.'

Mariette ducked her head and did not look her in the eye. 'My father's there as well,' Mariette muttered. Sabine paused, for a moment feeling guilty about her concern for her own family members.

'If you know anything, Mariette, tell me. I won't stand by and see my father and brother shot for something they would never condone and had nothing to do with.'

Still without looking at Sabine, Mariette snapped, 'I don't know anything'.

Sabine continued to watch focusing on trying to pick out the figures of her father and brother from the crowd of men. Would there be no end to this war, she thought as she watched boys she had been at school with, treated like criminals.

'I can't just do nothing. I have an idea', she muttered as if to herself.

'What can you possibly do?' Mariette hissed – by now clearly frightened herself. 'Just wait here, Sabine. With me. It's too dangerous to leave.'

'You stay here. Watch everything that happens until I come back.'

The friends hugged. Pulling her hands from Mariette's grasp, Sabine turned and left.

She ducked out of the town and took the longer route by Saint-Leon-en-L'isle, because it seemed safer. It was sometime later she hid her bicycle by the side of the road and began to run into the forest towards a popular *Maquis* hideout. She heard the click of a gun behind her and a challenge, 'Who goes there?'

She stood still. Hands raised.

'I'm looking for Hérisson.'

'And who are you?'

'Sabine. Tell him Sabine needs to see him.'

The man came close. She noticed the deadness in his eyes and that he wore an F.T.P. armband like Hérisson's, except it had a Spanish flag beneath the insignia.

The man pointed with his gun, indicating she go in front of him along a path through the dense woodland.

'Is it far?' she asked. There was no time to lose.

The youth did not reply, but before long they arrived in a clearing.

A lorry was parked there. Several wounded men were lying on the grass. Two fresh graves had been dug further to one side. Others were taking down tents and throwing the contents into the lorry. A man was shouting directions furiously in Spanish. As she walked into the scene, he turned.

'What the devil?' Carlos growled, his eyes narrowing as he recognised her. 'You. I told you never to—'

'It's urgent', Sabine blurted.

At that moment Hérisson emerged from one of the tents. He looked different. Tired. Anger crossed his face when he saw her, and she realised she'd made a terrible mistake.

Carlos glanced from her to Hérisson. Grimly he tossed him a rifle and said, 'I told you. Women are dangerous. It's your fault she's here. You guard her.'

Hérisson held the rifle in one hand and raised the other. 'Wait. We can trust her.'

The men surrounded her in a loose circle, all with rifles or pistols in their hands.

'Why're you here?' Hérisson asked. She shivered. He'd never spoken to her in that detached way before.

Struggling to come to terms with her lover's coldness, she focused on her father, her brother, her neighbours. The men she'd come to save.

'I need your help. In Mussidan, the *Boche* have rounded up innocent men. They'll shoot them unless they find out who carried out the attack this morning.'

One of those surrounding her thrust his face into hers. 'And what kind of *help* do you propose, *Mademoiselle?*'

'We have to do something', she pleaded.

'But exactly what? What do you want *us* to do?'

She looked away from the man's hostile stare towards the others who bore the same unfriendly look in their cold and exhausted eyes.

'Rescue them. Please.'

'*Mademoiselle*, we can't fight against Panzers.'

'But we can't just stand by and let them die.'

'Do you want us to go with hands-up to the Nazis. Is that why you've come here?'

Sabine swallowed. She was crying openly now such was her turmoil. They made her feel humiliated and stupid and frightened all at the same time. But what was she supposed to do? Nothing?

'Are you asking the Resistance to give in? To surrender?' Carlos asked harshly.

She closed her eyes and nodded.

He laughed.

Then the whole group broke into mocking laughter. When she opened her eyes, they were all laughing at her, every one of them. Except Hérisson.

'We can't do that. We have orders. We're about to liberate France.'

Carlos pointed at Hérisson and said, 'We can't let her go when she talks like this. She's too much of a risk. Guard her. It's your fault she's here.'

Hérisson stood straight. 'I can't. I won't.'

'Then we're going to have to execute her as a spy.'

Hérisson walked over to Carlos and said something Sabine couldn't hear. When they'd finished Hérisson directed Sabine towards a large beech tree. She obeyed, telling herself he couldn't really mean to execute her. But there was a tiny stab of doubt. He'd never treated her with such indifference before.

'Sit there. Put your hands behind your back', he ordered as they reached the tree.

'Don't you dare hold me as a prisoner', she shrieked at him, fire in her eyes and fury in her voice.

'You heard him. Do you want to get shot?'

'If you don't let me go, I'll never forgive you.'

'I'll live with that.'

She flinched at the sound of his voice, so cold and unfeeling, like a stranger.

He laughed in her face. 'You don't understand, though, do you? You don't know even my real name. You don't know anything.'

At that moment, in her frustration and anger, she hated him but she kept her mouth shut while Hérisson stood to one side of her, keeping her under his guard while the other *Maquis* cleared away the remains of their camp and treated their injured.

A sombre funeral was held for the fallen men. Afterwards angry shouts as Carlos vented his fury over the delay in arrival of the promised support.

The night passed slowly. She felt every beat of her heart as she wondered what was happening to her family. What was happening in Mussidan? She daren't fall asleep but could not have done so anyway. She and Hérisson glared at each other as the night darkened and then, eventually, turned to dawn.

It was now the twelfth of June, but what did that mean. What had happened in Mussidan?

A *Maquisard* approached and whispered something in Hérisson's ear. He stood up, taking a moment to stretch his legs. 'You can go now', he told her.

'I'll never forgive you for what you've done'.

'Go home, Sabine. There'll be no trace of us here in an hour. There is nothing you can tell.'

'If anything's happened to my father or Tomas ...'

'I'd never forgive myself if something happened to you. Take care.'

How dare he whisper words of endearment after holding her at gunpoint all night? She turned and would have slapped him, stopped by the look in his eyes. For a moment they were alive again, and flashed with life and excitement, like fireworks on Bastille day or sparks in the first autumn bonfires. But it was only for a second or two, then his eyes glazed over and became once again flat and dead like the world was now. That was what war had done to them all. She turned away from him and began to hurry down the slope to her bicycle. She might still be able to save her father and Tomas. It might not be too late.

'Stay alive', he called running beside her and grabbing her arm. 'I'll come for you when this is over.'

'Don't bother,' and she shoved him away.

She ran through the forest, tripping and falling. Brambles ripped at her legs, scratched her arms and pulled at her hair. She found her bike, and gasping for breath, she cycled like an Olympian back to Mussidan.

As she approached, the town was quiet. Mist rose from the river, and it seemed as if she were crossing the bridge into a ghost town.

Using walls and shadows, she crept round to Mariette's. Left the bicycle inside the door and moved up the stairs. All seemed quiet. Either everyone had fled or they were inside their homes, hiding. At the top of the stairs her fears returned with force as she saw the splintered door hanging precariously on its hinges.

'It's me', Sabine called, cautiously pushing the remains of the door aside so she could step into the room. As the door swung fully open she saw her friend crouched and trembling on the floor by the stove. The left side of her face was swollen and her hair tangled and unkempt.

'What happened?'

Mariette stared at her, no spark of recognition, clearly still in shock from the attack on her room and, by the look of it, on herself as well. She shook her head. In a faint voice, still with head down, she began to explain. 'They let some of the prisoners go last night. Mostly the older ones and the war wounded. I'm sure your father and brother got away. But it's been terrible. Terrible.' Mariette flopped down, for all the world like a puppet – lifeless.

Sabine crouched beside her.

'What happened, here?'

Mariette shook her head and still in a whisper, answered. 'I heard breaking glass and a ruckus in the street. Then a scream. I went down to try and find out what was happening. There were two men pulling Lillette down the alley. I tried to help but I couldn't. One of them followed me here. The noise went on all night. Screams. Yelling. Breaking glass. It's only got calm now. They must have gone.'

Sabine hugged her friend.

'I've got to find out what's happened to Papa and Tomas.'

'No, you must wait here. It's not safe.'

She took a grip of her friend's hands. 'I've got to. I'll be back as soon as I can. Don't go out.' Mariette shivered and shook her head, bringing her hands to her face, covering her sobs. As she reached the bottom of the stairs, Sabine paused a moment. Should she follow Mariette's advice and wait? It would be safer than risking violence, rape, or arrest, but still she couldn't. She needed to know.

Once in the street, she was aware of others emerging, but, like her, keeping to the shadows, ready to fade into the mist should they have to. They moved, all of them, in silence, towards the *Mairie*.

A group were already standing outside. Some of the women were weeping openly.

Edging up to them, Sabine asked, 'What's been happening?'

'It's been horrific,' one of them said, shock depriving her of language in which to be more specific.

'I watched as much as I could bear, said another.'

A third, more articulate than the others, told her 'Those scum from the North African Brigade marched one group of the prisoners away last night. The ones with their hands on their heads. We heard shots, and they haven't been seen since. When the men from the Brigade returned, under orders from Hambrecht and his side-kick Steiner they took *Monsieur* Grassin, the mayor and *Monsieur* Christmann, his assistant into the courtyard where everyone could see them. They tied them to chairs and demanded they tell them who the Resistance fighters were.' By now tears were streaming down her face but she stuck to her task. 'First they punched and slapped them. I could hear it. Every blow. Then, when they got no names, it got worse. Much worse. I could hear their screams of pain. It went on for hours. Hours. Finally there was silence. But that was the worst. The silence. They'd beaten them to death.' She directed her listeners to the bodies lying in front of the building, draped in blankets. 'Then the rest. It went on all night. Smashing windows. Women screaming. Men shouting, drunk, singing in German. I've never been so frightened in my whole life.' She pulled her cardigan around her, but she wasn't shivering from the cold.

"Our men have gone to find out what happened to the prisoners.' She nodded in the direction of the alley. 'They were led away by soldiers along the *Route de Bordeaux*, then they turned down the *Chemin de Gorry*.'

The woman began walking in that direction, and Sabine followed her, hoping to find her father and Tomas alive, yet fearing what she might see. The pathway led past the doctor's house and garden, and then on into fields and the farm beyond.

A man ran towards them, emerging from the mist. 'Go back', he yelled at them. 'I'm going to get the doctor.'

Another man appeared from behind the first, waving his arms. 'Don't go any further'. It was an order not advice.

'But my father', Sabine cried out. 'I must find out what happened to him.'

'He was released last night, with your brother', the man said. 'Go home. Now".

'But what happened to the others?' she pleaded.

The man just shook his head. Behind him, Sabine could see men laying out bodies in rows. 'How many were there?' she asked her voice trembling.

The other still said nothing, merely crossing his arms over his chest. Then, with a sigh, he said, 'Go home now, *Mademoiselle*. Your family need you.' As Sabine turned she saw Genevieve collapsed against the wall. Sabine put her arm around her supporting her.

'Let me see you home.'

They walked towards Geneviève's home. Rapid footsteps, someone running, put Sabine on alert, but Geneviève walked steadily on towards her front door as if nothing could possibly be dangerous anymore. The doctor appeared running towards them, carrying his bag. He paused, spared a brief look at Geneviève, then opened his bag. He took out a notepad and pencil, scribbled an address, and gave the paper to Sabine. 'Take this. Go there now. Get me help and transport to the hospital. Pray God there is still someone alive.' The doctor closed his bag and rushed off again, heading for the *Chemin de Gorry*.

Assured that Geneviève was safely home, Sabine glanced back to see the doctor working his way calmly along the row of bodies, bending by each one to feel for a pulse. She went to the address on the note, knocked on the door and was greeted by the frightened face of an older man. Handing him the doctor's note, he nodded, then closed the door in her face.

Sabine returned to Geneviève's home hoping to find out more of what had happened. She was there, with her mother who was sitting at the kitchen table crying.

'He never did anything.' She put her arms round her daughter. 'But they've killed him. I wanted to go to him. They said no. They'll bring him here.'

Sabine shook her head, utterly distraught. How could the God she'd been brought up from infancy to see as one of infinite love, allow an obscenity like this to happen. She had been so proud of herself handing out pamphlets and running messages and weapons. And this is where it'd all led. Bitterness flooded her. The damned *Maquis*. All that is, all that was, and all that she had been . . . it had come to this. The death of her friend's father. Bearing witness to the grief of her friend and her mother amplified her sense of guilt. It was as though she had pulled the trigger on all these innocent men.

She needed to get away, to be back home. To see for herself her father and brother really were safe, not buried in that mountain of corpses. As she picked her way through the streets, the pavements strewn with the glass from shattered shop windows, she knew that the little town had been given over to violation, and those who had done it had been given license to strip it bare. The revulsion rose within her. She stopped, bent over, and vomited in the gutter.

Once out of the town, the roads were unusually quiet. When she arrived, her parents were sitting at the kitchen table as though they had never left it. 'Where have you been all night?' her father shouted rising to his feet as she entered the room.

'Father, I was held prisoner.'

'They didn't touch you?' he said, grabbing her arms.

'No, not like that. Papa, *Maman,* please God, you're all safe. And Tomas?'

'He's fine. He's seeing to the goats.'

'Papa, I was in Mussidan this morning. It's horrific. They killed . . .'

Her body began to shake uncontrollably. Her father fetched a brandy. 'Drink this', he said, pressing the cup into her hands.

She gulped it down. It burned her throat. She managed to stop trembling and her father pushed her into his chair by the fire. He stood beside her, one hand on the back of it.

'After we were taken into Mussidan, we were divided into groups. I was with the older men. They treated those who had war injuries a bit better than the rest. When I told them Tomas was fifteen, they allowed him stay with me. Otherwise who knows what would have happened. He might have been placed with those suspected of being involved in the *Maquis*.'

'But I didn't recognise any of them', Sabine chipped-in without thinking.

'I would hope you wouldn't. Her father gave her a long look.. 'Who could know the grounds for their suspicion. The length of a man's beard stubble. His youth. They know they're losing the War. They seem to have lost all reason.' Papa paused, shaking his head.

'The second group were those they considered fit for work. They'll be transported to forced labour camps in Germany. We were in the last group. The one they let go. The Gestapo boss, Michael Hambrecht, and that bastard Schneider orchestrated everything. Hambrecht was staggering and obviously drunk when he arrived and considerably worse by the time we were allowed to leave.

It was him that decided which men were going where. His henchmen from the North Africa Brigade did the dirty work. Word went round that they'd been authorised by their superiors in Limoges to discipline fifty men, in reprisal for the eleven German soldiers who had died in the battle in the morning. We didn't know what that meant, of course. If anyone had told them who was involved in the attack, they'd have let us all go.

'Now. Why don't you tell me what happened?"

She took another large pull of the brandy and explained as much as she knew of the evening's events, taking care to leave out Mariette's attack.

'Promise me, Sabine. No more.'

Sabine nodded. The actions of the Resistance had nearly killed her father and brother. She could never forgive herself if anything she did caused harm to any of her family. And her parents, Tomas was their only son. They would never forgive her if she led him into danger.

Chapter 64

THE FOREST

Hérisson glanced at the rising sun. It must be nearly eight. If she didn't arrive soon, she wasn't coming. And what would that mean? She was his last hope.

A sound from the road, the steps of a pack animal pulling a cart. Someone was coming. Not Sabine on her bicycle, but maybe someone he could trust. Disappointment swept in a wave over him when *Monsieur* Georette appeared, his bent figure crouched over, reins wrapped around his hands, apparently dozing.

The mule continued steadily. It knew the way. *Monsieur* Goerette was a local black-marketeer. The Resistance had him in their sights as a *gouger*, one who fleeced those he bought from and overpriced what he sold. There was no way he could be approached.

Hérisson slipped back into the undergrowth. He'd have to wait a little longer. As the seconds passed, he was forced to consider alternative methods to deliver the message. To enter Mussidan himself was akin to a suicide mission. The garrison was as jumpy as fleas on a dog, but there was no time to make any other arrangement. And he daren't return to Carlos without completing his orders.

He was about set off himself when she appeared. He savoured

watching her for a moment. Her hair neatly rolled. Red lipstick, the colours of her defiance, and yet applied no doubt after she had left the farm, so as not to irritate her father. She was beautiful, more so than ever.

He stood up carefully. Using the trees for cover, he edged nearer, keeping just out of her line of vision. He moved when a breeze rustled the leaves, when a pewit called, when a hare burst from the undergrowth. Any noise he made was drowned by the forest. He was part of the woodland around him, invisible, breathing with the trees as if they were one.

When Sabine reached the foot of the incline she had to dismount. The weight of the basket laden with cheeses to barter for essentials was too great for her to be able to cycle to the top. She began to push it and it was then he moved, emerging from the forest just behind her. He encircled her waist with one arm and clamped the other hand over her mouth. She tried to ram him with her bicycle, but missed. The bicycle fell to the road with a clatter. Cheeses rolled from the basket and spiraled to a standstill.

In spite of her efforts to free herself, and she was surprisingly strong, he had no difficulty in restraining her and pulling her into the cover of the forest. He pushed her against a tree and pinned her there with his body, still with his hand over her mouth. He faced her for the first time since he'd aimed a gun at her. Sabine's eyes flared with fear, then with anger when she realised it was he. She kept struggling although she knew it was hopeless.

'If I let my hand free, will you promise not to scream?'

She nodded. He let his hand fall from her mouth. There was such hostility in her glare, he stepped away from her, leaving her free to run if she wanted. She brushed down her clothing and then strided to the road, towards her bicycle. She leant down, picking up the cheeses. Silently he helped her. Once the basket was full again, she climbed onto the bicycle.

'I have a message. It's vital,' he explained, unable to look her in the eyes.'

'I don't care. I've done with all that.'

'Please, Sabine.' He was begging now.

'I told you. I'm finished with all that. I mean it. And now you've made me late for market. I need to go. Now!'

He caught her arm. 'Please, Sabine, it's happening. This message could mean our liberation. I promise you I'll never ask again.'

She took a hand and lifted his chin so she could see his eyes. He couldn't hide his pain. The death of Sacha following the Mussidan raid and Lola's death from wounds afterwards had hit the brigade hard. Tears filled her eyes. "The town is dead. All those people. The funerals. Genevieve's father. They were innocent. For what?"

'We can't let their death's be in vain.'

Her hand dropped and took hold of her handlebars as if ready to continue her progress up the hill.

He reached out, putting a hand over hers and squeezing gently. 'It's the last time. I promise. I can't bear to put you in danger.'

'What is it you want?' she asked, turning to look him in the eye.

'Take this to the baker', he said, holding out a small, rolled-up message, just like the many others she'd carried for him before.

She turned an ear towards him to catch his muttered instructions. Then she stretched out her hand and took the vital piece of paper.

'Thank you', he said.

As she began walking away he called after her. 'I need you.'

She stopped in her tracks and turned. 'I meant what I said. Never again.'

'But I love you.'

She staggered back a step, eyes wide as though startled by his declaration. Then the anger returned. 'If you loved me, you'd never have held me at gunpoint. I'll never trust you again? You played with me. You wanted a courier and I'm just the fool that did it for you.'

'No, Sabine. I'm glad you're stopping. How could I ever forgive myself if something happened to you? I know you believe in freedom like I do. Give me another chance, I'll prove myself to you. Please, just one more chance.'

Her eyes flashed in anger.

'How can you even talk like this when you're giving me another message to deliver? Putting me in danger again. Putting my whole family at risk. If you really love me, prove it. Stay away from me!'

Her words shocked him, but he nodded. 'Promise me, you'll wait for me until this is over and I will stay away.'

'That works for me', she said.

She let him push the bicycle to the brow of the hill, walking by his side, both silent and deep in thought.

At the top she got back on the bicycle.

'I promise', he said reaching out a hand to her face and running a finger along her jaw line. 'I love you. I'll stay away. I'll fight for our freedom, yours and mine. Then I'll come for you.'

She pushed down on the pedal and the bicycle shot off down the hill. His heart felt as if it would burst. Overcome with emotion he shouted after her. 'I'll tell you my name. When you stand beside me, in church, at our wedding.' The wind caught his words and danced with them around the birch trees which lined the lane. She didn't stop or turn her head. He didn't know if she'd heard him at all.

He stood watching her until she was gone then retreated back into the forest. He would win her back. He had to.

To be continued

BOOK 2 RESISTANCE, EQUALITY
BOOK 3 RESISTANCE FRATERNITY

I hope you have been captivated by the lives of the occupants of Saint-Antoine-de-Double. Please take the time to leave a short review, it only takes a minute or too of your time and is a great way of providing feedback and encouragement to emerging authors.

NAMES OF VICTIMS

VICTIMS PONT-LASVEYRAS 16th February 1944

Paul Elie Gilbert BITARD
Albert Jean BORDERIE
Albert BRUN
Andre CADET
Pierre CHAZARIN 'Bricard'
Yves CROUZY
Maurice DAMIS
René DAUBISSE
Robert Aime DELAGE
Jacques DUBOUE 'Rabouin'
André Marcel DUPUY
André DUREDON
André Eugène Joseph ENAULT
Francois Louis Charles Pierre ENAULT
Jean EVEINE
Adrian FAROUT
Jean Gabriel Mathieu GARDES
Raymond GATINEL
Hermann GELBERGER 'Henri'

Roger GIRARDEAU

Raymond GRANGER

Raymond LAGORCE

Albert LAVAUD

Joseph LE JALU

Jean Marcel LOSEILLE

Francois MACHEFER

Pierre Louis MADRONNET

Pierre Henri MISSEGUE

Henri Joseph Albert PEYRAMAURE

Joseph POMPOGNAT

Noel POUYADOU

Paul SCHNEIDER

Raymond Georges SIMON 'Coeur de lion'

Robert SOUDEIX 'Courgnolle' and 'Spada'

12 Deported

Louis BARON

André BARTOU - Died in concentration camp (Mauthausen in Austria) 21st april 1944

Honoré BIROLET - Returned to France after liberated from camp 6th May 1945

Alexandre BOSSAVIT - Returned to France after liberated from camp 21st May 1945

Jean Pierre Henri DELAGE 'Jeantou' - Died during deportation march 1944

Roger DELON 'Le Catalan' - Returned to France after liberated from camp 2nd May 1945

René LAGUIONIE - Died in concentration camp (Mauthausen) 6th may 1945

Max MADRONNET 'Moreau' - Died in concentration camp (Mauthausen) 21st february 1945

Pierre Lucien MARCHAT 'Chevalier' - Returned to France after liberated from camp 26th April 1945

Léon MARSALEIX - Died in concentration camp (Mauthausen) 17th april 1944

Robert Maurice MAURY - Liberated from concentration camp 1945

Léon Jean PROMIT - Liberated from concentration camp 1945

Jean REMY - Liberated from concentration camp 1945

VICTIMS OF 11TH JUNE 1944 MUSSIDAN

RESISTANTS KILLED FIGHTING AT THE TRAIN STATION

Georges BLANCHARD

Jean GUERIN (age 35)

William HOFFMAN

Yves LEROY (age 19)

Jean MIGNON (age 22)

Henri RODE

Robert SUSSAC

Roger VIRION (age 21)

Two further victims not as yet identified

TRAIN DRIVER

Chiesa MARCEL (age 42)

HOSTAGES SHOT

Roger ALBOY (age 19)

Paul ARNAULT (age 45)

Albert AUBERT (age 19)

Louis AUBERT (age 47)

Georges AUDET (age 24)

Jean BEAUGIER (age 65)

Andre BIENFAIT (age 37)

Leon BLAES (age 25)

Gabriel BONDIEU (age 23)

Paul BOURSON (age 41)

Camille BUSQUET (age 38)

Ernualdo CAVAZZUTI (age 66)

Jean CHAUMEAU (age 38)

Robert CHAUMEIL (age 18)

Camille CHRISTMANN (age 31)

Camille CREYSSAC (age 27)

Marcel CREYSSAC (age 30)

Roger DELEBRET (age 21)

Charles DIEBOLT (age 16)

Rene DIEBOLT (age 37)

Georges DULUC (age 47)

Rene DUMONTEIL (age 18)

Rey DUMONTEIL (age 45)

Jean DUPUY (age 62)

Georges DUTEUIL (age 16)

Roger EYRAUD (age 18)

Jean FLAYAC (age 18)

Eugene FOLNY (age 35)

Felicien FOLNY (age 29)

Maxime GARDILLOU (age 20)

Roger GIRAUD (age 34)

Marcel GIRAUDON (age 36)

Raoul GRASSIN (age 53)

Andre GROS (age 44)

Joseph HERRMANN (age 47)

Andre LAFAYE (age 20)

Lucien HERSKOWITZ (age 18)

Clovis LONGAUD (age 45)

Pierre MARTAUX (age 50)

Eugene MATHRAT (age 31)

Jacques MAZE (age 17)

Pierre MEYTADIER (age 17)

Jean MONTAGNAC (age 17)

Edouard NICOLAS (age 24)

Emile NICOLAS (age 37)

Jean QUEYREAU (age 22)

Alphonse RENAUD (age 30)
Rene SCHUSTER (age 23)
Lucien VERGNAUD (age 18)
Max VILLECHANOUX (age 17)
Leon WINANT (age 17)

The Society for the Remembrance and History of the Resistance and the Deportation of the People of Mussidan are still trying to identify two of the victims of the massacre at Mussidan. Anyone having information or photographs which might help with that is welcome to contact me and I can forward the information to the appropriate person.

ACKNOWLEDGMENTS

A huge thank you to Alan Hamilton and Aaron Sikes for their advice and editing, Ann Fraser and Alison Simpson for their beta-reading, Viccie Corby, Janice Rayns and the rest of the gang at Bordeaux Writers for their help and encouragement, Pat and everyone at Dordogne Ladies Book Club who managed to take the time to advance read, Licarto at 99Designs for the book cover design, and my friends, family and children for all their encouragement and support.

In the course of my research for this novel I have referred to the following books which have proved invaluable:-

La Ligne de demarcation, by Patrice Rolli, published 2020, Editions L'Histoire en Partage.

Les Mussidanais dans La Seconde Guerre Mondiale, published by Patrice Rolli, published by Memoire et Histoire et de la Deportation en Mussidanais.

Defying Vichy, Blood, Fear and French Resistance by Robert Pike.

ABOUT THE AUTHOR

Eilidh McGinness is an emerging author of historical fiction. This is Eilidh's third book in the genre.

Eilidh was born and brought up in the Highlands of Scotland. She studied law at Aberdeen University, Scotland. Then practiced law for eighteen year specializing latterly in criminal defense. She then moved to South-West France where she now lives.

Eilidh has always had a passion for history and is fascinated by seemingly ordinary people who achieve extra-ordinary things.

She loves to hear from readers so please say hello or join her on social media where you can keep up to date with offers, giveaways and new releases.

🐦 twitter.com/eilidhmcginness

BB bookbub.com/profile/eilidh-mcginness

ALSO BY EILIDH MCGINNESS

THE CYPHER BUREAU

Inspired by the life of Marian Rejewski, the Polish mathematician who first solved the Enigma code, and the team of men at the Cypher Bureau-the novel follows their lives before and during World War 2

Praise for the Cypher Bureau

Captivating, compelling, fascinating-Iain Bayne, Runrig

An exciting and forthright novelisation- Crime Fiction Lover

For anyone interested in the topic and in the hardships of WW2 this book is fascinating-Jennifer S. Palmer.

JOSEPHINE,singer,dancer,soldier, spy

Inspired by the life of Josephine Baker, the woman described as 'the most sensational woman anybody ever saw. Or ever will.' By Ernest Hemingway. The fictional biography focuses on Josephine's actions during WW2 where she joins the French Resistance, ready to die for her beloved France.

RESISTANCE BOOK 2, EQUALITY

The Resistance are desperate for arms to battle the Nazi terror. Josette returns from Germany. The lives of the occupants of Saint-Antoine-de-Double becomes even challenging.

Printed in Great Britain
by Amazon